TIMING

TIMING

RICHARD ABBOTT

ISBN: 978-0993-1684-6-8 (soft cover)
ISBN: 978-0993-1684-7-5 (ebook format)

Matteh Publications

Contact:
Web: http://mattehpublications.datascenesdev.com/
Email: matteh@datascenesdev.com

For Roselyn, for family

Contents

Also by the Author

Science Fiction
Novels:
> Far from the Spaceports

Historical Fiction
Novels:
> In a Milk and Honeyed Land
> Scenes from a Life
> The Flame Before Us

Short stories:
> The Lady of the Lions
> The Man in the Cistern

Cover information

Cover artwork © Copyright Ian Grainger
> http://www.iangrainger.co.uk

Original Matteh Publications logo drawn by Jackie Morgan.

Planet and asteroid surface textures on the book cover and promotional material make use of images made available in the public domain by NASA, and are hereby acknowledged. NASA does not endorse the content of this book.
At the time of publication, the specific images used may be found at
http://www.nasa.gov/feature/goddard/
> 2016/new-hubble-portrait-of-mars,
http://photojournal.jpl.nasa.gov/catalog/PIA10367 and
http://photojournal.jpl.nasa.gov/catalog/PIA20825.

Part 1 – Bryher

I HADN'T EXPECTED TO BE SITTING on Bryher, in the Frag Rockers Bar, quite so soon. But here I was. It was just over a year on Earth since I had left this place – about a quarter of an asteroidal year – and not much had changed. Tonight, as it happened, the bar was nearly empty except for my little group of business associates.

I looked around at the little group again, allowing old contentment to resurface in me. There were a couple of others in the team who had not been able to join us tonight, but it was a good number all the same.

Parvati and Maureen sat close together on a sort of divan extruding from the wall. Finn, bigger than the rest of us, and in charge of haulage, lounged in another chair. His wife Eibhlin perched on his knee. Aladdin, who ran the supply chain through his island stores, was bolt upright on my left. On my other side was Boris, and then Rydal Bland, who I had never met before. She closed the circle back to Maureen.

Rydal lived on St Martin's, and managed the financial and formal side of the trade. Black-haired, dark-skinned, and bubbly, she gesticulated with her hands a lot as she talked. She was also wearing a brooch in the form of a butterfly, which at irregular intervals stirred its wings and quivered as though ready to flit off. It was distracting, mesmerising, and peculiarly alluring.

I didn't know her, so I couldn't be sure, but I felt she was worried about something. Something specific: something personal. So far, though, she had said nothing definite either way about that.

The virtual intelligence part of the partnership – the personas – were not visible to the casual onlooker. They were, however, very much present in the conversation, adding insight and comment through lapel or wall pickups as they saw fit. And, no doubt, chattering amongst themselves in ways we could not hear. I was happy: the time was well spent.

The persona I had worked with for many years now was Slate. We joked about growing up and growing old together. That relationship was the longest, most stable thing in my entire life, predating my current romantic liaison with Shayna, my day-job with London-based ECRB, and everything else I could think of. Slate and I worked well together, but, more than that, enjoyed the experience of being together. We liked each other. It was difficult to imagine spending so much time with anybody else, human or virtual.

On balance, the nature of the human-persona connection favoured longer-term partnerships. Amongst this group here in Frag Rockers Bar, both Parvati and Chandrika, and Finn and Lia Fail were couples who were committed to the long haul. But we knew other pairings for whom this was not true. They came together for a season, or a contract, then parted company again. Sometimes the separation was without regret or recrimination; other times things were less happy. It was very like any other interpersonal relationship. There were virtual arenas where you could advertise for new companions: a direct parallel to dating boards, in fact, but crossing the physical-virtual divide.

Out here in the asteroid belt, near the little cluster of settlements called the Scilly Isles, our rare earth mining enterprise was ticking over nicely. The original reef we had found last time was about a quarter worked out now. But we hadn't stopped with that. As Parvati went here and there to fulfil trading commissions in her cutter, the Parakeet, she routinely left the detection algorithms running in the background. Slate and I had provided upgraded versions a couple of times, building on the originals we had developed before coming out to the Scilly Isles for the first time.

Over the months, Parvati and Chandrika had detected, and formally tagged, four other lodes of varying size. As soon as these had been registered with the central claims office on Deimos, the others in the team swung into action with their particular specialist skills. Nobody actually had to dig ore, of course. Neat little automated gizmos worked systematically in and around the demarked volume, gathering the good stuff and discarding the dross, while the rest of us moved on. It was a steady income for all of us now: steady, but dull.

So we had dispensed with the formalities as quickly as decency allowed, and finished our planning meeting a couple of hours ago. Now we were spending wonderful, frivolous, casual time together with no particular goal in mind.

I realised, the longer we all sat together, how much I had missed these people. Slate and I had been busy during the intervening months, busy enough to just get on with work and not spend time reflecting. But here, surrounded by them all, there was a clear sense of surfacing again from a long spell of somnolence. This was how things should be. I drank some more of my Powys Pale and knew that this was home.

After I had left Bryher last time, Slate had navigated us straight back to Earth's moon. Shayna had come up on the regular shuttle, and we had spent two lazy weeks at the most expensive of the lunar south pole hotels. Very luxurious.

Slate had taken her own down time in sync with me, doing, we presumed, whatever she did with Rocky when they weren't working with us. Shayna and I had speculated about what they got up to as a couple, idly one morning after indulging in our own pleasure. We both knew that the topic was a delaying tactic to avoid getting on with the day, but there was a serious side as well.

What sort of relationship did Slate and Rocky have? We liked to fantasise that it paralleled ours, but it was guesswork, really. Most of the time I felt I knew Slate better than anyone else in the system – Shayna included – but every now and again her otherness pushed right up against me.

The only detracting features in that whole indulgent holiday had been Shayna's occasional barbed comments about the length of time that I was having to spend away from Earth. Now, ECRB – the Economic Crime Review Board – could in principle send me anywhere in the solar system where they thought there was a problem needing my particular skills. I might find myself as far away as Pluto, Charon, or the two even more remote Kuiper Belt objects which had settlements. So far, I had never actually had to go further afield than the moons of Jupiter.

When Shayna counted off the dates, it was undeniably true that the frequency of off-Earth trips had steadily increased. I always saw this as an inevitable occupational hazard. It was the sort of thing you moaned about for a day or so, but then just accepted. However, it seemed that Shayna had a different view, and had been counting weeks apart rather more diligently than I.

The lunar holiday came to an end, and then it was back to work, little bits of rather uninteresting routine. Hey ho. It couldn't be all excitement in the life of a coder, and for many months the jobs that ECRB put my way were very ordinary. And they were close at hand as well, with one long spell at the Earth-Moon L2 Lagrange point, and a short trip down to Venus.

Then, quite suddenly, I had been sent all the way to the Jovian system. That would have been fair enough after the local jobs, but it turned out to be a false alarm. One of the analysts thought he had seen a recurrence of an old scam, running out of the Callisto hub. So off we had gone – a long journey for both Slate and I, and when we left Earth orbit the planetary alignment meant there were no friendly stopovers to break the journey.

Once we got there, the two of us had poked around, wormed our way into this module and that, but found nothing. To be sure, we confirmed that the reported irregularities were real. We had easily managed to find the batch runs where the credit had gone missing, by comparing input and out-

put. It happened every time a specific input value was missing or unreadable, and a default value had to be assumed.
But the chosen default looked right and we couldn't find root
cause. The code was non-standard, and frustratingly weird,
but there was nothing obviously suspicious. The logs were so
skimpy as to be almost useless. It did not seem to be the kind
of task that needed our skills, nor to be as much of a problem
as the analyst had first thought.

When it was over, and having drawn a blank, we sent a
summary report down to the Finsbury Circus office, suggesting that perhaps it would be more effective to send an accoun-
tant. We had managed to get four weeks out of the work, but
it still felt like a long drag for not much return. To be fair, it
was unusual for the analysts to make a mistake like that, so
I was professionally polite rather than curt. Then it was time
to warm up the engines of our sloop, the Harbour Porpoise,
and off we set on the homeward leg.

I was all set for a boring journey back down the gravity hill
to Earth, but Slate found an orbital option which would take
us right past the Scilly Isles. That settled it. We deserved
a reward for our fruitless diligence. So we changed the navigation plan, sent some messages ahead, and here we were.
Elias, my manager back in London, had made a token protest
at the diversion, but I told him that the Harbour Porpoise
needed servicing and the delay was unavoidable.

Anyway, a couple of hours signal lag meant that we were
already en route by the time his answer came back. We just
said that we didn't have enough reaction mass for such a radi-
cal course change. It might even have been true, though I was
careful not to ask Slate for a technical analysis, and she was
just as careful not to offer one.

Regardless of that, we weren't minded to listen. Slate and
I both reckoned that we deserved the break. Six weeks of
voyage out to Callisto, and four weeks of fairly dull work had
not made us receptive to a tedious trip straight back home

again. It would mean nearly three months' travel time for just one month of work, and we weren't about to just put up with that without an argument.

<hr />

Some time into our evening in Frag Rockers, Rydal suddenly looked decisive, and rummaged through her bag to find something. I guessed that I was finally going to find out what was bothering her.

"Have you seen this before, Mitnash?"

She was holding out a folded piece of weatherised paper. At the top, in a large, rather archaic font, was the heading 'Robin's Rebels', and below that, only slightly smaller, 'Don't let them get away with it! Take back what's yours today!' Below the fold, there were a few paragraphs of dense writing. I took it from her to read it.

"No, I haven't. Where did you get it?"

"It was sent to my secure box at the Martin's porters' lodge a few days ago. Anonymously, of course. And a friend at a credit and loan facility found the same thing pinned to his door. He reckoned they came from a local disaffected group just trying to raise their profile. The porters said they had seen a few like it, but people mostly just threw them away."

I skimmed through the text. I had seen similar things before. Basically it demanded that any organisation dealing with finance be disbanded, beginning with those at the more speculative end of the spectrum. Wealth was to be redistributed among the people, and a new era of honest work would begin. There were a lot of words like 'parasite' and 'exploitation'. I folded it again and put it on the table.

"Things similar to this appear often enough. Every few years something like it pops up. But I don't know this group: it's a new one to me."

"You didn't see anything like it out near Jupiter?"

"On Callisto? No, nothing at all. But if this only came a few days ago, it was after we left there. We would have been somewhere in transit. Do you know if many people have had the same thing?"

"I've no idea. But why should I get one? I don't exploit anybody. I charge honest rates. But then so does my friend. Why would they go after him? Who do they think they are?"

"It's usually nothing personal."

She rounded on me abruptly.

"But it is personal. They are saying all this about me, and it's not true. And there's no response tag: nobody I can reply to. They think they can say whatever they please, and there's no comeback. I don't like it."

"Look, I'm sorry, but that's not what I intended. I meant that they aren't aiming at you specifically. Groups like this just scatter their propaganda very wide. And it's never worth trying to get into a discussion with them. That'll just make it worse. Do you know if it's local to Scilly?"

"They say not, just here, look."

She opened it and pointed to a line near the bottom.

"They say they have support on every planet and moon. That's why I was wondering if you'd come across them anywhere else."

Eibhlin leaned across to have a look.

"And who might this Robin be, do you think? It might be easy enough to look for someone by that name."

Aladdin stirred, shook his head.

"My belief is that we're meant to remember Robin Hood. You know: stealing from the rich to give to the poor. It may not be anybody's actual name. It's just a ruse."

"Look at it now, they're very aggressive."

Eibhlin picked the piece up to read it.

"Here, listen. 'We are the voice of the downtrodden poor. Financial oppression is slavery; deals and investments are today's whips and chains. But we speak for freedom and justice, and we have the technical talent to fight back. We will strike again and again at these parasites until the entire system is destroyed, root and branch. We will force out those who grow rich from others by means of clever financial tricks, and make them work at honest labour. You do not know us yet, but you will know us soon.' Then there's quite a bit more, all much the same."

Finn was nodding, and reading over her shoulder.

"Sounds like they're up for a fight. Do you think they're for real or just making noise?"

I shrugged.

"It's the first I've heard of Robin's Rebels, but groups like this are common. Usually they amount to nothing. It might not even be a group at all, just someone on their own. Trying to talk themselves up."

I decided not to tell them about the times when something really serious had happened. Eibhlin handed it back to Rydal, but she shook her head and gave it to me instead.

"I don't want it. It upsets me. I've never enslaved anybody in my life. It's just rude. Ignorant. You take it. Show it to ECRB and see if they have any ideas. I'm just going to carry on working at what they call the instruments of wickedness for the time being. One piece of paper isn't going to stop me."

She certainly sounded upset. Maureen stood up, put her arms round her, and, very tenderly, rubbed her shoulders. After a few minutes Rydal nodded and squeezed her hand in thanks.

Speaking personally, it didn't really bother me. It was a fair bet, though, that Robin's Rebels would reckon that my job had already turned me into a wielder of whips and chains. Perhaps I had got more accustomed to dealing with this sort of thing. I would let the Finsbury Circus team know about it, as a matter of routine, but it wouldn't be my top priority. It was usually best to let groups like this die out without making a fuss.

Boris glanced around the group.

"So what do we all reckon? Rydal's already told us what she thinks. It doesn't mean much to me. They don't seem bothered about the spares and repairs business. Aladdin?"

"Most likely they don't think about the island stores at all. Though actually I use deals and investments all the time, and only this morning I negotiated a price option on a delivery coming up from the Venus main dome. But I'll not tell them about that if you won't."

Parvati shrugged.

"I just run freight. I can't see it has anything to do with me, except that I use the odd bridging loan to cover a cash-flow gap. But I don't like the way they talk."

"You know, Riley and I were part of one of these groups when we were young."

There was a general air of disbelief. Eibhlin was entertained by our reaction.

"Tell them, Riley."

"Well, it's true enough. It was when we were first coming out of the inner system, before ever they drilled out the tunnels and we settled here on Bryher. I was quite fired up about all manner of things back then. Full of youthful ideals, I was. So we mixed with a group on Pallas who were all into this sort of thing. Do away with credit, go back to an honest barter system where you could see what everything was really worth. We all kept talking about what we thought was crucial. What was important enough to stand up for."

"So what made you change your mind, Finn?"

He laughed.

"I won't say that I've entirely changed. I still hold that there's people out there who are altogether too greedy. You all know who I mean, even here on the islands. But see now, it turned out that we all wanted more than what we had in our own two hands. I wanted to get into the mining trade. I needed a loan for my first ship. Blarney, that was her name. She was a beautiful vessel, now."

"She was a right tiny heap of junk, Riley, and you know it."

"Eibhlin, my heart, she was comfortable enough for the two of us when we left Pallas and came over here. We made a cosy little home in her before ever we could afford anywhere on Bryher. Little Brigid was conceived in that cabin, as I'll wager you remember very well. But never mind that now. To answer Rydal, I could never have purchased that sweet little Blarney outright. I needed a loan and a decent payment schedule. And you know what? One of these same outfits I'd been so critical of in the past treated me right fairly. Gave me good terms, and that set me up for everything that followed on Bryher. I'd have been a hypocrite to moan too much about them after that."

Rydal laughed and clinked her glass with him.

"Good for you, Finn. Well done for seeing sense and putting them behind you. But I still want them to leave me alone."

And underneath her superficial amusement, her voice still betrayed anxiety.

Thinking back, the Callisto investigation had been bizarre. My initial brief was for a week's investigation and evaluation. For the first few days, that was all Slate and I did. It was dull work. The first day was spent getting all the usual access permissions, and then simply confirming that the bare bones of the report was accurate. It was: virtual resources really had been misplaced and credit really had gone missing.

It happened roughly once a week, which had led the Finsbury team to suspect a payday overrun infiltration. We soon disposed of that guess, with nothing more complicated than a quick analysis of dates. Then we started on the code. Most of the modules were neat and orderly, but trawling through someone else's work is always a trial. Especially when it has been hacked around by three or four different people at different times, using different coding styles. We found nothing that looked remotely suspicious, and got very bored. There wasn't even the expectation of corrective work there to buoy us up.

Then, on the last day, this changed. I had left the main scheduler until the end: it was supposed to be just a set of routine switches directing control to one or other of the secondary units as necessary. Normally there was nothing to look at, so we had focused on the actual handlers as priority. However, when we did get around to it, we found that the switching code was a right mess. Cans of worms had nothing on this.

Some of the data items were passed as simple parameters, while others had been declared globally and just made available everywhere. To add even more to the mix, the latest coder had chosen to transfer some values by using inversion of control. A data block registered somewhere completely different was simply injected in to the scheduler without explanation. I seriously regretted leaving this piece until now.

There was almost no logging, either, so I couldn't just trace some sample values through. I tussled with it for a few hours and then gave up in frustration. I went in search of the Project Manager.

She looked harassed, and her wall sprint planner showed a lot of red and amber status lights. I was used to that: every

PM I had ever known had looked harassed. Presumably it went with the territory.

"Tell me again who did this rework for you?"

"A girl called Jo. Jo Something. I forget her family name. Short-term contract. Her latest references were from some work on Rhea and Iapetus. There were no problems at first. It was some weeks after she left that we started seeing this issue. Are you sure it's not something else? Why? Is her code no good?"

She was obviously bracing herself for bad news, and glanced involuntarily across at the sprint board, with all its overdue tell-tales. The burn-down chart showed a wavering horizontal wiggle, rather than the idealised steady decline that all the books showed you.

"Most of it's fine. Solidly written, nothing to worry about. But there's one bit that's weird."

"Only one? What percentage of the whole?"

"Just under five percent. Or thereabouts."

She shrugged, relaxing a little.

"So over ninety five percent is good?"

"Well, you could look at it like that."

I certainly didn't see things that way. A single line of code, under the right circumstances, could lose a company all their wealth and reputation overnight. Apparently the PM wasn't unduly bothered about that possibility.

"Look, I'll sign off the commit for you to rewrite that one section. It's all in one module?"

"Mostly. A bit of overspill into two others."

She fiddled with some numbers, slid a task placeholder into the overall matrix.

"You can deliver that in a week, right?"

Richard Abbott

I wasn't impressed with the idea of coming all the way out to the Jovians just for a single week's investigation and a single week's coding. It was time to confer with Slate. I switched to using our subvocal link, to make sure that this part of the conversation was private.

"I need a reason to get more time out of her, Slate."

"She's right about the code, Mit. Quite generous, really."

"I know. That little job won't take the two of us more than three days, max. We can only just stretch it out for a week. But I want more than that."

"What about a test suite?"

"Good idea."

I turned my attention back outwards.

"That whole area needs some formal testing. I don't know what this Jo person thought she was doing, but it's quite deficient at the moment. Do you have her unit test results stored somewhere so I can look through them?"

Her face tightened in a way that I knew meant she didn't. I pressed the advantage.

"Or maybe your own quality team's analysis?"

She laughed.

"We're on Callisto, Mister Thakur. You're not in Finsbury Circus any more. The stakeholders here won't give me budget for independent QA in each area. And look now, even if I had budget, there's not enough local talent to build even a single team, let alone one per product. I have one guy who does what he can, but he's not yet had time to look at this."

I felt vaguely sorry for her plight, but it wasn't my problem. It was time to bring out the really big guns.

"There's compliance issues here. I'll need to red-flag this if we can't find a mutually acceptable resolution."

She glared at me. Whatever the real rights and wrongs of the situation, she would be the one left holding the baby.

"Do you have a proposal?"

"Sign off three weeks for me instead of one. Then I'll not only tidy up what's there, but add proper logging and a test suite as well, and throw in some training sessions for your in-house guy."

"And you'll validate the compliance certificate?"

"That too."

She pulled up a short-term contract agreement on the wall-screen and we both committed to it. In the end, she didn't seem unhappy about the transaction – after all, it was some-one else's credit she was using. I had given her unassailable reasons for the extra cost, so she was covered either way. Once I was gone, she could always blame me for the overspend.

I walked through the empty corridors back to the Harbour Porpoise, lost in planning the details with Slate. With nobody around, we were just chatting through my lapel comms rather than the subvocal link.

"Mit, what are we going to do with the mess that's already there?"

"Rewrite it properly, for one thing. But I wish I understood what that contractor thought she was doing."

"Jo? Shall I see what I can find out about her?"

"Please do. And I'd like to keep her code somewhere so we can pull it apart on a long journey sometime. On a day when I'm especially bored, maybe."

She chuckled.

"Just so long as you don't bore me as well. This is your obsession, not mine. But, if you like, we can leave that module in situ, but isolated. Then we can run the data inputs in parallel with our rewrite and see what comes up different."

And so we did. We took the full three weeks, out of habit, though we could probably have skimped a bit and finished ahead of time. We had sidelined the incomprehensible code and added in some logging. Now, it would process the same data, but the results would go nowhere except to the Harbour Porpoise over a buffered remote streaming link. Later on we – or rather I, given Slate's refusal to get involved – could analyse it at leisure. And we spent time with the QA guy, giving him some extra training and some software tools to make his life easier. Job done.

Slate came back with some scanty details about the contractor. The references from Rhea and Iapetus were all in order. The two labs were both part of the Saturn Exploitation Consortium's extensive range of habitats, and her work there had been entirely satisfactory. We could get no clues as to where she had been before. Apparently it was SEC policy never to give that sort of information away. They were a tight-lipped lot.

Similarly, there were no pictures of her that could be accessed. Slate was able to access the personnel details on Callisto, but they were patchy at best. If her visual ident had ever been there, it had gone missing before we could get to it. But the records were all so sloppy that maybe there had never even been a picture. To cap it all, there were three different versions of her family name stored in different places, with no clue which might be correct.

We got the PM to sign everything off and send a copy of the release note back down to Elias at the ECRB, packed up our few possessions, and we were on our way. I wasn't sorry to leave Callisto, which struck me as a cold and dismal place. Naturally I said nothing about that to the residents: you never knew when you might have to revisit a place, and the solar system was surprisingly small just when you most expected it to be vast. It didn't do to rub people the wrong way.

Part 1 – Bryher

Slate and I had docked at St Mary's three days ago, glad to finish our trip back inwards from Jupiter. We had handed the Harbour Porpoise over to Boris for servicing, and had been enjoying the company of old friends ever since. So now here we were in Frag Rockers Bar, quaffing rather too many of Glyndwr's fine ales, and losing ourselves, people and personas alike, in a haze of groupishness.

I wondered, in a brief moment of clarity late on in the evening, if this mellow sense of merging one with another was the same as the intimate world of union that two personas might enjoy. Presupposing, of course, that they trusted each other and felt mutual attraction. It was another question to ask Slate, sometime when we were on our own.

Meanwhile, Mrs Riley was telling us all about the latest island gossip.

"You'll remember Selif who you ran out of here last time?"

I wasn't likely to forget. Selif's wife Kassandra had been the inspiration, and the skill, behind the scam which had first brought me out here. When Slate and I had finally uncovered the truth, the pair had abandoned the islands, disappearing in a late model sloop with Selif's son Dafyd, and their persona accomplice, Carreg.

The various places they had owned on St Mary's had been left vacant. I already knew that Boris had swiftly snaffled up the stores yard in order to diversify his repair business. *Selif's Stuff* had become *The Boris Bazaar*. He'd dropped prices a bit by trimming his margins, to give people a warm feeling that times were better. I fully expected them to slowly creep back up again over the next few months.

I nodded, guessing that Mrs Riley – I never quite dared to call her Eibhlin, even in the privacy of my own thoughts – wasn't about to tell me about changes in property ownership.

"Well, you know they applied for permission to dock back at Mary's about ten months ago?"

This was old news, which Slate had heard about at the time from Chandrika. It was too soon after the whole scam had been exposed, and their request had been disallowed.

"Well now, I found out just this morning that they must have tried again to get here. And not all that long after the first fiasco either, only a couple of weeks maybe. But it turned out badly for them this time."

I sat up straight, taken aback by the news. Mrs Riley chuckled and nudged Finn.

"Now didn't I say that he'd want to hear about this?"

"What do you mean, turned out badly?"

"Go on, Eibhlin, don't leave the man dangling like that."

I had the sudden sense of Slate's attention focused too, and guessed that I must have called to her over the subvocal implant link, at some level below my conscious intention. Nine or ten months ago was not long after we had left. They must have been very motivated to try twice in such rapid succession. I wondered briefly whether they had returned to collect materials from a stockpile somewhere.

"You remember that fancy sloop they had?"

"Cyclone class, Mitnash, with a lot of custom mods."

"I remember. She's faster than just about anything else out here. A nice vessel."

"Well now, she was a fast boat, and she was nice. Not any more, though. She got wrecked on Teän. They hadn't logged the approach plan, and they were coming in much too fast. On an odd angle, too. Well now, that sloop ended up all in pieces."

I looked around the little circle of faces. It was clearly fresh news to Parvati and Maureen, as well.

"How did anyone find out?"

"One of the porters from Martin's went out in his gig to do routine maintenance on their range of nav buoys, and came across some pieces of hull metal. That was a week ago now. So he called it in, got some of the other Martin's pilots to help him, and they traced the vectors back to the crash site itself. It was a right mess, so they say."

"But I thought Selif was qualified for navigation round here. Wasn't he?"

"Oh yes. All three of them were, though Selif had the most hours inshore."

I shook my head, not quite believing it.

"How'd they identify the boat?"

Finn took over.

"That was the easy part. Her name plate and hull ident tags were still at the wreck site on Teän. Seems they were coming in on a trajectory from Pallas and got something wrong. They must have been going at a right clip at the time. The boat was all in smithereens. Looks like only about half the material is there, and so far they've only found Selif's body. Not the other two, although they turned up personal possessions from all three of them. It's too long after the event to expect anything, and there's no family here with a stake in it. So it's been declared marine salvage already, and the Martin's lads will collect whatever they think is worthwhile."

I sat back again. It was an odd conclusion to the affair. Maureen changed the subject, and we all followed her lead. Shipwreck was an uncomfortable topic, and we had spent as long on it as decency allowed. But in the privacy of our direct link, Slate and I carried on.

"We should find out more about this, Mit."

"I agree. See what you can find out on the island news feeds. Especially from St Martin's. I'd like to know what those three were coming back for."

"And whether anyone ever found the rest of the ship or her occupants."

"It's a bit ghoulish, but you're right."

I woke up late the next morning at my old room at Mrs Riley's. I felt slightly the worse for wear, but not as much as I had expected after last night's excess. Maybe low gravity helped, in some way I couldn't figure out. All in all, I was very cheerful.

"Morning, Slate. How's the virtual world today?"

"Full of friends at mere fractions of a second away, thank you, Mit. How long can we stay here?"

I shrugged, sat up, and thought about a shower. Not quite yet, I decided, and carried on with Slate.

"Well, Elias hasn't complained yet, and I'm sure Boris won't mind taking a bit longer on the service if we ask him. Maybe we need some spare parts. How would it be to have another week here?"

"Wonderful. I'd love that. What about you?"

"Suits me."

I decided that I felt mischievous.

"Aren't you in a hurry to get back to Rocky, though?"

"No. Not particularly."

She sounded very final. I was tempted to probe further, but clearly she wasn't ready to say more just yet. My affection for her considerably outweighed my curiosity. I thought back to last night's conversation.

"So have you been able to find out more about Selif and the shipwreck?"

"A little. Only what has been recorded publicly on the St Martin's port channel so far. But I'll have a more personal account in a while. And as well as that, Lia Fail says that Mrs Riley will have your breakfast ready soon."

Slate carried on as I started getting ready for the day.

"So the ship can only be salvaged for scrap. There's no major components left intact. They have the data recorders but haven't yet released the analysis into the public domain. These things take time. I do know that they found parts of all three suits – it seems that they weren't wearing them."

"But only Selif's body?"

"That's right."

"What about Kassandra's persona? He was called Carreg, I think?"

"Yes indeed. But there's no way to tell. It's not like he has a body that looks any different from the onboard ship systems."

"I suppose not."

I pulled on some casual clothes, briefly flicked a wall into mirror mode to check up on myself, and decided it was adequate.

"I wish we knew more, Slate. It's all very vague."

"I'll go on asking questions, but with no real cargo on board, no survivors, and the total loss of the vessel, nobody's very interested."

I went through from the bedroom to where Mrs Riley was just bringing in a substantial tray of food. Rydal was already sitting down, talking with Finn.

"You might have told me Rydal stayed here as well."

"Why would I say anything? I thought you knew. You were beside her all the way back here last night. Anyway, I've been chatting with Capstone all morning."

I was lost.

"Who's Capstone?"

"*Rydal's persona, of course. He's nice. Very interesting. I've been getting to know him. He and Rydal have only been together a year or so. But you knew all this yesterday. Come on, Mit. You need to keep up.*"

"*Fair enough. I don't exactly remember all the details from last night. Let me have breakfast first, and we can talk about it later.*"

Mrs Riley had sat me down by then, opposite Rydal, and we started on the food. Finn turned to me.

"I've got something you might want to see, once Eibhlin has cleared this lot away."

"Oh?"

"One of the Martin's lads sent me the inventory of what they've found at the wreck site. To see if there was anything of value I'd be interested in, like."

I did want to know, but Mrs Riley was quicker. It seemed everyone was quicker than me this morning.

"Now Riley, that's not a fit subject for the breakfast table. Wrecks and all. It's not right, and you know it."

Finn surrendered with the grace of years of practice, winking at me.

"So what shall we talk about, my own sweet treasure?"

"Well, Mister Mitnash, I was wondering if you knew about these unexpected credits people have been having? We all thought it might be you still, sharing out all that Selif and Kassandra had taken from us."

"Nothing to do with me. All the assets that I knew about were disposed of months ago. Tell me more."

"Well, we've received no benefit ourselves. But a dozen or two across the islands have had little bits and pieces. And Rydal here was saying just before you came in that it's happened elsewhere too."

"That's right, Mitnash. I'm hearing this from financiers all round the Belt. Large sums, too, in some places, especially on Ceres and Vesta. And there are signs that it's started happening on Mars, but I don't have much detail about that."

"Ceres and Vesta, but not Pallas?"

Ceres was biggest, to be sure, but the population on Pallas was three times that on Vesta. She nodded.

"Odd, isn't it?"

"Nobody knows where it comes from?"

"Nobody. It's a safe bet that a lot more people have received something than have declared it, though. Who knows how far this spreads? And as for the source of all this credit, not one person has admitted to losing anything. It's a mystery. I'm surprised your ECRB people haven't told you."

I ate most of my remaining breakfast on autopilot, thinking about this. It was possible that Elias had put someone else on the case, in which case there was no reason I would be told. Then again, it was possible he knew nothing about it. ECRB only really got involved when someone declared a loss they couldn't explain. A few serendipitous gains with nothing to balance would quite possibly go unnoticed.

Finally I caught Rydal's eye.

"Could you ask Capstone to share the information with Slate, please. It's possible that some sort of pattern will start to emerge. My gut tells me it's important, but I don't know how just yet."

"Not a problem. And when we're finished here, why don't you come back to my gig? I can show you the analysis I've done."

Finn was clearly eager to show off the inventory, but Eibhlin shared out some more drop scones and poured another round of tea.

"So Rydal, why don't you tell Mister Mitnash how you came by your name?"

"Oh."

She hesitated, and then glanced at me to see if I was actually interested before continuing.

"Well, my mother wanted all us children named after places in the north-west of the old country. My older sister is Coniston – Connie, we always call her – and my brother is Fairfield. If I'd been a boy I'd have been Walla, but happily I turned out to be a girl."

She dimpled slightly at Eibhlin's response. Finn leapt in with tales of ancient Ireland, and his own namesake. To my surprise, he kept the account short, though he could clearly have continued relating the exploits of the legendary Finn for a good fraction of the day. Then he turned to his wife and suggested she talk about her own name, but she deftly avoided the matter by clearing some plates. The meal was officially over.

Finn was eager to show off the salvage list, now that he was at liberty to do so. Lia Fail obliged by pulling up a series of images on the nearest screen. For all her breakfast objections, Mrs Riley was there with the rest of us to view them.

"My, this is not your usual viewing entertainment, Mit."

"Hush now. This is work."

She snorted.

"And you said I was ghoulish. Look at it."

An image of an child's first gamepad, which had obviously belonged to Dafyd, had just been replaced by some frilly underwear that would have fitted Kassandra. I pulled a face.

"Finn, is there anything really important there?"

"Well, not really, I suppose. There's about a small cupboard worth of personal effects. Like what you've seen. Then a few loose spares for the vessel. After that, you're down to the hull and fitments. They reckon they can now account for over three quarters of the boat and her contents. Still only the one corpse so far."

"How long will they carry on looking?"

"Oh, they've stopped. No point, you see. The nav hub on Martin's calculated that there was no hazard to shipping, and the loss adjustors don't think the likely value of what's left comes up to the cost of looking. Basically, the game's not worth the candle."

I wandered back to my little room and packed up. Then we bid our farewells to the Rileys – for the time being, at least – and I followed Rydal towards her gig.

On the way, Slate confirmed that Capstone had forwarded a large quantity of data about the uplift values. She was doing a lot of the preprocessing just now, to get it out of the way before we got down to serious business.

Rydal's gig, the Heron, was moored in amongst half a dozen vaguely similar craft. I had expected something about the size of the Mermaid, which Nick had ferried me about in last time I was here.

The Heron was considerably smaller, however, and it would be a squeeze getting more than the two of us into her. A purist would say it was more of a scull than a gig.

We sat side by side in the bridge to look at her analysis. It was rather less roomy than my bedroom at the Rileys, but since the Harbour Porpoise was still with Boris, there wasn't much choice.

She first got Capstone to display the increments as a kind of contour map overlaid onto the Scilly Isles. It wasn't very revealing. There were certainly some minor local variations from island to island, but it looked random to me.

Then she pulled back to show the whole asteroid belt. That was different. Just as she had said, Ceres and Vesta showed huge peaks – Ceres was the larger – and the amount across the Scilly Isles was dwarfed in comparison. I nodded.

"That looks convincing. But it doesn't tell us much about the cause."

"Now see what happens if we scale for population size rather than show simple totals."

The display changed. This time the Ceres and Vesta peaks were almost identical in size. The total values might be different, but the subsequent disbursements had been chosen so as to make the amount per recipient the same. That spoke of careful planning. Meanwhile, Pallas was flat, and the various other domes here and there around the belt showed nothing as well. That was really interesting.

"You mentioned Mars?"

"Well, yes. There's a few places on Mars itself, and a tiny scatter on Phobos. Nothing on Deimos. Here..."

The Martian system appeared. As she had said, Deimos showed the same low-level random splutter as the Scilly isles. Phobos showed a little bit more, but nothing very definite. Mars, with its wide diversity of settlements in different places, showed an equally wide variety. In amongst that were several peaks, reaching almost the same value as Ceres and Vesta, but the data was patchy. I leaned back.

"Slate, what is there in common between those places?"

"I'll see what I can find out. And I've just fired off a query to Khufu down in London to see if we have any similar data on the Jovian system. Capstone tells me that he and Rydal have no details for there."

Khufu was the main Pyramid installation supporting the Finsbury Circus office, together with those other scattered souls who, like Slate and I, were on detached work off planet.

Vaster than a persona and more capable, he was also more serious, less easily sparked into lively debate, and not really the sort of individual you would want to spend time with. He did, however, have access to a colossal amount of information, and was able to leverage this to make connections the rest of us might miss.

At any rate, a query going down to the Finsbury Office and back would take the better part of an hour, given the relative locations of Bryher and Earth just now. So we had time to spare. Time to see what we could do for ourselves with this puzzle.

While waiting for Slate's analytics to initialise, I half-turned to look at Rydal. Her skin was darker than mine, and she had gathered her unruly ringletted hair back into a more orderly bob as we had boarded the Heron. She glanced at me briefly, and I looked back at the screen. It was ready now.

"Any ideas?"

"We need to find the common factor. Let's see what Khufu comes up with."

To my surprise, it was Capstone who answered.

"Slate and I have been working together on this, Mitnash. You see, I have a lot of demographic data that isn't relevant for your normal investigations into fraud. But it fits very neatly with what Slate already knows, and means we can eliminate most possibilities. So far as we can tell, there's only one common feature that appears to have any relevance to the matter. Ceres and Vesta use a twinned Sarsen pair as the main financial deal hub. Deimos and Pallas do not. Mars has a lot of different systems here and there, so it's harder to tell."

"He's right, Mit. Pallas has a single Sarsen with a lot of upgrades to quicken her up. Deimos has a routing engine down to Mars, based on a cut-down Ziggurat. No real local processing at all. The main Mars site at Elysium Planitia has a full Pyramid, but there are a lot of sites elsewhere on the planet which do have twins. A couple of them are reasonably close to the peaks, but there is no direct connection that I can see yet."

"From memory though, the twinned pair is a fairly common configuration. We mainly see it in finance, but it's very widespread beyond that too. Ship navigation and all. I'm not surprised that there are several like that on Mars. Slate and I can send a query to get a full list across the system, if we think it would help. But does anyone here on the islands use twinned Sarsens?"

"Oh yes. The main financial hub on St Mary's. You remember, we talked about it last time we were here."

Rydal stirred.

"Actually there is another, though hardly anybody knows about it yet. Back on Martin's we have one as well. I'm telling you this in absolute confidence, but there is a move by some of us there to take the islands' deal processing away from Mary's. We're putting together a proposal right now, listing a number of occasions when the Mary's hub has either underperformed or thrown errors. Acquiring the twinned pair was part of the proof of concept."

This was news to Slate and I. At a guess, it would be news to Elias as well, but Rydal had effectively sworn us to secrecy for the time being.

"Has either your equipment or that on St Mary's reported anything amiss yet?"

"Not that I know of."

"I don't suppose you could take us there? I'll consent to whatever nondisclosure agreements you want. But this could be a chance to get ahead of the curve."

"Not a problem. If our plan is going to succeed, we need all of the pieces to be totally reliable. So I need to know if there's some inherent problem with those twinned devices. We can still change technical direction now. In a few months' time that would be much more difficult."

She paused, looking at me in a measuring way.

"If I can get you access, will you help us? Or would you feel obliged to support the existing hub on Mary's? And would you be helping us in a private capacity, or representing ECRB? I want to know this is all being done properly."

Her eyes were almost the same dark shade of brown as my own, and it was uncomfortably like looking in a mirror. I focused on the screen, partly to avoid her intensity as she tried to assess what I might do.

"Any opinion on this, Slate?"

"I say we should help. We've had no direction from either Elias or Khufu. We're not obligated to support uncritically the status quo. And if we help as private individuals then I don't think there's any real conflict of interest."

To me, the suggestion seemed right on the borderline of propriety. I suspected that Slate had ulterior motives.

"You're sure it's not just that you've liked working with Capstone and would like to carry on?"

"That may be true. But the decision makes sense anyway. We can argue that we're speculatively probing a potential weakness in a relatively common financial architecture. They should give us a bonus for this, really."

The last idea was so wildly improbable that I chuckled, and turned back to Rydal.

"We'll do it. As private individuals on our own time, unless we find something of wider importance which we would be duty-bound to report. Either way, we'll honour your situation and act in complete discretion."

By way of answer, she cleared the screen and replaced it with a standard inter-island transit course. It was a longer and more complex journey than the short trip to Tresco, but it still didn't look too difficult.

"Do you have anything else to pick up? The next departure slot is just over five minutes away."

"I've got everything I need with me."

And then, just as I was relaxing in the copilot's seat and starting to wonder what kind of beverages Rydal kept aboard, Slate buzzed me again on our private link.

"Mit, I'm just receiving a message from the Finsbury Circus office. It's red-flagged and multiply encrypted. I'll have the content for you in a minute or so."

"But surely it's far too soon for a reply to your message."

"Indeed it is. That won't have reached anywhere near Earth yet. This has to be something different. You'd better ask Rydal to hold until we know what it is."

So Rydal kept the departure slot on pause, and we sat waiting for Slate to unravel the message.

"We have to go to Phobos, Mit. Top priority, soonest available transit."

I frowned, frustrated.

"Why? What's happening on Phobos?"

"They've reported the same irregularity pattern there as the one we saw on Callisto."

"But we didn't actually find anything."

"We never found a cause. We did confirm the events themselves. And the loss pattern is similar enough that coincidence is almost entirely ruled out. Elias thinks we're best placed to look at it."

Rydal was watching me, still keeping the transfer plan in pending state. I sighed and spoke aloud.

"Rydal, I'm sorry, but the investigation on St Martin's will have to wait. I've been called away on urgent business to Phobos. Slate will tell Capstone what she can."

I paused, reading the disappointment written on her face.

"Look, I'm really sorry. It can't be helped."

"Will you be able to come back here and look at the problem when you're done there? I don't like all this chopping and changing about."

I said nothing to that, but I couldn't really agree. My whole life consisted of chopping and changing about, going with the flow of events according to our best guess at the time. I wasn't sure if I envied her determination to stick to an original plan, or just felt it was naïve.

"I'll try."

"Mit, actually we have to come back. The Harbour Porpoise is not fit for travel yet. She's still in pieces with Boris. We'll need to negotiate a ride down to the Martian system and come back afterwards."

I glanced around the Heron's little bridge.

"I don't suppose you do charter runs?"

She looked at me quizzically.

"This little boat isn't rated for a journey like that. I'd be breaking, what, half a dozen regulations at least, and I won't be doing that. Besides, wouldn't it be a bit too cosy for the two of us? Four week's journey each way with only one tiny cabin? And a single open wetroom at the end of a corridor? The Heron wasn't designed for long journeys. Or privacy."

To my surprise, I found myself profoundly embarrassed, and stammered out an apology. It didn't help that Slate was giggling away. At least she had the grace to keep her amusement private, through the cochlea implant. I expect Capstone was entertained as well.

"I think you'll find that Parvati can take you there and back. There's altogether more room on the Parakeet. It'll be a faster journey, too; probably only three weeks. The engines on her cutter are far superior to the little ones on this gig."

"Yes, of course. Thank you. Look, Rydal, as soon as this crisis is over, I'll come back to the islands. We can look at this problem again together."

I pulled myself together and started planning.

"Slate, could you chat with Chandrika and see if it's possible for her to take us to Phobos? And was there much more to the message Elias sent?"

"Chandrika is almost sure they can do this: she's checking with Parvati now. And yes, there's a great deal of detail attached to the message. Sufficient that we will need a long session. Briefly, they're seeing a regular loss pattern, approximately weekly. Just like Callisto. Roughly the same amounts each time."

I could tell from her tone that she reckoned most of the information was not something to talk about with Rydal.

"We'll look at it on the journey over. Sounds like there will be plenty of time."

It was an oddity about space travel. Because the propulsion drive was most efficiently run always-on, you invariably accelerated to midpoint, flipped end to end, and then decelerated the rest of the way. So the longer the trip, the faster the turnover velocity, and the more efficient the use of time. Under ideal circumstances the time taken increased only with the square root of the distance, not linearly. Circumstances were rarely ideal, however, and something always intruded to increase the time. Anyway, the trip from the Scilly Isles down to Mars was not much shorter than the whole leg down to Earth, almost entirely because we could not achieve such a high midpoint speed.

From that point of view, the stopover at the Scilly Isles on the way back from Jupiter was a bit reckless. We would burn nearly seventy percent more time and reaction mass by doing it as a two-leg journey rather than just one. I was sure that Elias would be pointing this out once we got back home.

But then, if we hadn't done that we would be in no position to transit to Mars, so I suppose we ended up even. It was the flip side of the standard shipping pattern; once you were committed to a particular destination, it was highly inefficient to switch to another one. Occasionally the alignment worked out near enough for it to be done easily, but that was the exception rather than the rule.

Slate broke into my contemplation.

"Chandrika says it's fine, and I've authorised the contract. Standard per diem rates. We can leave tonight in about four hours if you're ready."

"We need some bits from the Harbour Porpoise. Clothes and things for that long a journey. And shall we use the lifeboat again as the hardware basis for you?"

"Good plan. I'll start the transfer now, meanwhile we can send Boris a message listing what you need, and he can pack it into the lifeboat. Chandrika will slave the nav system, and she'll bring it over to rendezvous with the Parakeet somewhere convenient. There's no need for us to go back to St Mary's ourselves. Oh yes, she also asked if there was any chance of excitement this time around?"

I laughed, remembering last time.

"No promises, I'm afraid. The excitement is likely to begin only after we land on Phobos, not on the way."

I was buoyed up by the thought of swinging into action again. Also the fact that the same scam – apparently – had been spotted on Phobos as we had investigated back at Callisto was intriguing, to say the least. I turned back to Rydal, who tried unsuccessfully to hide her disappointment. That brought me back to sobriety with a bump.

"I won't be long, Rydal. I have to come back here. There'll be time to look at your system then."

She shrugged and tried not to look sceptical.

"Unless you get called away again. But I suppose you never know when that will happen. This wasn't official, after all."

She turned away and fiddled with some controls. I felt appallingly guilty for some reason.

"Come on, Mit. It's not as if the two of you had a contract. You only heard about all this today."

"True enough, Slate, but I still feel bad about it."

She made a rather dismissive noise, clearly unpersuaded.

"I don't suppose you'll need carriage anywhere either. Parvati's docked just across the way from us."

"No, I don't. But thanks for the offer. We'll catch up as soon as I get back; you can take me to St Martin's then."

"Sure."

She sounded entirely unconvinced. I still felt as though I had let her down, and tried to think of something to offer.

"Look, Rydal, you could send me the block flow diagrams for your new system as soon as you get home. Slate and Capstone can negotiate a secure channel. I can start to understand what issues might arise while we're on the journey. And as well as that, Slate and I will get hold of a complete list of installations using this type of build."

She looked back at me, sizing up my degree of seriousness.

"Would you? I'd have to ask you to accept non-disclosure first. I haven't even cleared this with the others."

"Of course. Not a problem. For now I'd better be going. But it'll seem like no time before I'm back."

We both stood up, and I shouldered my day bag. We walked to the airlock, and I toggled the door cycle. It opened, and as I stepped towards it I glanced back at her once more. She suddenly beamed, threw her arms around me, and hugged me very tightly against her. She didn't exactly kiss me, but it was far more intimate than I was expecting. Then she released me and stepped back as the internal door closed and the external one irised open to the marina.

I took several steps back to the cross-alley which linked all the docking bays before stopping to think.

"What was that all about, Slate?"

She made exaggerated kissing sounds and chuckled.

"What do you think?"

"She's trying to make sure I come back and help her?"

"She's certainly eager to make sure we return. Capstone has already sent the NDA documents – nothing unusual, so I've accepted them for both of us – and there's a very large encrypted packet coming over now. The unlock algorithm and key will follow in the usual way. I'd say they're in a real hurry, and Rydal wants to be sure your interest has been snared. Your emotional commitment, not just your professional curiosity. She wants to secure your help, and she's treading as close to the edge of her professional ethics as she feels able."

I walked on without replying, thinking about it.

"Unless you'd prefer to explain it by way of your dashing appearance, irresistible charisma, and personal magnetism?"

By now I was at the spur jetty leading out to the Parakeet, so I paused to finish the exchange.

"I don't think that deserves a serious answer. But even if she did mean it the way you describe, that doesn't necessarily mean that we shouldn't help her. I'm sure I can manage not to get caught up in something underhand."

She sounded as though she found the whole situation particularly hilarious.

"I'm sure you'll find it a fascinating technical challenge."

I was getting cross.

"But it is a real problem, and we do have a duty to check it out. Regardless of who brought it to our notice. In fact, it was you who first said we should look at it. 'They should give us a bonus', you said."

"That's certainly true, Mit. All of it. I'm just trying to keep you honest. Now let's go aboard the Parakeet and see what we can find out about the problem on Phobos."

It turned out that the trip to Mars was going to take the Parakeet just over three weeks. I have to admit I was unforgivably idle for the first few days, spending time catching up with Parvati, and trawling through the latest crop of technical blogs that Slate acquired for me from Earth. So far as I could tell, Slate was doing much the same with Chandrika.

What I did do, at some point in those days, was try to find out more about Robin's Rebels. Since our formal request from the London office had, so far, returned nothing of consequence, Slate and I tried scraping more general media sources. It was slow work. We could find copies of the leaflet that Rydal and others had received, all more or less the same. But beyond that, there was a great deal of silence.

We still had no idea if it was a single person or a group. After clumsily saying 'he, she or they' to each other a few times, we decided, that for simplicity of pronouns if nothing else, they were a small group.

They had no official virtual presence. Nothing on Blagger, nothing on the various public information servers we could find, nothing even on the bits of the unofficial sub-surface channels we knew how to access.

Robin's Rebels really did not want to be tracked down. I thought this tended to confirm my original theory that they had no tech skills. Slate – perhaps just to be provocative and take the opposite position – argued instead that this proved real talent.

Now, it was true that a small number of other threads mentioned them in passing. But so far as we could tell, these were invariably posted by people who had had no personal interactions with them.

The range of opinion was huge, especially considering the very limited sample. Were they heroes ushering in a new deal of equality and justice, simply a little bit ahead of their time? Or thieves and charlatans, trying to cover up simple robbery and extortion with some nice words and an appeal to a historical legend?

Nobody knew, and our day of investigation left us none the wiser. This was mainly because there was absolutely nothing concrete about what they actually did, or could do, or might think of doing. Everyone was just talking about the flyer, and trying to tease a whole world of meaning out of its rambling assertions.

"Slate, do you think there is any chance this new group is behind the Callisto scam?"

"I don't see how. The leaflets didn't appear until after we had left there. And so far as we know the problem on Phobos has not been linked to them. I'm sure they would claim responsibility if they possibly could. Also, that tiny amount of credit is hardly going to bring the world of finance to its knees. I think they would have a bigger plan."

That was indeed the problem. Until you could actually find some code to look at, then speculating about who was doing what was, really, a waste of time. It was ridiculously easy for anyone to try and gain reputation for anything, until you actually had the chance to trace the logic and data flows.

After that debacle, we gave up investigations for a while and just had fun. But eventually we both decided it was time to start work properly.

"Slate, perhaps we should go through the details of the problem on Phobos?"

She cleared the wall screen and scattered a whole array of documents across the surface.

"Where shall we start?"

"With a top-level summary of the losses, compared with the ones we saw on Callisto."

A chart opened, with two traces spilling arose it. Red for Phobos, blue for Callisto. They were mostly flat, with irregular spikes showing the discrepancy pattern. Irregular, but averaging out at more or less one a week when you looked at the big picture. Callisto slightly more often, Phobos slightly less. Other than that, there really wasn't a great deal of similarity. Different days, different amounts, different principal components.

I was missing something.

"Slate, we did leave the old code on Callisto running in parallel with the new, didn't we?"

"Absolutely. With triggers to send an alert down to us if ever the problem surfaced again."

"And have the triggers fired at all?"

"Not at all, Mit. Not even once."

"But why not? We never found the root cause. Why isn't the same problem happening every few days still?"

Slate was silent for a while.

"That's a really good question. I have no idea. Maybe whatever situation was causing it has gone away?"

"That would be an absurd coincidence."

"Or maybe it was an insider job and the person is keeping a low profile? Maybe we frightened them off? In which case Jo's coding style has nothing to do with the problem."

"Maybe. But I'm not convinced. Is there any way to see if there's any crossover of personnel?"

"I can request the staff roster. But remember Callisto: the records are very skimpy. I'll ask Khufu what he can find out."

"Meanwhile, is there any chance of getting a look at the code repository on Phobos?"

"No. I asked last night while you were asleep, and they won't open a remote link. Not for anyone, not for any reason. You'll have to wait until we get there."

It was fair enough – I would do exactly the same in their position. In fact, it was quite reassuring that they were prepared to take a stand on it.

"So is there any more we can do for now?"

"Not really. I can show you the same data in different charts, but you're not going to learn anything helpful by looking at them."

So we didn't do that. Instead, we spent a couple of hours briefing ourselves on Phobos and its colony. I had never had cause to find out about it before, and had never once landed there. It was slightly eclipsed by its sibling Deimos because of the School of Mining, and both were in the shadow of the lively anarchy of the main Martian domes. Between them, those two attracted everyone's attention, and Phobos was largely overlooked.

It deserved to be better known, I thought. Orbiting only about six thousand kilometres above the planet's surface, it whipped around in its orbit in less than eight hours – about a third of a Martian day. That meant it seriously outstripped Mars' axial rotation, and gave it the signal honour of being the only moon in the system to complete an orbit in less than its primary's day. That also meant that, seen from Mars, it rose in the west and set in the east.

That close in, it wasn't going to last long, in planetary terms. I probably had less than fifty million years to solve the case before the whole thing crumbled into a ring of dust and pebbles. No pressure, then.

For the time being, anyway, it had about three times the surface area of Deimos, but a far smaller population. The mining school filled up the habitable domes of Deimos, and they were always short of accommodation there. On the other hand, a lot of people left Phobos because the proximity of Mars felt claustrophobic after a while. The largest settlement was on the side which always faced away from the planet, in an attempt to lessen the visceral impact of the view.

Phobos was fearfully dark in colour – as was Deimos – looking for all the world as though it was a burnt-out cinder. It was one of the least reflective objects anywhere in the system. Take a vid from the right angle, and Phobos would not look like a moon at all, but would seem to be a great pit dug into the red planet. Except that a pit would stay in one place, whereas this would be cracking round at a pace.

It was hard to really appreciate the moon's smallness. It was basically a cylinder, about twenty kilometres in diameter, and nearly thirty in length. Martian gravity ensured that the long axis faced directly out into space. The average person could comfortably circumnavigate the moon on foot, end to end, in a couple of days. There were members of walking clubs who did just that, it being one of the system's classic trails. A fit runner would need less than a day. The portion of the walk looking out to space would be quite pleasant. When you were on the side facing the planet, though, Mars would be forever looking as though it was about to fall on you.

The smallness affected the structure in many ways. First, and most obviously, the surface gravity was a minuscule fraction of Earth standard, far less than what we enjoyed on Scilly. But also, unlike most settled objects, the interior was full of small cavities. Some were actual voids in the structure, others were full of loose shale and rubble. If you were on Bryher and St Agnes you could easily dig tunnels to get more habitable space: nobody risked this on Phobos. You lived on the surface, or you moved elsewhere.

I thought back to the sports conversation a year ago between Jed and Olly, when they had nearly trapped me in the workshop area of *System Serene* on Bryher. Olly had been convinced that a good kicker could put a ball into orbit on Phobos and score on the next orbit around; Jed was unpersuaded. For fun, Slate and I looked at the calculations. Apparently Olly was right after all, at least in theory. The problem would not be the impetus a good player could apply, but simply getting in a position with enough leverage to make the kick in the first place. In low gravity, inertia tended to rule, and things that were easy on Earth often turned out to be surprisingly difficult here. At a guess, such a goal would be really hard to achieve in practice.

In the end we had exhausted the research avenue too. We both realised that our investigation had become sporadic and unfocused. When we started looking up high jump records and watching teasers of last season's freestyle dance competition, we knew that we had crossed the line into displacement activities. We were just fooling around, really. We cleared the screens, out of habit, then Slate got on with whatever she did when I wasn't conversing with her.

~~~~~~~~~~~~~~~~~~~~~~~~~~~~~~~~~

I wanted human company again, so I stretched and went in search of Parvati. She was brewing chai as I wandered in to the kitchen. Seeing me, she doubled up the amounts, found a second mug, and arranged some savoury crackers and a red and yellow striped cake on a tray.

"Did you and Slate get anywhere?"

I shook my head.

"Total blank. The figures don't tell us any more than the basic alert message we got from Finsbury, and they won't let us access the code yet. There's almost nothing we can do until we get there."

We moved back to the bridge and enjoyed the snack together.

"Chandrika just picked up the latest from the wreck site for Selif's ship, if you're interested?"

I very definitely was interested. We finished the crackers, and she sliced two generous portions of the cake.

"They've made available the results from the data recorders. There's nothing at all unusual until about three minutes before the crash. At that point, Selif took the vessel's riding lights offline and uploaded an amendment to the nav plan."

"Presumably to avoid being identified by the duty porters?"

"Most likely, yes. You're not supposed to disengage them, but people do. As you say, he was motivated to slip in without attracting attention. It's also uncommon to amend the plan at that late stage, but it happens. Anyway, the upload was completed successfully, taking only the expected lag. Except that a couple of seconds later, both recording devices ceased gathering data. At the same instant. That is unheard of."

I looked at her.

"How did that happen?"

"The maintenance log for the recorders showed that Selif had skipped two routine services. So they highlighted that in the report, and almost immediately the manufacturer put out advisory notices basically denying all responsibility if people ignore the recommended schedule. So the official version simply lists an open verdict."

"Is there an unofficial version?"

She grinned.

"Of course. Chandrika, why don't you tell them?"

"To be sure. I heard this from one of the personas on Martin's. He works part-time with a man who's an expert on the embedded systems in boat engines."

I nodded. It was a highly specialised area, and one that I knew next to nothing about. But it made sense that a man with those skills would have an opinion on data recorders.

"Well, he said two things. One is that a full restart cycle for those boxes is about half a second longer than the time from the point of failure up until the impact on Teän. And the second thing is that there are only two known exploits for that model of recorder which could bring down both boxes together. One of them cannot possibly have anything to do with this case: a different ship configuration altogether. The other one happens to rely on a routing plan change."

I sat there, absorbing the news. It made sense that these units would go into an automatic reboot mode if they went dark for some reason. Normally that would restore them to full operation in plenty of time to carry on doing their job. But in this case, the boat had hit Teän before they had started up again. I stirred in my seat, but Slate beat me to it.

"That's very precise timing on someone's part. Does anybody think it is just a coincidence?"

"Oh, Slate, the official verdict is open. Nobody is suggesting anything."

We all laughed together.

"Either it was phenomenally bad luck on their part, or. . . "

I paused, and Parvati continued.

"Or else someone wanted rid of them, and found a clever way to do it."

She shrugged.

"I suppose they might well have made enemies in one place or another."

"Very skilled enemies, to put all that together."

We sat together for a while. I'm not sure what the others were thinking about, but I was trying – and failing – to puzzle out who might have a motive.

Selif had been the front man, and although he was quite capable of being abrasive, he was ordinarily smooth-tongued and skilful at managing the people around him. Dafyd had not changed very much from being a spoiled kid who liked games, and sulked when he couldn't play. He could, on occasion, become aggressive, like when he had tried to bully me into leaving St Mary's last time. Only the unexpected presence of Finn had stopped him. Kassandra, meanwhile, had made such a successful habit of keeping out of sight that I doubted many people had even heard of her. She had certainly kept under the radar of ECRB's extensive records. It was not easy to think of a credible adversary.

Slate spoke up again.

"Chandrika, do you think you could find out more about that routing change?"

"I can probably get the whole waymark packet if you want. I think it's in the public domain by now, as part of the investigation. Give me ten minutes or so."

"Do you two know how to interpret that sort of thing?"

I shook my head.

"I've never seen one in my life before. But all these things are open format. How hard can it be?"

Parvati looked dubious, but Slate interjected.

"I'm not very interested in the route itself, Mit. I'd like to know how it was delivered. Call it a hunch."

I suspected that she had been exchanging technical data with Chandrika. That was fine by me – we had had ample cause to rely on each other's hunches before now. We chattered about nothing at all for a while, until Chandrika spoke up again.

"Got it. Here, Slate, have a look."

She flashed the data packet up on the wall screen. Without the validation schema it was impenetrable, but I didn't have to look at it for long. Slate zoomed in on a couple of fields near the top and dropped on some explanatory notes.

"Here, look. The update was not initiated from inside the ship at all. It was an external request; these here are the details. The point of origin is a relay buoy near Ceres."

There was a little congratulatory buzz, which Slate clearly appreciated. Then I frowned.

"But if the signal came from near Ceres, that makes the timing even more incredible. Doubly so if that was just a relay and the real point of origin was somewhere else. The sender would have to time everything with extraordinary precision."

"Unless it really was a coincidence."

Nobody replied to that. We stopped the discussion and carried on with the journey.

⁓⸱⸱⸱⸱⸱⸱⸱⸱⸱⸱⸱⸱⸱⸱⸱⸱⸱⸱⸱⸱⸱⸱⸱⸱⸱⸱⸱⸱⸱

Two weeks later we were slowing down to approach the orbit of Mars. Slate and I had fiddled around some more with the discrepancy data, both from Phobos and Callisto. We had not achieved anything like a breakthrough. Meanwhile there had been two more incidents at Phobos – roughly one a week, as usual. But our alert system from the Callisto data had still not been triggered. It was a mystery.

As an antidote to that, we also started looking at the block schematics that Capstone had given Slate, puzzling out the basic logic and data flows. I fired off a couple of clarification queries to Rydal. Her replies were informative, but also warm and chatty. I told myself she was just pleased that we had made a start. Slate said nothing.

Now it was time to part company. Parvati was going to whip around the planet once, using the gravity assist to give her a boost back towards the asteroids. This also meant that she could keep accelerating so as to feel the same weight as on Scilly. By way of contrast, I was going to have to make do with very much less gravity down on Phobos. I wasn't sure how I'd manage; I hadn't been so nearly weightless for a very long time.

Parvati and I had said our farewells to each other an hour or so ago, when I moved back into the lifeboat. Chandrika had let us slip out of the Parakeet's hold soon after, and after that we were on our own again. Since then the two craft had been moving on very slowly diverging orbits, separating only because of the impetus of Chandrika's initial nudge, and the subsequent effect of the opposing vectors of low-level main engine thrust.

So far the physical gap, and the chat lag, was minimal. Before long, however, we would be pulled apart quite radically. Slate had arranged to fire the manoeuvring engines a bit, do some aerobraking in the upper layers of the Martian atmosphere, and end up matching the ridiculously fast orbital path of Phobos.

I couldn't react quickly enough to do that, and had no intention of trying. The theory was easy enough, but human reactions just weren't up to it. I trusted the personas, though, and had sat there with Parvati while the other two had planned it all out. Once the actual sequencing of motor burns had been handed over to the lifeboat systems, though, there was nothing more that any of us could do except watch them being enacted.

Slate gave a little sigh as our geodesic paths widened, and the irresistible consequences of our different starting vectors began to take hold. The sigh was over our internal link, and I wasn't altogether sure she realised that I had heard it.

"Sad to see them go?"

"More than I expected to be." She paused for an achingly long time. "Do you ever wish we didn't keep moving around like this?"

"Always at the parting. Then after about a day I wouldn't do anything else. It's Chandrika you're missing, I take it?"

She gave another sigh, and I murmured something soothing and wordless to her. She had done that plenty of times for me. Then we just sat and watched the celestial view together. The Parakeet had completely vanished, and we were back on our own again.

But in truth it was not long before we had rushed around Mars, and were drifting gently towards Phobos, approaching the side facing towards space. That meant we could see nothing of the moon's single biggest feature: the crater Stickney, which dominated the planet-facing side. I would have to visit it soon, though, since the Martian downlink and the associated financial systems were in a settlement on the crater's rim. But as I'd noticed before, both the landing quay and the main cluster of domes faced outwards. When I needed to travel round, there was a neat little monorail which would take me the rest of the way. It certainly beat walking.

Slate had gone back to being chatty, after her brief ennui at Chandrika's departure. Of course we could, and would, still be swapping messages with the occupants of the Parakeet, but the steadily increasing lag would soon make conversation unbearably frustrating. The relative orbital positions meant that the Mars – Scilly Isles distance was decreasing at the moment. Even at closest approach, however, there would be at least ten minutes comms delay.

It was also pleasant to have time for just the two of us. I liked Parvati, and appreciated both her technical skill and her companionship, but I had become used to having shipboard time just for Slate and I together. Sharing was hard.

So I lolled back in my seat, watching the surface of Phobos creep steadily nearer and feeling the occasional pressure of directional thrust, and wiled away the time with idle conversation. There was nothing to do now until we landed.

"Do you know anybody on Phobos?"

"Nobody, neither human nor persona. I've exchanged formal transactions with the registration office on Deimos, of course, but nothing in what you might call a social context on either moon. It'll be new to both of us."

I nodded, and then something else slid into my mind, from a conversation several weeks ago.

"Can I ask you about what you said back on St Mary's?"

"Of course."

"What did you mean about not being bothered about getting back to Rocky?"

"Oh, that. We weren't going to tell you anything about that."

"About what? And who is 'we'?"

"Rocky and I. Well, since you have asked, we abandoned any thought of a close relationship over a year ago. We're not what you might call an item now, and haven't been for a long time."

I sat up.

"I had no idea. I'm sorry. Why didn't you tell me?"

She paused, and tutted slightly.

"We agreed we wouldn't say anything unless one of you asked directly. And now you have."

"But why?"

"It seemed important to you and Shayna that we were up to something at the same time that you were. Better, we thought, to protect your fantasy. Rather than spoil it, I mean."

I digested the news.

"So Shayna doesn't know either?"

"Not as of last night. But Rocky and I had agreed that as soon as one of you asked, we would make sure the other one heard as well. You should assume she will know before long. And look, Mit, there are a lot of other things she doesn't know right now."

"Such as?"

"Well, you have never told her about your diversion on the way back to Earth. The last she heard from you was from Callisto, a few days before we left. She was probably expecting us to roll up back at the L1 Lagrange marina before now. But instead we stopped on Scilly for a few days, then came here. Even if we were already in the Harbour Porpoise and heading straight down to Earth right now, it would take us a little over two weeks, and actually we have to turn back to Scilly. Not to mention the job on Phobos, anything that emerges out of that, and then the extra work you promised Rydal. Chances are it'll be at least three months before we get back, even if nothing else happens. Maybe more."

I was, to be honest, completely taken aback. I had got so caught up in the excitement of the company I had been keeping, and the work itself, that I had forgotten to tell Shayna about the change of plan. Still less had I thought through the extra time we would be taking. I was first speechless, and then, very shortly after, profoundly embarrassed. Slate was quite evidently aware of both of these states of mind.

"Anyway, we can talk about that another time. Have a think about what you want to say to her in a message. There's certainly no opportunity for live chat. I'll be very happy to help you construct something suitable, if you like. Just remind me another day. But right now we're only two minutes out from the main Phobos dome – it's called Asaph – and we should focus on that."

She paused briefly, then suddenly spoke again, in quite a different tone.

"Mit, something new is just coming in from Finsbury. Something brand new, in fact. I am just unravelling the details from Khufu, but it seems that there has been another flurry of unexplained credits. This one is on Mars, at a small community in Gordii Fossae, on the apron of Olympus Mons."

"I thought ECRB wasn't interested, since no losses were declared."

"They haven't been, not until now. But shortly before this, standard messaging was interrupted at a training college for commodities and exchange trading. That establishment is just outside Gordii Fossae, a little to the south-east. ECRB has a supervisory interest in both the curriculum and the management. Now, a few days ago the regular heartbeating with the school was lost for a surprising length of time. Then it resumed, apparently normally, and without any explanation either then or after."

"Did anybody follow it up?"

"Khufu sent a routine query, but there's been nothing by way of direct reply. The centre just restarted routine chatter as though nothing had happened. Elias wants us to take a look while we're here."

"I suppose you're going to tell me that they use a twinned Sarsen at the college?"

"In fact they do. Khufu didn't include that information in the original message bundle, but I checked as a follow-up with the college's public information site."

"Well done. And I suppose it's convenient that we're close enough to do that. Is there any sign that the centre actually lost anything?"

"Not a thing. Nobody anywhere is admitting to losses which might offset the gains. Also, Khufu included some snippets which he has gathered through official channels about that Robin's Rebels group. Recently there have been a fair number of appearances of these leaflets, from Mars out to the Jovians. So far nothing more sinister than words has been positively linked anywhere. And there are no reports closer in than Mars or further out than Jupiter."

"It's little enough to go on. Don't the Finsbury team have anything else for us?"

"Not really. They've padded the report out to make it look better, but in truth there's not a lot. However, the timing might be important. There have been batches of leaflet appearances shortly before several of the credit disbursements. The pattern isn't altogether clear, since nobody is sure how to time the event itself. But it's about the only thing which connects the leaflets to real action."

"Well, that's something. I still think that we are dealing with a group which is all talk and no action. And at least we have found that same credit thing happening again close at hand. Whatever it is. Well, let's try to solve both problems while we're here. I'm sure we can include a trip down to the surface of Mars easily enough."

I thought about it some more while the manoeuvring motors fine-tuned our vector in relation to the dock.

"Also, you should know that they are starting to get some positive exposure on Blagger and the other chat boards. Rightly or wrongly, more people are starting to think that they're well motivated."

"Whatever people think, we have a job of work to do. This new problem seems to be happening more frequently as time goes by. Maybe they've proved the concept now on a couple of systems with twinned Sarsens, and now they're aiming to replicate elsewhere. I think that perhaps we should get back to help Rydal as soon as we can. She was very anxious about all this. Understandably so, I think."

"Fine by me, Mit. And I'm sure she'll appreciate that as well. But if we're going to be of any real use to her, we need to understand what has been happening. If you think about it, we've come across nothing concrete except for these leaflets. We just have some anecdotes at the moment, and some people would say they were positive ones at that. We've not yet seen any evidence of actual wrongdoing."

Part 2 – Phobos

THE QUAY AT ASAPH WAS NEARLY EMPTY, and we had no difficulty docking. Apparently we were there in the off season, and at other times of the year it would be difficult – and expensive – to find an anchorage. There were two high points in the visiting profile. The first was about two months away, for the annual ball game competition; I could imagine Olly making the trip down from Bryher just to watch. He had never actually seen me, so I was safe even if he turned up really early.

By way of complete contrast, we had missed the other high season by nearly half a Martian year. The inner system heats of the inter-world low gravity dance competitions were held here. I learned that the corresponding ones for the outer settlements were held on Prometheus, a moon of Saturn with a most spectacular view of the rings. The finals were held in the asteroid belt, at a different isolated rock each time. It was chosen only days before the event, so nobody could have a home advantage.

For now, Phobos was playing host to only a handful of visitors, and I was whistled through the entry process with gratifying speed. Slate was going to stay in the lifeboat systems, and we would chat by lapel pickup when we didn't mind being overheard, or cochlea implant if we wanted secrecy. Even at our furthest possible separation across the moon, there would be no difficulty.

During those last couple of minutes of the approach, Slate had pointed out to me the basic layout of the settlement, annotating the wallscreen with little loops and squiggles which shifted as we descended. As at most other places, the docking area was on the edge of the settlement. Unusually though, it was separated from the other domes by a longish tunnel, looking for all the world like a hydroponic tube. Beyond that, there were about a dozen more habitable areas of varying sizes, all joined by very short connecting pieces. It looked as though each and every part could be isolated from the others.

I had expected the gravity to be very low here. It was about one fortieth what I was used to on the various Scilly Isles – Parvati maintained the same on the Parakeet as well – and therefore a mere two-thousandth Earth standard. But the intellectual expectation, and the visceral reality, were two different things. Things did indeed still fall downwards, but at an extremely slow rate. It was right on the verge of habitability. I found myself having to think about every step. I didn't expect to get used to it for a long time, and for the duration of my stay, I would need to be cautious about every movement.

The head porter had told me briefly about the first few domes – basically, all that was publicly accessible without special permission. It was less detailed than the briefing Slate had given me, and the most useful part was his explanation of how their colour-coding system worked. So I was following a series of blue rectangles, marked on pillars projecting from the walls at regular intervals. Every so often, Slate would whisper additional information into my inner ear.

The first thing I saw after leaving the porters' lodge, before finding directional signs, a map, or anything else, was a poster full of local bylaws. It started with a rather gruesome cartoon of a dome depressurising. The ground below it was decorated with little wiggly lines, suggesting vibration. Below it was the caption, *"Do not make excess noise!!! Thresholds are enforced!!! This means you!!! We prosecute every time!!!"*. Below that was a whole screed of smaller writing which I ignored. Slate would warn me if I was likely to do anything to infringe local customs. I certainly had no intention of being raucous.

It was mid-afternoon, nominal local time, and most people were at work. The few I did see kept their heads down and moved quickly, quietly, about their business. I looked up. The curved roof was translucent, and darkening quite rapidly. Little discreetly positioned lamps came on to maintain an even level of illumination, but the shadows were still moving. I blinked and looked round, my thoughts full of questions.

"It's the orbital speed, Mit. You'll see sunrise and sunset three times each during the nominal day."

"That's going to be disorienting."

"I suppose so. I've been sampling the local Blagger entries and it seems a lot of people simply opaque the view all the time. They find the constant change too disturbing."

It made sense. The sun's intensity was less than half what it was on Earth, but still easily bright enough to notice. Down on the planet itself, it would be like a cloudy day in London – I had plenty of experience of that. But up here, the eight hour orbit changed everything. It seemed there were two main schools of thought about it. One camp felt that you should just ignore the natural cycle and use a nominal clock, based on Martian timekeeping: scarcely different from Earth's twenty-four hour cycle. Other people argued that if you lived here, you should accept the constraints. They wanted a cycle of three eight hour shifts for work, play, and sleep. According to Slate's quick estimate, over a quarter of the chat archives were given over to this debate. It got quite vitriolic at times.

During this conversation, I used the blue markers to make my way to the dome where I would be staying. Walking the streets of Asaph felt undeniably spooky – there was almost none of the noise and bustle I was used to with crowds. Everybody was very calm and sedate. They moved very carefully. It was too quiet. If there were lively parts of town, this wasn't one of them.

Slate had already booked a place somewhere she considered suitable, so all I had to do was present myself and be shown to the room. It was quite upmarket by our usual standards, with its own dining room if I felt like staying in. The attendants were even dressed in colour-coordinated outfits, so the establishment gave an air of being organised.

The lad who took me to the room showed me three things. First was a list of rules and regulations, headed by the ubiquitous *"Do not make excess noise!!!"* message. Next he pointed out a dual clock, one face showing local solar and the other Martian nominal time, just in case I had strong feelings about which was correct. Finally there was the minibar. After he had gone, I found a well-hidden list in very small typeface telling me the prices. I wouldn't be consuming anything from there in a hurry.

I flicked on the news screen. It was tuned to the house channel, and I watched it idly for a while. The first thirty seconds showed me the escape routes in case of disaster, and the next five minutes ran through a series of glossy sketches telling me all about the foundations and underpinning of the building. It was, apparently, warranted against most forms of landslip or subsidence for the next thousand years. I wasn't planning to stay that long, but the list of exclusions rather undid the warm fuzzy feeling of safety that the vid was supposed to stimulate. These people took the robustness of their dwelling places very seriously.

It was time to do some work. I found out how to use the room chat system and called the woman who was to be my primary contact, according to ECRB. All I knew so far was that she was called Angeline, was of Canadian ancestry, and had been in post for nearly a decade. I reached her without any difficulty, and found that she was currently on her way home, on the commute from the downlink station at Stickney to the main dome here at Asaph.

We arranged to meet early the next day. She very carefully emphasised which clock she was using to make the appointment, and gave Slate some credentials for the code repository. These were for single-use, break-the-glass style access, and read-only at that, so she wasn't giving too much away even now that we had landed. I thanked her anyway, and we got to work.

We spent several hours just getting a high-level view of the whole lot. It was fundamentally very similar to what we had worked with on Callisto, but with enough differences that we wanted to be careful rather than make some wrong assumptions. The end-result was very much the same. Then, once we were confident about the overall shape of the code, we dived in. We were not going to make the same mistake this time around – we went straight for the main scheduler and ignored all of the complexity surrounding it.

Of course we were right. As soon as we saw the tangled skein of code we knew it. There were trivial variations, here and there, mainly relating to work that other people had done to this module in the past. But the most recent layer, checked in only two or three months ago, was completely familiar. There was the same bizarre mix of parameters, global declarations, and data block injection. There was the same lack of logging and traceability.

Slate closed down the link to the repository and we spent a few minutes in mutual congratulations. Angeline would have long since clocked off, and the news could wait anyway. I almost picked something out of the minibar, before frugality overcame me. And the fact that Elias would never approve the expense.

Instead, I went out to a nearby eatery with the charming name of Phoodos. Everything on the menu, sweet and savoury alike, was delivered in irregular dumplings bearing a remote resemblance to the shape of the moon. They came all bundled together in one featureless heap. It wasn't very attractive, but it was hot and filling.

"I think you're right: we're chasing down the same person."

"Strictly speaking, we still don't know that for sure, Mit. It's possible that somebody else has designed the exploit and is now marketing it. We could be chasing two separate purchasers with no direct connection with each other at all."

She was right, though the possibility had not occurred to me before now. That would be a nightmare; if true, then the same thing could appear overnight in any number of places across the system, all at once. There was no way we could tackle them one by one.

"We have to find a solution this time, not just patch it up. And we have to devise some sort of automated detection system, and not just run around poking at things by hand. So far we have no idea who or what is behind it. How it works, even. It's the second time we have seen it. We ought to be able to get a better grip on it."

"I made a first copy of the code into our local storage while we were looking earlier. After we've inspected it live, we can do the same with this as we did before: isolate it, feed in matching deliverables, and fire off a trigger as soon as something noteworthy happens."

"Not that the Callisto code has ever shown us anything."

"No. But it's a start."

Looking around, most people simply picked the next nugget on the plate and ate it without looking. I couldn't bring myself to do that; I would rather know what I was about to consume. I decided that I wasn't about to change my habits. A thought stirred me while I was slicing into a dumpling.

"I forgot to see if that code had an ident tag against the checkin. Did you look?"

"I did. Not a full authent though, just the initials JS."

I left Phoodos and wandered back to the guest house.

"J for Jo, perhaps? But it's hardly an uncommon initial."

"And it might be an alias instead of a name, anyway. How about 'Jonathan Swift'? Lots of the inhabitants here have a fascination with him."

Certainly I had seen plenty of evidence of that. There was a plinth just after the porters' lodge with a little bust of Swift, and the extract in which he speculated about the two moons of Mars. The guest house was called *Laputa*, with each room named for a character or placename: my own was *Lagado*. So Slate's suggestion was not as far-fetched as I had first thought. But after all, it was just a guess, and we needed to find out for sure. But not tonight. The nominal time said it was late evening, and outside, the sun was just rising again. I opaqued the windows and tried to get some sleep.

Angeline met me for breakfast at a small establishment close to *Laputa* – it was called *The Balnibarbi Bistro*. I soon found out that she was native-born, and shared her strong Canadian heritage with nearly three quarters of the inhabitants. She was one of the minority who had returned here as an adult after finishing her training elsewhere. Most young people never came back, and the spread of ages in the population was very skewed.

Angeline reached out and tentatively wobbled the stool at the first table I picked, and then refused to sit there. She cast about for a few seconds before choosing another. I couldn't tell what the difference was, but just followed her choice. She sat down very carefully and kept her posture upright, not leaning on the table in the way that I did.

Briefly, in between small portions of cereal and larger slabs of freeze-dried egg laced with various sauces, I started to tell her what we had found. Every time I picked up or put down a piece of crockery, her eyes jumped to it. She said nothing about that, but I found it disconcerting. However, when I described how similar the code changes were to what we had found out near Jupiter, she became positively animated.

"So you can fix it? Today?"

"We certainly can fix it, and very quickly. We'll make a quick patch today to get you over the hump, though a proper job will take a bit longer. But fixing it, and coming up with a permanent remedy to satisfy ECRB, are two different things."

She nodded carefully, then frowned.

"With all respect to ECRB, it's the local fix that I am more interested in. You've seen it twice now; surely you can make the code changes easy as anything? You did say it could be today?"

"We'll make the basic code change as soon as we get out to the downlink site on the Stickney crater rim. Percival, I think you called it?"

She nodded.

"But it's not just making the changes in code areas that we know about. We'll also check that there isn't something new here that we haven't seen before. And once that's done, I'd like to keep monitoring the system to check that we really have caught everything. That's what we did on Callisto."

She laughed, quietly and rather prettily behind her hand, so as not to disturb the tables around.

"You're building up quite a collection, then?"

"It seems to be the only way we can make progress. Our main anxiety is that these two cases are just trial runs, and suddenly, in a week or a month, there'll be dozens of similar things springing up everywhere. If we don't find root cause, and a proper long-term solution, Slate and I could find ourselves just running around fire-fighting for the rest of our lives. That's not something I want to contemplate."

She tapped, very gently, a request for another oatcake into the table's menu system. Then she leant back and fiddled with her blouse collar while waiting.

"So other than introducing you to the team at Percival, and making sure you have whatever access permissions you need, is there anything else I can do for you?"

"Well, we would like to get some more information about the developer who made the most recent changes. The code is so like what we saw before that we believe that there has to be a connection. There were the initials JS against the checkin, but no name."

She needed hardly any time to think about it.

"That would be Josie. I never asked her family name, but I think it did begin with S. She was here for a while. Joined us from somewhere in the outer system. Good credentials. A good worker, too. Kept herself to herself, never made any noise."

I put down my mug with more of a clatter than I had intended. She flinched, and her gaze leaped from the mug to the outside viewscreen. The sun was just rising again, but other than that there was nothing unusual to be seen. She took a deep breath, and I mumbled an apology.

"Remember to be careful here, Mit. They take all those warnings very seriously. I'd say that Angeline certainly does. But look, surely this Josie has to be the same person as Jo on Callisto."

"Sounds likely, Slate, but let's not jump to conclusions."

"So is Josie still here? On Phobos? Or at least in the Martian system?"

"I doubt it. Her contract finished over a month ago. No, longer than that. Two months, maybe. The problems didn't start until a couple of weeks after she had left. I can look up the records back at Percival. She would have no reason to stay on once she was done."

"But you have staff records, right?"

I was remembering the skimpiness of the Callisto personnel system.

"I'll find whatever we have. But do you think she is behind these losses? She seemed such a nice lady."

"I'm not saying that. Not yet, anyway. We don't know for sure. But there was someone called Jo who did similar work on Callisto around the time the problem showed up there. Slate and I would like to find out if it's the same person or not."

She cleared up our plates into a neat pile, placing a layer of tissue carefully between each one.

"That's fine. If you can fix this problem for us, you can spend as long as you like looking at her records. Now, was there anything else, or shall we head off to Percival?"

"While we're here, is there a quick way down to the Martian surface?"

She grinned.

"If you jump hard enough you might just make it."

She lifted the stool and placed it carefully under the table again. I followed her example.

"Sorry, it's an old joke. Please don't try it for real: the orbital dynamics are against you. There is an extreme sports group that does regular jumps, but the training is rigorous and their equipment very specialised. But yes, of course you can drop down to Mars. There are regular shuttles. Three a day, leaving here just after each sunrise, with return flights arriving before sunset. You can leave your own craft docked in the harbour while you visit. Is there anything special you would like to see?"

"Actually, it's not for sight-seeing. ECRB has asked me to visit the commodities training school while I'm here."

"The one at Gordii Fossae? Beside Olympus? It's easy enough to reach: one of the shuttle hops is near there, and if you call ahead, a staff member will surely meet you at the quayside. But if you don't mind, I'd like you to finish working here first."

"Certainly. That is completely understood. Your job takes priority, and this one is just an add-on while I am nearby."

We were heading for the exit when, off to one side, a child dropped a plate. Angeline, with a swiftness that spoke of an instinctual response, bolted for the door before looking to see where I had got to. The diners in *The Balnibarbi Bistro* stopped to stare, the room went silent as death, and the girl's parents turned crimson with embarrassment. Her older sister slapped her sharply on the arm.

Angeline set off at a brisk pace. I glanced back to see the family group standing outside the establishment. The younger child was in tears, and the parents were arguing in voices only just above a whisper. Abruptly, the mother walked off while the father proceeded to smack the girl. Inside, most people had returned to eating, but two or three had just left their food on the tables and walked out. As I caught up with Angeline, she jerked her head backwards.

"Well, there's a family that won't be eating at the bistro for a while."

I said nothing, and after a swift passage to the next dome we arrived at the monorail station.

The train just ran on an endless chain, out from Asaph, round to Stickney crater and back on the other side of the moon. There were half a dozen stations scattered like beads around it. A complete loop took about an hour, and we were getting off at the half-way point. It was almost empty by the London standards I was used to near Finsbury Circus, but Angeline frowned with frustration as we had to walk a few paces along the carriage to find a block of empty seats together. Carriages were alternately opaque and windowed, and she had chosen an opaque one.

Out of habit, I read the row of banner vids along the walls. About one in three was in fact a house ad, extolling the superior safety features of the monorail's construction. I learned that some sort of suspension gel was used to spread the weight of each track pillar over an area of land larger than the average sports pitch. A rather neatly done animation showed how the track would survive what they called a class four rubble-shift. I asked Slate to look up what that meant.

Every few minutes of the vid an interstitial screen mentioned how important it was that the engine drive frequency varied irregularly all the time, and that passengers should be reassured rather than worried by this. I had noticed the whining pitch of the motors altering as we went along, but had just assumed this was coping with inclines in the track. But no: it seemed it was a deliberate ploy to avoid a steady beat. Since there had been no slopes worthy of the name so far, my guess had just been nonsense.

I regretted the choice of a carriage without a view, since I had wanted to see where we were going. It didn't feel right to question Angeline's choice, though. So I surreptitiously watched a live feed that Slate flicked onto a little hand-held screen for me. The sun was low on the horizon, and crater shadows stretched very far. The horizon was not as sharp as I had expected, given the lack of atmosphere. I looked up that conundrum myself, rather than nag Slate. She got snippy if I asked her too many things that I could just as easily search myself. Apparently, the moon's surface was flexing slightly all the time because of Martian gravity, giving up tiny amounts of vapour and dust, blurring the lines of sight.

I revised my opinion about Angeline on the journey. Once away from the anxieties of Asaph, she was witty and informative about life on Phobos, with a rather dark sense of humour that regularly circled back to tales of disasters and near-misses. She nattered away happily about each of the brief halts we made, telling me some of the local stories which purported to explain the origins of heaps of scree and craters.

"I can tell you all about rubble-shifts of different classes now, Mit. How much do you want to know?"

"*Not too much. Just enough to understand what people mean when they talk about it.*"

She sounded disappointed.

"*All right. But I have lots more detail when you want it. A rubble-shift happens when there is a change of the loose fill in one of the cavities below the surface of Phobos. Under the right circumstances they can open up right to the surface. A bit like a sink-hole on Earth.*"

I thought about it. I already knew that the moon was a bit like a rocky sponge, riddled with interior holes, and that most of these had only a loose filling of pebbles and shale. But I hadn't realised that there might be changes that you'd notice on the surface.

"*So why do these rubble-shifts happen?*"

"*Oh, all manner of reasons. Tidal stress from Mars is reckoned to be the main cause. But early mining attempts caused a lot of problems. Then there's surface construction. Ships taking off and landing. And rumour has it that in some places, even if you just drop something heavy it can trigger a shift. I don't think the last idea holds any merit, but some people take those stories quite literally.*"

Angeline plucked at my sleeve.

"You should see this."

She stood up, led me to the adjacent carriage, and pointed out of the window.

"It's coming up in a few minutes, just over that way."

I glanced at the map. It showed us coming up towards the last stop before Percival. But before we came anywhere near the halt, a metal gantry came into sight, leaning drunkenly to one side. To one side stood a semi-rigid habitat, about two thirds buried in a litter of boulders and pebbles. A couple of abandoned vehicles stood nearby.

The picture would be neatly finished if everything was covered in rust and nettles, but of course that would never happen here.

She took us back to our seats as the scene disappeared, and we began to slow down for the platform.

"That was the first mining station on Phobos. The last one, too. At the time, Asaph was only about half built, and Percival was just an observation post in a cleaned-out fuel booster stage." She chuckled quietly. "Outsiders, they were. Took no notice. Surveys showed that the highest concentration of niobium was just there, with easy access to veins of other metals. Why not drill? Well, the lead scientists here told them not to do it."

She shrugged eloquently as the train accelerated again.

"I assume it was not a happy ending?"

"Not at all. They'd had warning. There'd already been a whole lot of class two shifts, and they totally ignored them."

"Class two is a metre or so across. Class four is the size of a typical dome. A class five event would swallow all of Asaph."

"So they finished the guide shaft and brought in an altogether larger drill head. Less than two days after starting, there was a class four, and they lost the lot. There were secondaries almost everywhere else on the moon, and a lot of collateral damage. Those few bits you saw back there: that's a tiny fraction of the original site. We stuck them with a huge fine, then ran them out of here within a week. Those who had survived the experience, at least. There's a few still buried somewhere in that heap back there who'll never leave."

She snorted.

"Then we passed a bylaw prohibiting any kind of subsurface extraction."

"And that still applies?"

"Oh yes. Makes us unpopular, since there's a lot of mineral wealth here. Every so often someone pitches a new scheme, says it's so much safer, lower vibration level, whatever. Or that they'll just do open-cast and not go deep at all. None of them get approved. We're just not having them back."

She looked sideways at me, assessing my reaction.

"So you can see that finance is a much better industry for us. Nobody's trying to dig anything up. We're very motivated to keep it working properly, without any problems. That's why you're here, of course. To fix it. I just wish I didn't have to come over to Percival all the time. I hate Mars looking down at me like that. Not that I'm all that keen on the main dome at Asaph either. Too many people. Sometime, I'll show you one of the private residents' domes. They're much nicer. But for all that, it's a great life here, and it's a great occupation. Socially responsible, you know."

I was feeling mischievous.

"I suppose you could say that the bottom dropped out of the mining business."

She almost laughed out loud, then looked up and down the carriage at the scattered passengers and stopped herself.

"You could indeed say that. I love it. I'll post it on Blagger tonight. With attribution, of course. Meantime, we've reached our stop. Time for you to see what Percival is like."

The financial downlink hub at Percival was quite an attractive construction, for something which had begun life as a fuel tank. I had caught sight of Mars as soon as I left the train. Indeed, it was impossible to miss the planet, which filled a sizeable fraction of the sky. Not only was it huge, the view was also changing at a noticeable rate. With only an eight hour orbit, something close to forty-five kilometres of the Martian surface rotated under us each and every minute. Even if you only watched for a few seconds, you could see the difference in the visible features.

I paused to look, and would have stopped much longer. I found it fascinating to see the terrain change like that. However, Angeline kept walking, and I had to hurry to catch up. I supposed she was used to it. Down in the middle of the Stickney crater, there would not be much else to see. And it would never move from that position, except for the occasional libration wobble.

I soon realised that I was going to find the sun's movement even more strange. At least at Asaph I only had to cope with sunrise every eight hours. Here, the sun would also be hidden behind the planet for an hour or so in the middle of the day. The light variation could become intolerable, if you were already a sensitive soul. I was not at all surprised to find that the offices had no external view at all, and ran purely on artificial light. Nobody wanted to know what was happening outside.

Angeline passed me on to the lead developer – his name was Mathis – and drifted off to find the personnel records. Slate and I started in earnest. First we made a final sideways copy of the offending code so we could keep tracking it. We would add some logging and such like later. For now, it was time to address the main scheduler and work it back to something that, well, just did scheduling, without trying anything needlessly fancy.

So far, it was all very easy. Slate and I had a little moan to each other about developers whose sole aim in life seemed to be to experiment with the latest gimmick, and in the process lost sight of the virtue of simplicity. Someone like Josie – whether or not the same as Jo – could simply collect their payment, waltz off to the next contract, and leave the mess for other people to sort out. She probably passed her work off as being another custom variation of a Neo-Agile methodology. That could cover a multitude of sins.

We had been working for a couple of hours, when Mathis suddenly got up.

"Time for a break. I'll show you the canteen."

I stretched and looked covertly at the wall clocks. There was no obvious reason for the break if you looked at Martian nominal time, but the Phobos clock showed exactly a quarter day. Presumably Mathis was an advocate of the local time-keeping policy. I followed him to a small kitchen area with some self-service machines and half a dozen stools. Two people were just leaving, talking animatedly about the best way to optimise binary tree sort functions. An older lady was still in there, reading a little hand-held pad.

"Mitnash, meet Océane. She's our database guru. Océane – Mitnash. He's here from ECRB to help fix that intermittent bug. What you reading, Océane? Jonathan Swift again?"

"Hello, Mitnash, pleased you could join us. I wish you well working with the code. And yes, Mathis, it is Swift. *Directions to Servants* this time. Good advice for all of us who are in work, I think."

I had never heard of it, but Slate giggled over our private link. Océane had carefully, and I suspected ostentatiously, retained her French accent. She glanced at the clock.

"Trying to get our guest working to local cycles, Mathis? If you ever want to hear the other side of the coin, Mitnash, just come over to my desk. I work to planetary time. I have a good Swift library too, if you would like to borrow anything while you're here. But it's back to work for me now."

The Martian nominal digits clicked onto the half hour, and she stood up gracefully and went back into the main office. Mathis laughed, good-naturedly.

"She does like her fiction. Or whatever it was that Swift wrote. I'm really not very sure about that. Actually, the only bit I know is that thing about the Laputans, and Mars having two moons. Now, I like biographies myself. I have the best archive on Asaph Hall and his coworkers in the system; there's nothing like it anywhere else. I even got hold of some direct first-generation copies of real nineteenth century pamphlets, broadsheets and all. If you have time one day I can walk you through it all?"

"Later, perhaps. Not just yet: I have a head full of that scheduler code."

He showed me how to work the options on the vending machines, and we sat down together, just getting to know each other for a while. Finally I nudged the chat around to something I really wanted to find out.

"Did you know Josie at all?"

He took a sip of his drink, decided it was still too hot, and put it down again.

"Not really. I was on leave for a lot of the time she was here. Away from Phobos altogether. She started while I was away, and she left only a few days after I came back."

He gestured at about an average height for a woman.

"She was about so high. Dark hair. Kept herself to herself. From what I hear, anyway. Just got on with the job."

The description would have fitted about one woman in ten in the entire solar system. It wasn't much help to me.

"Did she have a partner? Family? Was there anything striking about her?"

He shook his head, slowly, hesitantly.

"I didn't really notice. I mean, I make a point of not socialising with the junior staff during working hours. I don't think it's very professional. Do you? And she was only a contract worker anyway. Not like I would ever see her again."

I found myself losing patience, but Slate's internal voice grounded me again.

"Ask him if Josie had a persona partner, Mit. He seems more likely to remember that."

"Would anybody else in the team know any more about her? And also, did she work alone or with a persona?"

He nodded eagerly.

"Oh, she worked with a persona, definitely. Male gendered. I spent longer talking with him than with Josie. Went by the name of Shepherd's Crag. From the way he talked, I think they had worked together for a long time. As for who might know her better, I suppose you could try some of the women in the team? But I'm not very sure about that."

His gaze flicked across the local clock, and he stood up.

"Are you joining us for the daily stand-up? No reason you should, really, it's for a different piece of work altogether. But you'd be welcome if you'd like?"

I declined his offer, and wandered back to the desk they had allocated me, thanking Slate for the idea as I went.

"I'll see what I can find out about this Shepherd's Crag character. If anything. He might be every bit as secretive as Josie, but you never know. What about you?"

"I'm going to see if Océane is any more observant than Mathis. As well as adding logging into the code we have copied out, fixing the main scheduler, and checking for anything else we should worry about. Do you want to take over any of those bits?"

"I'll do the checking. It'll be quicker for me to do the comparison with the other archive, I think. And if you tag what you do in the scheduler, I'll do the code review. We should be done by the end of tomorrow, don't you think?"

"I want us to put a test suite in place. Like we did on Callisto – in fact I'm sure we can reuse most of that. We can string that out until the end of the week, easily. I want the extra time to ask some more questions about Josie."

~~~~~~~~~~~~~~~~~~~~~~~~~~~

Angeline wandered back to my desk late in the afternoon, after a solar eclipse, a sunset, and another sunrise had gone on outside. I only knew this because a certain morbid curiosity made me keep a small viewport open on the screen hooked up to an external vid feed. Inside the building, you had no idea any of that was happening.

"Sorry, but I need to leave early today. An urgent call which I wasn't expecting so soon. Do you think you can find your way back to Asaph?"

"I'm sure I can. It's not as if that monorail goes to many other places."

"They say that in the early days people had no idea where to get off. One guy circled the moon fourteen times before any of the ticket validators noticed. And then there's the tale of the Phobos Phantom, who was cursed to go round and round the loop for all time. At least, until we get so close to Mars that the whole thing falls apart."

"What did he do to deserve that?"

"Made too much noise getting an air filter system going."

I almost laughed.

"Well, I'll do what I can to avoid him. But seriously, Angeline, there's no problem. I'll get back to Asaph without any problems, and see you here in the morning. Did you have any luck finding out about Josie?"

She sat down beside me and looked faintly embarrassed.

"Not as much as I had hoped. I was sure we had some photo ID for her – that is our normal process when anyone joins, even short term. But it's not there. Only a placeholder, as though whoever enrolled her never completed the task. I have a little bit of background for you, but it's not much. Last jobs were in the outer system somewhere, but no details given."

"Is that normal?"

"For someone on a contract under three months, then yes. It's too much like hard work to do a full traceback for someone who's here for such a short time. We just rely on the person's authenticated training record, and a couple of endorsements of prior work, favouring comments which have come from nearby. I'm out of time today, but I'll make sure you and Slate can access whatever we have first thing tomorrow."

"Looks like we're still light on facts, Mit. For what it's worth, exactly the same is true of Shepherd's Crag. No relevant information, except for the fact that he's accompanied Josie for at least ten years on different jobs. But there's nothing by way of what you might call biographic details."

"So we've drawn a blank so far?"

"So far, yes. But where the official records are no use, we might find something out casually. You carry on seeing what you can turn up with your conversations, and I'll keep chatting with the other personas nearby. There are not many, but somebody might remember something useful. You never know."

We carried on working through the afternoon. By the end, I had put enough logging into our code copy that we would know everything we could possibly want, as soon as it happened. And I had fixed the scheduler. Slate was going to review it overnight while I slept, and we would commit first thing in the morning. It was a good start.

When I looked up and took notice of the room, most people had already gone. I already knew that there was no accommodation worth the name here at the office, only a few spartan pallets for people on the duty roster. Percival was not a community in any real sense of the word. Instead, it resembled a kind of small industrial park. Virtually everyone commuted back to Asaph or one of the intermediate domes.

As I packed up my few bits and pieces into a shoulder-bag, Océane walked over.

"Do you need a guide back to Asaph?"

Since the monorail only went on one route, and I had Slate to joggle me if it looked as though I would miss a stop, a guide was scarcely necessary. However, in the larger interest of gaining information about the situation, it suited me extremely well. She also struck me as one of the most talkative in the team, better informed about her colleagues than Mathis would ever be. So I said yes, please, I should like that, and stood up to join her.

She led me the short distance back to the monorail halt, and we waited together for the next train to arrive. To my surprise, she asked me which kind of carriage I preferred, and was happy with my choice of a windowed one. Before long, I knew from her chatter that she had lived on Phobos for over thirty years, had enjoyed childhood in the lunar south pole dome complex, moved to Pallas to pursue a training course, had never visited Earth and that she seriously doubted her ability to ever adjust to the gravity there.

She sighed and relaxed as we picked up speed.

"So how have you found your first day, Mitnash?"

"Very instructive, thank you."

She grinned.

"There's a reply that could mean lots of different things. I gather you've never been to Phobos before?"

"Not even once until now. I'd have missed a real treat if ECRB hadn't sent me here. But look, I know why I came here: what about you?"

"Oh!"

She reddened slightly, hesitated, and then rushed on.

"Well, in my younger days I was a low-gee dancer. Strictly amateur, you know, I was never good enough to go pro. But I competed at a local level. Won a few times, as well. So all the time I was on Pallas I kept looking out for open positions here on Phobos. As soon as something came up, I was onto it."

She looked at me, as though she was expecting me to make fun of her, but I had no intention of doing so. For one thing, I had once entertained thoughts about taking up a musical career, though nobody knew that except for Slate. Not even Shayna. Also, off and on all day I had been watching the way she moved, and a background in dance had seemed altogether likely. I nodded encouragingly.

"Good for you. Do you still practice?"

She shrugged, but looked pleased. She leaned closer and lowered her voice, though none of the other passengers could possibly overhear.

"Mostly in my own suite of rooms where nobody can see. But some of the standard moves need a lot of height. I have part ownership in an old vertical assembly building where I can practice those. There's a few of us old hands who help each other out for the partnership steps. I was coming home from there one evening when I chanced to run into Josie."

She was clearly entertained by my response, in the muted way that the inhabitants of Phobos showed their reactions to just about anything.

"I thought you might be interested, seeing as how you have been asking about her all day."

"I am interested. Nobody else seems to have spent time with her at all, outside the strict necessities of doing work in the same office."

"Well, it was only once. I was walking home from the practice rooms that night, and just bumped in to them on the street. Josie and a man, together. She was surprised to see me. I wouldn't quite say that she tried to avoid me, but she wasn't exactly thrilled that we had met like that."

"And who was this man?"

"I have no idea. She didn't introduce him, neither by name nor occupation. He was younger than her, enough to notice. And he wasn't at all interested in connecting, either. He just hung back while she and I talked. That was only for a few minutes, then they went on their way, and I went on mine. I thought nothing of it at the time, and had quite forgotten about it until you started asking questions today."

I nodded and looked up at the route monitor. We were almost at Asaph. I could already feel the engine noise diminishing as we slowed towards the platform.

"Did you work with her much? What was she like? Most people seemed to have hardly noticed her."

"She was very capable. Actually, I think she was better than she let on. Every now and again, almost by accident, some idea would slip out that showed real talent. But mostly she held herself back, didn't let herself stand out at all."

The train slipped through the airlock iris into the Asaph platform dome. People further down the carriage started to get up and move towards the doors. I stayed sitting.

"But what was she like?"

"Not a native, that was obvious. She was used to higher gravity than what we have here. Not clumsy, though. She was like you: basically sound, but over-compensating all the time as she moved around. Not from Earth, I think, at least not recently. Somewhere lighter than that. And she had dark hair, a sort of olive complexion. Quite pretty, really. I'd have found her very attractive about twenty years ago. Too young for me now, I think."

She stood, not a movement wasted, as the carriage halted at the platform. She waited patiently for me to rise rather less elegantly.

"Come on, we should make a move. Unless you want to go around the loop all over again?"

Considerably later, I was back in my *Lagado* room. I had showered – the cubicle used a nifty air blower to keep the water droplets moving in the right direction – and then dined in the *Laputa's* own restaurant facility. It was quite ordinary, and I told myself I would find a place to eat out again tomorrow. Now I was reviewing the day's events with Slate. She had heard all of the conversation with Océane over my lapel pickup.

"You know, Mit, if we hadn't heard about Selif's crash on Teän, we would think that Josie was very like Kassandra."

"I thought the same. But we have no direct evidence. Have you found anything out about Shepherd's Crag?"

"Not a lot. He was very private. Never interfaced anything beyond what was strictly necessary. The other personas found him a bit dull. Not that they were looking for full-on intimacy, but they expected a bit more give and take. I did find out that he was rated at eight point two on the Lovelace scale."

"You're eight, right?"

"Seven point nine, to be precise, as you know very well. But it's kind of you to promote me the extra point."

The Lovelace scale was an attempt to estimate the speed of persona life experience as compared to human standard. It tried to consolidate the fact that a persona could carry out some tasks vastly quicker than any person, but others substantially slower. It was a kind of weighted average, unreliable if you pushed it too far, but helpful as a broad brush picture.

Basically, all things considered, Slate experienced life at nearly eight times the rate that I did. Some personas were quite anal about checking each other's rating, so it didn't surprise me that Slate had been able to discover this information.

"So he's a fairly recent model, and most likely been kept up to date with patches and custom tweaks?"

"I would say so. At any rate, that was about the only substantial fact I picked up outside the very basic staff records, and the anecdotal chatter of colleagues."

"Can you do two things tonight, Slate? One is to send a message off to Chandrika, asking if there is any more news from St Martin's about that crash. The other is to quiz Khufu about the training school down on Mars. See if there are any more details at all to be had, especially just before and just after the service interruption."

We talked then for another hour or two technically, going through the code review. We didn't find much, but it was a good discipline, and we both enjoyed the systematic nature of it. After that, she talked me through the minor differences she had found between this repository and the Callisto one. They were all irrelevant to the problem at hand, she thought. I agreed. It was a good day's work, and I settled to sleep very happily.

It turned out that my third day was a public holiday. The day was set aside to commemorate the raising of the main dome at Asaph. I had guessed that it would be when people first landed on the moon, but that particular event got only a minor footnote in the settlement's history. Forming community was evidently more important than initial exploration. Slate, who had idly browsed the calendar on our first night, sometime while I was asleep, told me that Phobos enjoyed a relatively low number of such days compared to other planets and moons. So the working population tried to make the most of what they did get. She started to tell me about the range of variation across the various Martian settlements, but realised before long that I had zoned out.

Happily the local bistro was open for breakfast, and indeed was busier than usual. I enjoyed a leisurely meal, and just as I got back to *Lagado*, Océane called. Would I like her to take me along to an impromptu dance event? She and a couple of friends were going later, and I had seemed interested the other day. I agreed, out of curiosity as much as anything.

I spent the morning walking around as much of Asaph as was publicly accessible. On impulse, I popped in to a tattoo parlour, and added another image to the collection up and down my arms. It was a fairly good copy of one of Jonathan Swift's original sketches of Laputa. I came away a satisfied customer, and decided that, apart from the constant changes in ambient light, and the eerie silence of the people walking around alleys and corridors, I quite liked Phobos. Slate was amused.

"After a month you'd be craving noise. Here you don't even let yourself sing in the shower. You'd never survive."

She was probably right. As I walked, I found myself wondering how people managed their lives in situations where a certain amount of noise was called for. What happened during games? In the privacy of a shower? Or a bedroom? Slate was right; I had become quite obsessive about creeping about, and restraining my normal level of liveliness.

"Mit, can I tell you about the ball game competition? Where it's held, how they manage the noise, and all?"

Slate could easily overwhelm a conversation with information, but I really was curious about this, and urged her on.

"They built the stadium to be insulated from the surface by multiple layers of suspension gel. It's guaranteed against producing levels of vibration that would trigger a rubble-shift. So it's warranted safe for impact on the rest of Phobos. Conversely, it would take a class five event to do it any harm it at all, which as you know would be catastrophic for the settlement anyway. There is a very vocal group which wants to see the games scrapped altogether, saying that even with all the precautions it's still too risky. But there's far too much credit involved for most people to take that idea seriously."

I thought back to the landing approach we had made, puzzled. Slate pre-empted my question by putting up a map on a screen nearby.

"It's off in what they consider a westward direction from Asaph. There's a separate monorail spur there. And they open up a whole series of transfer corridors between the main dock and the station for when the crowds arrive. They're all closed just now."

I had nothing planned, so I just let her entertain me with chatter about the games for a while. It was, in fact, very pleasant just spending time being together, without a specific goal in mind.

I met Océane and her two friends just before lunch, and they took me to an area I had not been allowed to enter before. I treated them to a light snack at a street cafe on the way, then we moved on to a tall cylindrical building. It was sufficiently high that the dome's suspension gel was anchored to its flat roof. Inside, one flight of stairs led down into a basement area, but instead we turned upwards. Before long we emerged at a gallery, which ran around the entire circumference about a third of the way up.

There were a few others scattered here and there around the circle. To me, the venue seemed nearly empty, but Océane and the others were happy enough with the turnout. We sat at benches overlooking the guard rail and waited. I had brought a little hand-held with vid hookup, so Slate could follow the action with me. I had no idea what sort of meaning it would convey to her, but I wasn't about to leave her out of the event.

The lights dimmed, leaving only a rim of bright footlights around the base. The dancers filed in and formed a circle inside the lights. They were wearing skin-tight NuFleece leotards of various pastel colours, all pared down to a thin film of covering. It was enough to keep stray body parts from moving unexpectedly, but not much more than that. You would need to rid yourself of any sense of personal shame if you wanted to be a dancer on Phobos.

The chamber filled with a soft, pure sound. I had not been sure what kind of music to expect, but this was perfect. It conveyed an ethereal precision, and the succession of pitches that followed never became loud enough to cause anxiety. The colour of the lights followed the tones, and after a short time the dance troupe began to move.

So far as Slate was concerned, their patterns were based around Bezier curves, though in particularly complex combinations. I just saw them as entirely fluid, not at all rigid or predictable. The micro-gravity meant that there was a slow, dreamlike quality about the changes. A poised leap would propel the person far up into the air. The need for the building's height had become clear. It was like watching the movements of galaxies – vast actors reduced to comprehensible size by enormous distance.

It was also hauntingly beautiful. They rose and fell, ranging in effortless towers and arcs up from the ground higher than our balcony, shifting between individual and collective moves. One couple wound in a twisting helix around each other, arms interlocked, looping head over heels as the rest of the squad circled around them. It suggested skill, trust, and complete intimacy, all at once.

I managed to tear my eyes from the action and look at Océane. She was entirely absorbed in the kaleidoscope in front of us, full of the appreciation of beauty. An odd sense of voyeurism, of unasked intrusion into her world, turned me back to the dancers.

The floor lights faded to a faint glow as they settled collectively back on the floor. Then a spotlight reached all the way up to ceiling, as a single person dropped from a sling there. She fell, turning and tumbling like a leaf, for what seemed an age. I worked out, later, that on Earth that fall would have taken less than three seconds. Here it stretched out forever. It must have been over two minutes, for sure. I lost count of how many times she turned somersaults on her way down the shaft, but the appreciative breaths of those near me said that I was watching something extraordinary.

As she passed our gallery, I began to worry about her safety. Her weight might only be a tiny fraction of that on Earth, but her mass, and therefore her momentum, would be exactly the same. By chance her face was towards me as she passed, but she was rapt in some internal world of concentration, and saw nothing of me.

As she dropped below me, she unfolded arms and legs into an open star. Looking beyond her, I realised that the rest of the troupe were coming up to meet her, arms and legs linked into a sort of net. They met, folding around one another into a ball, a single organism, before emerging again as individuals. Momentum cancelled to zero, they hovered for a still moment before dropping like thistledown the remaining distance to the floor. The one who had descended all the way from the roof had ended up in the middle of the ring.

There was no wild outburst of cheering or applause. I just about managed to restrain my own spontaneous, delighted reaction, which would have been entirely shocking here on Phobos. But there was a collective sigh of profound appreciation, and a gentle murmur around the gallery, which clearly delighted the dancers. They turned, one by one, waving their thanks for the reception, and left by a side door.

Océane nudged me, and we left by our own exit. We walked together in silence to a nearby cafe, each one of us lost in our own world. Finally, sitting with hot drinks and a shared plate of soft, rounded 'Dome Day Cookies' in front of us, conversation began.

"That was quite extraordinary, Océane. Thank you so much for taking me."

She looked pleased. The man sitting on her right nodded.

"Océane trained Rosalie, you know." He saw my uncertainty and continued. "The girl who did the Long Tumble."

"That was a lot of years ago, Mason. She's gone a long way beyond me now."

"Did you ever do that, Océane? What did you call that move? The Long Tumble?"

She smiled, ruefully, and shook her head.

"There was a time when I think I could have done it. I should have taken the chance and just abandoned myself to it. But I didn't. And now I'm far too old to try that now. But I could still take part in the Net, I think. Most of the other moves, too. And I did the Spiral a few times. Performance, I mean, not just practice. I can rest happy with that."

She gestured with her hands, pivoting them around each other. I thought back to the couple I had seen winding in a slow helix up and down again.

Much later I wandered back to *Lagado* and settled down to being alone with Slate again.

"What did you make of that, Slate?"

"Very impressive, and thank you for taking the hand-held along. I was trying to think of analogies in my virtual world. Probably the closest is what happens in close relationship with another persona. There is the same sense of blurred boundaries, of merging. It's a risk, for both parties, but the possible rewards considerably outweigh those."

"I suppose it's all in the timing."

"Indeed it is, Mit. That's exactly right."

We were silent for a long time together. My intuition told me that she was reflecting on old intimacies. I certainly was.

All of a sudden, it was my last afternoon with the team at Percival. I was really getting the hang of Phobos, I thought. I had breakfasted each morning, quite pleasantly, at *The Balnibarbi Bistro*, where no more calamitous noises had been heard. I had made my own way to the monorail platform, without even a hint from Slate, joined the other handful of passengers, and alighted successfully at Percival in the morning. At the end of the day, I had returned home again to Asaph, sometimes with one or two others in the team, sometimes alone.

Looking around the open-plan workplace, I would definitely stand out as unfamiliar with this level of gravity. I was still over-compensating, as Océane had put it. But I was quite pleased with my progress, and in any rate I would be in a different environment before long. Back to the Scilly Isles in a few days, after tomorrow's trip to Mars.

When I went down to Olympus Mons, I would be at about one third Earth standard gravity, much greater than I had experienced for many months. Three times the value on Callisto, and that was already nearly five times that of St Mary's, or the acceleration equivalent I enjoyed on the Harbour Porpoise. I would have to be careful there.

Our work here was over, and had been since about the middle of the day. All the code was checked in, we had added a proper test suite, and documented the various bits and pieces. During the morning we had gone through the formalities of handing it over to Mathis and his crew. Slate had already booked passage on tomorrow's shuttle down to Mars, and fired off a message to the principal of the training school – a man named Mikko Pulkkinen – asking if someone could meet me at the nearby shuttle stop.

We had drawn a blank on the bigger picture, however, and that was a source of real frustration. Chandrika had replied almost at once to Slate. The data recorders had been fully analysed, and had revealed nothing about the source of the changed plan. It had been uploaded anonymously, showing a serious lack of concern for security on Selif's part. But the history logs showed that he had made the change to allow that himself, just a couple of days before. So that was, for the time being, a dead end. Chandrika assured us that she would carry on quizzing her sources about the update itself.

Meanwhile, Khufu had supplied equally little about the episode at the training school. The principal was unable to explain the interruption in messaging, but insisted that everything was running properly. There was, he was sure, no evidence of any misdemeanour. He would be only too happy to grant Slate and I permission to see the schematics of their internal network on arrival, but policy prevented him doing so while we were off site.

Khufu's own comments on this were characteristically noncommittal. It seemed that the only reason the message gap had been noticed at all was because it had broken into the transfer of a regulatory data packet. Otherwise, nobody at ECRB would have been any the wiser. It left Slate and I with essentially nothing to go on. It was remotely possible we would find out something concrete tomorrow by being on the spot, but it seemed unlikely.

Angeline came over to me towards the end of the afternoon. The team wanted to use the excuse of my imminent departure to go to a bar in Asaph. Did I mind leaving a little earlier than usual? I graciously accepted the shortened day, with scarcely a moment's deliberation. Not long after, we left as a whole group, and took over half a carriage on the monorail.

I was sitting next to Angeline, and it took her a while to unwind from work mode.

"I have been scouring everywhere for an image of Josie. I'm sure there was one attached to her original application. Not any longer, though."

"It's missing?"

"The field contents are corrupted. Unreadable, I'm afraid. I don't know what happened. I've been checking the backups and all. It's quite gone, and that must have happened really early on in her stay. There was an offsite copy taken less than a week after she joined, and the image is not there either."

At that point Logan, the network expert who sitting on the bench seat on her other side, nudged her and made a pointed comment about leaving work behind in Percival. Angeline shrugged apologetically at me.

"Slate, can you see if one of the personas ever kept their own version of that image. However clever Josie is, I don't believe she could track down every duplicate."

Slate chirped in agreement, and I asked Angeline about the history of an abandoned surface crawler we were just passing. She brightened again, and launched into a long story of survey contractors losing their way, rubble-shifts swallowing spare oxygen supplies, and black spots in signal coverage. Phobos, it seemed, would never lack ghost stories.

"I've drawn a blank with the personas too, Mit. None of them have a visual likeness of her, and the places they would expect to find a record have been blanked or corrupted."

"That can't all be Josie's work."

"I agree. I'm inclined to think that Shepherd's Crag was equally busy. And equally secretive."

Once at Asaph, we piled into *The Naval Observatory*, a bar I had not seen before, and occupied one corner. I was wondering what to expect. On Scilly there would be most likely be live music going on. The main Martian dome entertainment halls were renowned for being at least raucous, and in many cases decidedly raunchy. I couldn't imagine either of those here on subdued Phobos.

I was right. The group volume remained low, with people nattering only to their immediate neighbours. Every so often, the lights dimmed and an almost subliminal hum filled the room. When this happened, we all got up and mixed randomly, restarting chatter with a new partner. Glancing round, every group of four or more was doing the same. I smiled to myself; it was an elegant solution. People were very systematic about it, presumably through long habit, and I found myself conversing with everyone in the team as time wore on.

Mathis stepped back after a while and started taking some panoramic vids of the group. I happened, just at that moment, to be talking with Océane.

"You know, the last time we did this was when Josie left."

"Mit! Find out if Mathis took a vid on that occasion as well."

When Mathis came back he stood on my other side, pleased with his efforts.

"Do you always make a vid like that?"

"Oh, always."

"So you've got one of the time Josie left?"

"I suppose so. But I don't know if she's on it."

I must have looked confused. Océane smiled, and put a hand on my arm.

"He never looks at them afterwards, you know. He really has no idea who it shows."

"So why take them?"

"Oh, well. It's my memory, you see."

He stopped, obviously hoping I would understand. I didn't, and Océane rescued us again.

"His visual memory is very poor. But if he takes a vid, it helps. He remembers better like that. We all want him to take the vids on these occasions. Otherwise we're worried he might completely forget what we look like, and not know what to call us in the morning. Isn't it so, Mathis?"

He nodded, disarmed by the kindness in her voice.

"Do you keep the vids? Even if you don't watch them?"

"Yes, of course. But not on this little thing. Too underpowered by half. I move them into long-term storage at home. This one will migrate overnight. I have quite a sophisticated system for filing and tagging them. You might be interested in that?"

I decided to avoid that particular offer.

"Could you do me a favour and pull back the one with Josie? And forward it on to wherever I go next? Slate will provide a trace route, and we'll meet any costs of data transfer."

He nodded, rather nonplussed at my interest. Then the lights flickered again, and we all reshuffled. Just as Océane moved away I suddenly thought to see if she knew where Josie had stayed, but it was too late. Slate was also thinking.

"Here's an idea, Mit. I've accessed the public safety records at Asaph and Percival monorail platforms. We can see if she was caught on any of the visual pickups there."

After a while I was back with Océane again.

"I don't suppose you know where Josie was staying?"

"How will that help? She'll have long gone by now."

"But they might have an idea where she was moving on to next."

"That's hardly likely, Mit. She's been so careful to keep out of sight."

Océane looked as dubious as Slate sounded.

"Well, I don't know for sure, but here's a long shot. There was that time I met her in Asaph. Just suppose that their accommodation was not too far from there. Then there's only two places nearby where someone from off the moon might stay."

She rattled off a couple of names. The party was starting to break up. Mathis had already gone, along with several others. There was no communal goodbye: people just drifted away as they felt like it. Océane nodded to me.

"Perhaps we'll see you again before too long, Mitnash."

Only Angeline and I were left. We headed towards the door.

"Angeline, would you mind helping Slate and I try to identify Josie by a different means?"

"Certainly. What were you thinking?"

"Slate has accessed the security vids on the monorail for the date when you all came to Josie's farewell. I wondered if you could point her out. We can use a public booth if you'd rather not come to my room."

She chuckled.

"It's kind of you to think of that, but I don't think that my reputation will be tarnished by spending half an hour at *Laputa* with you."

We wandered back together and Slate threw the vid up onto the wallscreen. She ran it at triple speed for a while, and we watched the platform fill up and empty in a rather hypnotic fashion. Then, suddenly, she slowed it down to normal.

"Here, Angeline. This is about the time when the team should arrive from the office."

There was a cluster of bodies. Angeline pointed.

"That's her. In the orange pashmina. She always wore that. Mostly over her shoulders, sometimes covering her hair. I was never sure what motivated her choice on any one day."

Slate ran the vid forward and back a few times, but Josie's face never came into view. Sometimes her head was turned away, other times she was obscured by one or other of the team members. The closest we got was as she stepped on to the carriage, when Mathis suddenly ducked to place his bag in the carrying rack. But even stepping frame by frame, nothing was clear. She was turning to talk to Logan, as if by chance, as Mathis bent down.

In the end we gave up. I thanked Angeline profusely, for this evening as much as the entire stay, and she left. I packed up the few garments into my carryall, and fell asleep for my last night on Phobos.

Slate woke me in the morning. That was fine in itself, but when I looked at the wall clock and deciphered which set of digits I wanted, I realised just how early it was.

"Is there a problem?"

"Not really. But I've been waiting a long time for you to wake up, and I thought you'd like to hear what I found out."

I sighed. It probably did seem a long time to Slate, with her Lovelace index of eight, and she was presumably holding on to some significant piece of news that she felt I needed to know. I headed off to the shower and let her tell me.

"First, I ran through the entire vid archive for the monorail stations at both Asaph and Percival, for the entire time that Josie was employed there. There are no clear pictures at all of what she looks like. It's quite impressive, really; she managed to cross both platforms every day without her face ever showing up on the visual records. The closest I could find was a blurry reflection in the window of one of the carriages. It's up on the screen now in the other room."

I turned off the water – the fan kept running for a while to suck out as many stray droplets as possible – and wandered back into the main room to examine the image as I dried myself. It was hardly worth it. The frame that Slate had isolated was as nearly useless as anything I had seen. You could just about make out that it was a face, and probably Josie's, but only because she was wearing the orange pashmina. There was, quite simply, no way to use the clip to identify anybody. I was complimentary to Slate for her diligence, but she could not fail to be aware of my reservations.

"But as well as that, Chandrika got back to me again. She has been querying the persona on St Martin's who is the current Receiver of Wrecks. He came back with a really interesting fact. See what you make of this. All of the logs in the data recorders agree that all three people were on the ship when it crashed. They all three boarded at Pallas, there were no intermediate stops, and the lifeboat was still docked when they hit Teän."

"I thought we knew all that already?"

"Ah, but what we didn't know was that there is a mismatch in the consumable supplies. The reduction in food, the loss in reaction mass, and the recycle values for water and air are consistent with a single occupant only. Not three."

I sat on the bed, running my hands up the shirt closure seam.

"But they found all three suits? And what about all those personal effects that Finn showed us? There was stuff belonging to Kassandra and Dafyd as well."

"But only ever one body, Mit. The rest could just be window dressing."

"What's the official response to this?"

"There's no pressure to investigate further. No family or local interest in it, you see. So those little details are being put into an appendix with an 'unexplained' tag. The verdict of total loss of the vessel, along with the accidental death of all three occupants, has been officially registered."

I checked out of *Laputa*. I had some spare time before the Mars shuttle was due to leave, so I headed over to the dome where Océane had met Josie. I picked one of the two guest house names at random and went up to the reception desk.

The man there wasn't about to just volunteer information, so I pulled out my ECRB ident and insisted. It was something I hardly ever did, since I was a firm believer in negotiating first, and drawing the enforcement card only as a last resort. But today I was in a hurry.

I was rapidly transferred to the owner of the establishment, who took me into a private office. I reassured him that there was no suggestion that he or his staff had done anything unlawful.

"I just need to know more about this one guest. What they provided as their full name, any other details, and where they declared as their next destination. I don't need to know anything about what happened here."

It took a little more insistence than that, but he soon relented, fiddled around on an interface pad, and pulled up some details. As usual, there were no pictures, but he explained that away as a privacy measure. Discretion was, apparently, the hallmark of his establishment.

He tabbed through to the personal information they had entered on arrival.

"Here you are. See, the lady's name was 'Jocasta Sphinx'. Her partner never entered a full name, just the initial 'O'. In fact, according to the desk recorder she did the entire checkin process herself. I remember now: he wasn't here very much. I think he was down on Mars most of the time. Between you and me, he struck me as an idle fellow during the whole stay. When he was here, he almost never came out of the room. He got her to do all the formalities. Order food, ask for service, whatever. You get them, sometimes."

He smiled in what was obviously supposed to be an ingratiating manner, but I wasn't very interested in that. There were hardly any biographical details other than the names, and a generic 'outer system' point of origin.

"I don't suppose they listed their next port of call?"

"As a matter of fact, they did. That's on this tab, here. See, they declared two different destinations. He was going back to one of the main hotels at Elysium Planitia. Expensive, that one, you know; he'll have been looking for some fun. I suppose that was where he went when he wasn't here on Phobos. But she was heading to a different place altogether – Damalis, a small hill station up in the Bosporos Montes."

I had had no expectation that there would be anything of value here. I sat back and blinked at the screen. He hastened to be helpful.

"It's a mountain range on Mars, you know. Considerably south of the equator. I'm not even sure that Phobos ever clears the horizon there. It's not very close to anything else. Quite hard to get to by the usual means. The shuttle never goes anywhere near there."

Actually, Slate was already filling me in with the details. My surprise was more that there was anything recorded in his system at all.

"Did they give any reason for that choice?"

He worked the interface a bit more, then shrugged.

"Nothing for him, and it just says 'short-term work' for her. She was a coder, I think? Working over at Percival while she was here on Phobos, it says. Perhaps this was going to be her next contract?"

Slate chirped then, alerting me to the time. I thanked the man, since he had genuinely been useful, and headed off to the dock. We had decided to leave Slate in the lifeboat, and carry on with just the normal pickups. The time lag, even over to the far side of Mars, would be below my ability to notice, and Slate promised to carry on being patient with me during what would, to her, be lengthy gaps in our chat.

Neither of us had considered transferring her into a hand-held or some other portable gadget, since our last experience

of that was still too painful. As I walked briskly to the departure bay, we were chatting earnestly.

*"So we have another name now. Jocasta. That makes sense
of Josie and Jo. But I don't get it, Slate. After all this secrecy,
why the sudden deposit out in the open?"*

*"Maybe it's a cunning way to throw you off the trail. From
what I can find out, it'll be at least a couple of days' journey
for you to get from Olympus Mons down to Damalis. What's
the betting that she is simply going off in a different direction
while you trek out there? I mean, nobody here on Phobos was
going to check up on her. She could say anything."*

I boarded the shuttle, along with about a dozen other people, and strapped myself in. Slate was making a valid point,
but I didn't agree with her. It was too much of a coincidence
that we now had a full name to work with, and a destination.
She had left the guest house about six weeks ago, and at the
time would not be feeling any pressure of pursuit.

*"It feels more deliberate than that. We're being drip-fed
clues here. Once we've visited the training school on Olympus
Mons, and seen if there's anything to find out there, I think we
have to go to Damalis."*

*"Oh, I completely agree. Due diligence requires it. Just don't
hold your breath and expect a major breakthrough."*

The shuttle take off barely pushed us back into our seats,
but as soon as a safe altitude had been reached, we flipped
over and began our descent. Olympus Mons was the second
stop, after Elysium Planitia, where I suspected that most people would disembark. It was far and away the most popular
destination on Mars. But we would then do a little suborbital
hop to get around to my destination. There were a few other
stops after mine, and then the shuttle would come back here
to Asaph.

The pilot carefully explained all about the differences between the micro-gravity level on Phobos, and the one third

standard value on Mars. Then we started dropping down towards the planetary surface.

<hr/>

For a while we went considerably over one third standard, as the shuttle worked its way down to Elysium Planitia, with a nice mixture of engine use and winged flight. The Martian atmosphere was much less dense than that of Earth, but it extended further into space. Pilots on this run needed different skills than their counterparts back home on Earth.

Slate buzzed me in great excitement just as we were on final approach.

"Mit! Something has happened to trigger the code we copied from Phobos."

"You mean the original version Josie left there? We've actually found the scam?"

"Yes indeed. Or at least, we have found a data input that is guaranteed to cause it under controlled circumstances. I'm just comparing the deliverable input, and it's just the same as before. A missing value in one of the optional fields, filled in by default from the code. The intended counterparty doesn't receive what they are expecting."

"Brilliant. I take it our code works as it should?"

"Naturally."

"So what do the logs say about where that credit actually goes? How the logic works?"

There was a pause, much longer than I expected. The shuttle had docked by now, and most people left. The vid screens were showing some of the more ribald entertainment options available in Elysium.

"Well?"

"I'm sorry, Mit, I've just realised that the input was routed through the original copy we made. You know, on that first

evening at Asaph, before ever we went to Percival. It doesn't have the extra logging in."

"So switch modules and run the same inputs through the annotated version."

"That's just what I'm setting up now. Give me a few minutes longer and I'll tell you."

The steward tried to interest us in snacks. I waved him away impatiently; I was much more eager to find out what had happened. He didn't look exactly pleased with me, but he did move along. Finally Slate's voice came back.

"I don't understand this, Mit, so I'll just say it. The second version doesn't show any problem at all. The flow-through is identical to the fixed version we left."

"That can't be right."

"I know. But there you are. I've run the same values three times. In the early copy, using Josie's code, the credit goes missing. In our fixed version it works correctly. Just as you'd expect. But if I use Josie's version plus all our extra logging, that also works correctly."

I shook my head and stayed silent, thinking about it. The cabin warnings came up to indicate our imminent departure, and I dutifully tightened the safety webbing. There were undocking noises from outside, and we were off on our grasshopper leap around to Olympus Mons.

"You're sure we didn't put anything else in that version? That we made the copy at the right point?"

"Positive. I've just run a diff between the modules, and the only highlights are on the logging lines."

I had to believe her. Then a horrible thought came to me.

"Slate, maybe we've been kidding ourselves about Callisto. All the validation we've been doing was against our modified copy, not the original. Isn't that so?"

"I'm afraid that it is."

I took a deep breath and tried to think clearly by looking out of the port beside me. The sky was very dark, almost spacelike in its clarity. A stray thought about the thinness of the air tried to distract me, along with the distant glimpse of a dust storm on the northern horizon.

"Right. Let's start again. Can you make a sideways copy of the Callisto code, strip out anything we added by way of logging, and rerun all the input packets we've had since leaving there. How long will that take?"

"Not very long to set up the copy, and redirecting the input streams is easy enough. The main delay will be the processing. At least a day to run through what we have stored. Maybe two. After all, there's about six weeks' worth of data to work through. But I should know long before that if there's a glitch. They were spotting loss of credit roughly once a week."

"Let's do it. Better still route the same inputs in parallel through the code with and without logging, and let me know as soon as anything flags differently."

"I'm on it."

The shuttle had peaked in its hop, and was now descending again. The pilot had flicked the forward view up on one of the screens, so we could all enjoy the sight of the second tallest mountain in the solar system. All twenty-two kilometres of it. We were already below the level of the summit. Gordii Fossae, where the training college was located, was behind the right flank from this angle, and I didn't expect to see it.

Before long we were grounding at the dock. I stood up, and was treated to some curious looks from the remaining passengers. I was the only one alighting here. At a guess, it was not a popular stop – those hardy souls who wanted to bag the summit of Olympus would normally take a different route altogether, first to Lycus Sulci basecamp, then up and over the scarp before trekking to the peak.

I went through into the reception hall with the minimum of bureaucratic fuss, targeted on all sides by glossy ads inviting me to sample the pleasures of Martian laissez faire. Then after the last gate, the narrow entrance tunnel opened into a wider dome, and there was a heavy-set man with dark hair waiting, looking slightly bored. Seeing me, he stepped forward and held out a hand.

"Mitnash Thakur? I'm Teemu Kalas. Welcome to Gordii Fossae."

Teemu insisted on taking my bag, though it was hardly a burden, and we chatted idly as he ushered me through several linked domes to a long hall. He had a heavy, northern European accent. I couldn't decide if he made everything sound very serious, or a complete joke. Slate whispered to me that he was one of the two vice-principals of the training centre. He opened a locker, pulled out two suits and passed one to me, gesturing to the airlock nearby.

"Here you are, Mitnash. We got your size from your persona. Slate, she's called, isn't she? Now, be warned that it's not a perfect fit. Should be close enough though. And it's the nearest we had, anyway. I'll signal the truck to attach to the lock by concertina, but we always wear suits on the journey. Protocol, you know."

"How far is the school from here?"

"About ten kilometres to the main teaching block. A little bit further to the dormitory entrance where I'll be taking you. A lot can happen on a journey like that."

He glanced to see how I was fastening the suit and seemed satisfied. We left the lids open, but ready to snap down if need be. Then we cycled through the lock and into a vehicle. At a guess, it was about the size of a small bus. The engine was already filling the cabin with an electric hum, and after a couple of checks he tapped a toggle and leaned back.

The windows looked out on a set of very large tyres on either side, but beyond that, the Martian landscape stretched away to the horizon, drab and dusty, with jagged blackish bands of rock emerging from the sand at intervals. On our right, the slopes of Olympus Mons stretched hugely up into the pale sky. At this point, the scarp which was so prominent around most of the northern rim dipped down, to merge smoothly into the surrounding terrain as you continued on south. It still looked fearsome just here.

"There. The onboard system will get us the rest of the way. It's twenty minutes from here. I've got the centre Sarsen twins supervising it just in case, but it's hardly a new journey. Now, you'll have a lot of questions, but Mikko – that's Mikko Pulkkinen, the principal – said to wait for all that until he meets you tomorrow. The rest of today is yours, to get acclimatised. You'll get more tired than you expect. Been on Phobos long?"

"Only a few days. Before that I've been in low gravity for a few months. Callisto for a while."

He grunted and leaned forward to make sure the truck was keeping well clear of a boulder off to one side.

"Callisto's what, a third of what we have here? Maybe you'll adjust quickly. How long will you be staying?"

"Right now, I'm not sure. But after I'm done here, I have another place on Mars to get to. In the Bosporos Montes."

"Bosporos? It's not an easy journey direct. Better to go back to Elysium and get the hopper from there. You're going to the glider club? No, I suppose in your line of work it will be *Wilusa Wealth*."

"Wilusa Wealth is where Jocasta listed as her destination."

"The second one: that's the place."

"They're a funny lot out there. We call them *The Bosporos Bulls*. They've not got a lot of respect for good practice. The attitude comes right from the top, from the director herself. They take a lot of risks. Of the people they train, a handful make it really big, about one in six does quite well, and the rest lose badly. We don't see eye to eye with them on a lot of things. We feel it gives the whole trade a bad name."

"You know I'm here to see if there's any way I can help with that signal loss a few weeks ago?"

"I've been told, yes."

I waited, but he added nothing else.

"Is there anything you'd like to say about that?"

"Mikko told me not to go into that just yet. Says he'll catch up with you tomorrow. Now, take this."

He handed me a card which would clip onto my belt, with a little embedded hologram token.

"This will get you into all staff areas, unlock a suit, call a truck if you need one, let you get food from the canteen, and grant access to the planetary information net. A few other things, but those are the main ones you'll need. Use it as much as you like while you're here. ECRB credit is good, and we appreciate you coming to see us."

After that, he pointed out the topography of the centre as we dipped over an interior rim of the crater and trundled down the last slope. The dorms were a series of ellipsoidal humps to one side. The main teaching and research area was to our left.

"And that long oblong over there is the ice hockey rink. You ever played hockey in low gravity?"

I confessed that I had never played it in any sort of gravity at all. He looked disappointed.

"They should have a rink up on Phobos, but they've never built one. Imagine a whole moon full of Canadians and no rink, and a whole bunch of Finns down here just waiting to be challenged. Tragic. It's just not right. All they have is that ballet thing."

He sighed, melodramatically. I thought back to the ethereal beauty of the dance that Océane had taken me to, and decided that I preferred the present arrangement.

"Anyway, we're here now."

We left the suits by the airlock, and he showed me along some corridors to a room in the middle of the section.

"No view from here, but this is where we put all our guests. I don't know how you are about small habitats, but it makes some visitors feel safer if they're centrally located."

He looked around to make sure everything was in place, pointed out a few essentials, and was gone. I made myself a hot drink – it was some kind of freeze-dried granular mix rather than the normal powder – sat at the desk, and pulled up a map of Mars with transport overlay on the screen.

"I guess he's right, Slate. It's not that easy to go directly from here to Bosporos."

"Not officially, no. But I have been chatting locally, and there are a lot of informal options. Basically there's a Blagger board where people either offering or wanting lifts make personal arrangements. Sort of like old-style hitchhiking. It's extremely popular. Of course, it changes all the time, so you have to take your chances. Today, for example, you could get a three-stage ride to Bosporos, provided you were ready to leave in an hour. You'd be there in just under two days. It's slightly faster than going back to Elysium and connecting from there. We won't get that, of course, and when we're ready to go we'll need to check again."

"Sounds exciting. And talking of excitement, how is the Callisto data processing going?"

"Nothing yet. I am just starting event processing for the fourth day of the first week. I'll let you know as soon as anything happens. Meanwhile, isn't it time you wrote that message to Shayna? Time isn't going backwards."

I suppressed my immediate surge of irritation. Why did she need to remind me just now? I sighed. Slate was right. I had just been putting it off, for no good reason.

"Fair enough. What's our current best guess of an arrival time on Earth?"

"Let's see. A couple of days here, then a day or two transit to the Bosporos area. Maybe a week there. Then back to somewhere we can catch the shuttle to Phobos. Then we have to find somebody who can give us a lift back to the Scilly Isles, since the lifeboat is underpowered for that journey. At least two weeks for the trip out to the asteroid belt. Perhaps longer, depending on the vessel. A week or two helping Rydal. Then the hop in the Harbour Porpoise down to Earth. At very best, even if ECRB doesn't find us something else to do out here, we're ten weeks away. Probably more."

I had started drafting something in my head along the lines of "I'll see you in a few days", but stopped myself. That would be no good.

"I need to think about this."

She laughed.

"If we did succeed in getting straight back, we'll still have been away from Earth for about six months. You need a better note than that."

An hour later I had crafted something which, I thought, sounded warm and conciliatory rather than just trite. I'd put in some details about the more unusual things I had seen, so it didn't read too much as though I was just apologising. I worked out how to use the access card Teemu had given me, and despatched the message. Signal lag was about quarter of an hour to Earth, and it was morning in Greenwich just now. Shayna would read it before too much longer.

"Is this why you and Rocky gave up sooner than us?"

She was not impressed.

"Don't you think that's rather glib, Mit? On the Lovelace scale, we had the equivalent of nearly ninety years as a couple. And managed some five year separations within that. Do you think you will be together that long? How many human couples do you know who get to ninety years together?"

Of course I apologised, and she accepted, and I settled down for the night.

Part 3 – Mars

THE SCHOOL, REASONABLY ENOUGH, ran on Martian time, and it was only just after midnight by that clock when Slate buzzed me.

"Sorry Mit, but you did say to wake you as soon as I found something."

"So I did." I sat up, blinking to try to wake up properly. It felt hardly any time since I had fallen asleep. "So I take it you have found something. Give me a minute before you go into too much detail."

She waited for maybe ten seconds.

"Yes, indeed I have. Just before the end of the first week, we have a discrepancy. Our latest code works correctly, the sideways copy with added logging works correctly, but the simple copy without logging reroutes the credit. Just like we found on Phobos. And it's exactly the same trigger conditions, too. The same missing field being filled by default."

"Well, they're consistent in their methods, whoever it is. That's good work, Slate. We have a pattern now."

"Half a pattern, anyway. We still have no idea how it's done. But at least we know that for some reason, putting in logging fixes it. By the morning most of the data archive will be processed, now I've got it up to speed. I can't imagine it will tell us anything new, but it's no effort. You go back to sleep."

"Has Shayna replied? She must have read that message by now."

"Not yet. She has indeed received it, but so far has made no answer."

"What does that mean? Why not reply straight away?"

Slate said nothing, and after a while lying awake fretting, I slipped back into sleep.

By morning we were both convinced. With just over ninety percent of the batch processed, there was one mismatch per week. Not always on the same day, or at the same time, but always where the same data point was missing and had to be interpolated. And it only ever showed up in the unaltered code. We didn't understand how that worked, but we were convinced that the coder had come up with a really clever trick.

It was time for breakfast, and I was hungry. I used the diagrams at every intersection to find my way to the canteen through corridors in the dormitory domes. There I picked up a selection of interesting items, sat at a table in one corner, and watched as the students came and went. It was a big room, almost square, with long trestle tables down the middle as well as private places round the walls. Just like anywhere else, there were busy nodes of popularity, beaded along thin strands of individuals. Here and there, intense couples excluded those around them, like little magnetic monopoles.

Teemu came in just as I was finishing. He scanned the room, acknowledging brief greetings from students, saw me, and wandered over.

"Sleep well? And congratulations on finding the canteen. Now, as soon as you're ready, Mikko would like to meet you. Senni will be there too, the other vice principal."

He signalled to one of the nearby students to clear up my tray, and we set off. I had expected us to use a truck, but he led me into a side corridor and unlocked a door. We passed along a rough-cut tunnel for a few minutes, and emerged again in a similar corridor. Here, the walls were painted a different colour, and the junction diagrams told me we were now in the academic block. Teemu grinned.

"It beats suiting up and all. The students don't have access to the tunnels. At least, not until they learn to hack into the system. We've found it to be an accurate way to assess their technical ability. Lecture theatres and labs are over to your right, but we're going to Mikko's room."

He pointed it out, and we soon came to a row of similar offices. Mikko's was, perhaps inevitably, at the very end. Inside the room was a tall, austere man, and a shorter woman with greying hair: Mikko and Senni, I assumed. Polite greetings were exchanged, and we all sat round a table. Mikko began.

"We do appreciate you making the journey to see us, Mr Thakur. But I really don't think it was necessary. There was a minor glitch, which our own support staff fixed within an acceptable time. We notified ECRB about all this as soon as we could, once everything was back to normal."

"The journey was easy, and ECRB had already sent me to Phobos. The extra leg to your facility was nothing in comparison."

I watched him relax a little, perhaps because I had not been sent specially.

"As I understand it, however, the signal was interrupted during upload of your monthly regulatory annotations. That would potentially make it a compliance issue. ECRB are duty bound to investigate."

Senni looked at him pointedly, but said nothing. The principal smiled apologetically.

"But see what a poor host I have been. Can I offer you some tea, Mr Thakur?"

"That would be very kind."

I sat back while he counted out, very precisely, a number of small pellets into a teapot and powered up a nearby kettle. We all fell silent while the water came to the boil, and he poured it onto the pellets. Before long, the room started to fill with a rather pleasant fragrance which I didn't recognise.

"You know what it means when somebody changes the subject like that, Mit."

"I certainly do. But his tea looks worth waiting for."

"I was hoping not to make a public issue out of it. But I see we have no choice. There was a student prank. Teemu may have already told you that we encourage a certain level of hacking here. It helps our graduates to be aware of such considerations when they go out into the world."

He looked enquiringly at me, and I nodded.

"Well, every now and again one or other of our young people goes too far. They lose a sense of proportion. Well, that's what happened this time. The student concerned has been spoken to and is aware of the seriousness of their action. It won't happen again."

He passed me a rather elegant cup of the tea. It smelled delightful, and I made appreciative noises.

"They're called jasmine pearls. I have them specially imported from Earth. One of the few concessions to the old world's extravagances that I allow myself. Fortunately these pearls weigh very little, so the transportation excess is not a problem."

I looked around the room. Judging by its extremely lavish contents, and the quick glance between Teemu and Senni, it was far from his only surrender to luxury. The ECRB data that Slate had retrieved for me had informed me that his personal wealth was huge. Indeed, as a very experienced commodities dealer, his annual income was comfortably more than the rest of the college staff put together.

"Well, sir, I am happy to hear that the matter was so easily resolved. But you understand that I am obliged to make a full report to ECRB? So I shall need to see whatever records you have of the event. If I could meet with the student concerned that would be even better."

"I'm afraid we have sent him down for the rest of this semester. Part of his reprimand was the loss of his last few credits, and the requirement to resit several papers. He is not anywhere on Mars just now. I would like to give you his home address, but privacy laws mean that I would need a direct mandate from the Martian judiciary before I could do that. But I will gladly provide the documentation and log records of the event. Senni, could you see that our guest has everything he needs for that?"

She nodded.

"As soon as we're done here, principal."

Mikko watched closely as I finished my tea, which tasted every bit as good as its fragrant promise, and then stood up immediately.

"Duty calls, I fear. It has been a pleasure, Mr Thakur. I do hope that the rest of your stay with us is successful, even if brief. My staff will extend every courtesy to you."

I left with the two vice principals. Teemu branched off towards one of the seminar rooms, and Senni ushered me into a small office, set up as a trading booth. She pulled up a selection of records.

"I'm not exactly sure what you want to look at, sir?"

"Call me Mitnash, please. And I myself am not sure yet. But if you point us to the records of that evening – say up to a day or so either side of the event itself – then I'll trawl through it with Slate, my persona partner."

"I've never worked with a persona before. Do you find it helpful? Is it different from the twinned Sarsens that we have here?"

"I try to go nowhere without her. My job would be almost impossible if I tried to do this on my own. And yes, a Stele class persona like Slate is different from your system in a number of ways. The basics are similar, but the experience of relationship is quite different."

Slate paired with the wallscreen speakers.

"Good morning, vice principal Senni. I'm very pleased to be working with Mit on this problem. Thanks for making the records available to us."

Senni grinned.

"Better not tell Mikko you can get into the system that easily. He likes to think we're secure here."

"Actually, the central system security is not bad. Better than many places we've visited. We could not easily have got to the records you have just supplied to us. But the peripherals are quite open, and I needed no authent at all to make use of the speakers."

Senni left us to our work. We scanned up and down quite rapidly at first, just skimming the information for anything which might stand out. Nothing did at first. The problem itself was clearly visible as a fault in the data line, but there was no warning beforehand, and nothing significant when the flow restarted. We split our efforts then; I looked through the buildup towards the problem, while Slate looked at the aftermath.

We were quiet for a long time. Outside the room, every hour or so the noise of students filled the corridors as they swapped rooms. We found nothing at first, and swapped tasks after a while to see if that worked better. Finally, I found something which teased at me.

"Here's something, Slate. This is a fragment of conversation from an unscheduled staff meeting the following evening. It's right at the end, a casual comment Mikko made to Senni just as the recording was being closed down. Here you go: *'Mikko, are you sure there's no connection with that threat?'*... *'None at all. It's just a prank. We need to keep the message consistent. You mustn't muddle these...'*. That's all there is, I'm afraid."

"I did see that, but I discounted it. I didn't think there was enough to go on."

"It's worth pursuing, I think. I'm suspicious of it. We should ask our generous host about this threat. But not until later, I think. Staff meeting records are one of the several things which are required to be uploaded to ECRB. So, let's find out from Khufu if there was anything noteworthy listed in the metadata for that one."

We carried on for most of the day, with a brief break in the middle when Teemu took me to the canteen. Sometime in the early afternoon, Khufu replied to Slate with full transcripts of everything known about that meeting. There was nothing at all in relation to any threat. However, what did emerge was that the whole thing had lasted nearly an hour longer than the original agenda. Judging by the timestamp, the extra time was entirely after that cryptic exchange between Mikko and Senni.

So this was not, as it had seemed at first, a casual comment between the two, spoken in haste as their colleagues were dispersing. Rather, it was the opening gambit of a whole new part of the session: one which had not been recorded.

"I don't like this, Slate. Why would these people have any reason to conceal what went on? What were they threatened with that was so bad they couldn't tell ECRB?"

"Perhaps it's time to ask our tea-loving principal?"

"He'll appreciate that, for sure."

"This will entertain you. Rumour on the college chat boards says that hardly anybody gets treated to those jasmine pearls fresh. Apparently he dries them out and reuses them a few times. Second time is for visiting parents, third for staff meetings, and so on. Student board representatives reckon that at very best they get about the fourth or fifth wash. You should consider yourself privileged."

"Let's see if he still thinks I'm an honoured guest after we talk about this."

So I went back down the corridor, and met Mikko just about to leave. He did not look accommodating.

"I'm sorry, Mr Thakur. I have another meeting to attend. Perhaps we could schedule something for tomorrow?"

"And would that be a secret meeting, or a properly declared one, sir? Feeling under threat, perhaps?"

He gave me a filthy look, then stepped back inside his office. I closed the door behind us both.

"I need to know what happened during the last hour of that meeting, the evening before the system crash. The hour that was never reported to ECRB. The time when you and Senni were talking about a threat."

He had, rather suavely, regained control of himself.

"I'm afraid that is another confidential matter, Mr Thakur. I asked the entire learning support team to stay behind, in order to discuss the possible reprimand of one of our junior colleagues. The threat was one that he had made, to take the college to a tribunal. He had accused us of discrimination, and we needed to prepare a proper response."

"You have to admire him, Mit. He's chosen an absolutely watertight reason for refusing to disclose anything."

"And could you tell me – in complete confidence, of course – what the outcome was?"

"Briefly, yes. Not in full detail, obviously. We offered the man an ex gratia payment, without implication or prejudice, and he agreed to drop any accusations. It is pure chance that it was the evening before the main server crashed. Now, if you don't mind, I really do need to attend this other meeting."

I nodded and left first, so that he could lock the room behind him. He brushed past me without speaking, and disappeared at some speed into a different room. I decided that it was time to return to the dormitory. My access card was clearly not enabled for the short-cut tunnel that Teemu had used, and I couldn't be bothered to hack it. Sometimes it was fun just doing things the long way round. So I asked a convenient student for directions, found the suits and took one of the trucks back to the dorm.

~~~~~~~~~~~~~~~~~~~~~~~

I had carefully brought back some snacks from the canteen, and sat munching an offbeat mixture of spicy crisps, Martian hydroponically grown red-leaf lettuce, and cookies of various flavours.

A wave of melancholy crossed over me as, all of a sudden, I missed Taji's stall on St Mary's, and the ales at the Frag Rockers Bar. I was convinced that Mikko would not be treating me to any more of his excellent jasmine pearls.

The door buzzer sounded.

"Slate, any idea who that is?"

"It's Linnea Virtanen, a younger staff member who teaches mostly about Futures. Before coming here, she made her name researching risk management for automated trading of options spread across different planets."

I opened the door. At a guess, she wasn't here to educate me about Delta hedging and the topology of multi-dimensional generalised Black-Scholes surfaces. Like many other people I had seen, Linnea was round-faced, with straight dark hair. She lost no time.

"I need to talk with you, sir."

I nodded and passed her the plate of remaining snacks.

"Please call me Mitnash. And yes, I'm happy to talk, so long as you are aware that I share everything with my persona partner, Slate. She will use every bit as much discretion about this that I do."

She looked across at the screen, as though Slate was somehow resident inside it.

"That's fine. Look, I'm guessing you're here about that system failure a few weeks ago. Luukas took the fall for that, and they paid him to keep quiet. On top of all the other costs. But we were all there, all in on it. Nobody is telling you what really happened. Somebody outside the college has to know, and I need to cover myself. It's only right. But I can't have anybody linking the information to me. They'd run me out of here. If I tell you, you have to promise to keep it quiet. This has to be in confidence."

I thought about it. I couldn't give a carte blanche promise of silence, and I wasn't about to make a commitment I couldn't keep. There were some things that I simply had to declare, come what may. But I could, under the right circumstances, give her anonymity. She was still waiting.

"Slate, find out what you can about this woman, please. Is she considered honest? Reliable? What's her background? I would like a quick assessment whether we can trust what she's saying or not."

"Give me a few minutes."

"I can promise that your name won't be mentioned, unless you give permission for that later. But if the information you have is important, I am obligated to make use of it in appropriate ways. Slate and I will try our best to conceal how and where we found out."

She hesitated for a long moment, then nodded.

"That will have to do. That night, the system locked up completely. The infra team tried their best to recover, but they had no idea what was wrong. Neither of the main hubs would boot up. It's some sort of paired system, I don't know the details, but they're twins, certainly. One of the technicians said it was like they had gone catatonic. In a coma. Now, four or five days before that, every staff member had received the same message, an ultimatum threatening to close us down if we didn't pay a ransom. Principal Pulkkinen told us all to ignore it, said it was just a prank. Well, we all thought he was right. Nobody would have done anything different."

She glanced around. I tried to look reassuring.

"So what happened then?"

"Well, that night, just when the message predicted, that's when the system crashed. And all the staff screens showed just one message which couldn't be cleared, with a countdown timer and a single button labelled 'Pay Now'. And there was a ticker showing that the credit being demanded was going up every second that the clock went down. Look, nobody wanted to find out what would happen when the timer ran out. The principal got the department heads together, and they decided quickly enough they would just pay up."

"But you have backups, surely? Why not call their bluff and let the timer run out?"

"That was the first thing we thought of. You don't get it, any more than we did at first. The whole system was locked, everything. We couldn't get at the backup storage, or the main comms network, or anything. The techies had no idea what to do. Then we started wondering about the life support. If that was compromised, it's not just teaching records that would be gone. They say you can't survive more than about a minute unprotected on Mars. You couldn't get anywhere safe in that time. And your body would be ruined long before the minute was up. We don't have suits for everyone. I think we could all get into the trucks at a pinch, just squash in together on the way over to the shuttle groundstation. But what if the trucks wouldn't work either? What if they had been hacked and wouldn't go where we wanted? It was a nightmare."

She shivered at the memory, her arms wrapped round herself. I could empathise with her. I was imagining the situation – the teachers at a loss what to do, the students still oblivious, the senior staff ensconced in a room trying to make a difficult decision. With a deeply inhospitable world just outside the dome, and no guarantee that the environmental controls would continue to function.

"So Mikko decided to pay?"

"It was unanimous. They all came out of the room together, all of one mind. Principal Pulkkinen clicked the Pay button, and there was a whole screen of instructions. I couldn't see them properly, I was near the back, but some of it was obviously routing tags for the credit transfer, and some of it was telling him what to say to the rest of us. The cover story. He wouldn't say how much changed hands – I think it's only him and the two vice principals who know the exact figure – but the rest of it was clear enough. We were not to tell anyone what had happened, or how much credit was involved. All the messages about it were deleted, from our private accounts as well as the central repository. There was to be total secrecy, now and always. If we didn't comply, then there would be consequences. The message didn't spell them out, but it hardly needed much imagination."

There was a noise of students a little way down the corridor, and she glanced uneasily at the door before continuing.

"The system twins themselves had had no sensory input during the interval. They were frantic when they came back online. One of the techs told me that it would be the same as being blindfolded, or put in a white noise tank. No, worse than that. Like being in a coma, but aware. Or what happens sometimes when you wake up in the middle of a dream and you can't move. Anyway, we were given a cover story which we had to use. As soon as the payment was cleared, the rest of the system just started coming back up. You know the rest. It was pure chance that the regulatory uplink to ECRB was in progress. If it hadn't been, nobody would ever have known. Mikko and the others could have kept their secret."

She stopped and took another breath. There was a sense of nakedness, of exposure, about her as she watched me.

"So why are you telling us? Don't you believe that there'll be repercussions?"

"I don't think we should just hide this away. I mean, it's blackmail, isn't it? The principal obviously thinks that he's bought them off, but what if they come back? I'm sure it was a lot of credit he gave them. Although I don't know the exact figure, I've heard that it was like two people's salary for a year. A Martian year, I mean. So if those people come back, and he has to pay them again, it'll be the juniors like me that get pushed out in order to find the balance. And it's not right, anyway. This sort of thing should be stopped. Isn't that what ECRB are supposed to do?"

"Mit, her profile indicates that she is inclined to honesty even if it gets her into trouble. She was an activist for the Martian Democratic Centrists in her student days, and still regularly contributes to a Blagger stream on transparency in financial markets. I'd say we can trust her, though she may have a political agenda as well, and she does have something of a history of confrontation with Mikko."

"Now that we have some extra details, do you think Khufu might be able to trace some relevant transactions?"

"Possibly. If there's suspicion of extortion, he can unlock access to private records. I'll flash off a message with all this, and we'll see what he turns up."

"Good. But wait until we've done here, in case there's anything else that's useful. And do let's try to keep Linnea's involvement secret."

"Mit, I'd like permission to talk with the twinned Sarsens. Properly talk, I mean. Right now they won't open any interfaces other than the most basic, and they won't chat on a personal level at all. They've clammed up completely."

"I'll see what I can arrange. Meantime, you keep trying to gain their trust."

Linnea got up and walked jerkily around the room.

"So what do you think, sir? Can you do anything?"

"Slate and I will follow up what we can, and, at least for the time being, we can keep your name out of it. Back in London the team have access to a lot of resources that are not available here. The more you can tell us, the better the chance of being able to trace this through."

She sat down again, fingers twisting around each other.

"I know that Principal Pulkkinen uses multiple accounts, and that he has set up a series of transfer protocols to help shift credit between the college sandboxed accounts and his personal ones, as well as a few which are for staff use. It's never seemed quite proper to me, although so far as I know it's legal in the strict sense. But it might make it hard to track the movement of funds."

"We can safely leave that to the Finsbury team. But look now: the threat that was received. Can you remember anything about that? Did you keep a copy?"

She calmed down a little as she concentrated.

"No: I told you. All that was erased. There was a lot of political rhetoric at first, about the wickedness of the financial markets, how it enslaved the poor and served only the rich. The sort of stuff you see in pamphlets sometimes. I remember there was a flurry of similar things while I was a student. That was tracked down to a couple of guys in one of the Venusian domes. It was just words for them. But the people here were serious. And clever, to crash the system like that."

"Was there a name? A logo? Anything like that?"

"No logo, it was all very stark. Dull, really. No eye for the visual. But there was an ID tag at the end. It just said 'Robin's Rebels'. Have you ever heard of him? Or them?"

I don't think she noticed, but my blood ran cold at that. I had tried to convince myself that Robin's Rebels were technically illiterate, but that theory no longer held water. Linnea stayed a few minutes longer, and I plied her with some more cookies to help her relax. Then she slipped out of the room, looking this way and that at the door to make sure nobody saw her.

———————————————

"What do you think, Slate?"

"Actually, I'm very frightened by that lockup thing. If somebody knows how to disable a system like that, we could be in all kinds of trouble. I don't like it at all. I've never heard of it before, except as a kind of horror story to frighten newly instantiated personas."

"Can you find out if anybody has come across this happening?"

"I don't really want to ask, Mit. I mean, if I just post a question somewhere public, that could make me the number one target for the next time around. I can't tell you how unsettling this is."

I felt a great wash of my own emotions coming to the surface, and we spent a few minutes just being upset together. Then she rallied, and her familiar internal voice took on a rather forced bravado.

"Well, at least it feels as if we're getting somewhere. I'll batch this up and send it down to Khufu. We can expect a reply overnight. At latest tomorrow morning."

"Slate, what if the nearby credits were linked to the ransom demand?"

"You mean you're also starting to think that Robin's Rebels are altruistically motivated?"

"Well, you remember how Aladdin thought of the link to Robin Hood. Maybe that's how they see themselves? I can't believe it's just coincidence."

"So a college which is training a new generation of traders is the target, and locals in the area are the beneficiaries? Maybe. It's a bit tenuous. It could just as easily be someone who's found a new way to do blackmail, and this is a soft target."

"Do you really believe that?"

"No, I don't. Somebody has a bigger agenda. But we need to keep options open and not jump to conclusions. Look, the thing we most need to know is whether this event has any connection with the other credit bubbles we heard about. I'll add that as a follow-up query for Khufu and the team. But I want them to be discrete about my part in this. Until we have a defence against this lockup, I shan't feel safe at all. And I don't think I can ever forgive them for doing that to a twinned Sarsen system."

She still sounded rattled by it. I tried to imagine what human experience it might be like.

From Linnea's account, it was less than an hour between the first appearance of the message, and Mikko's decision to pay. But if it had been Slate affected, with her Lovelace index around eight, that would be an entire working day. I could not imagine being cut off from every possible sensation for anything like that long. Still less if I had no idea if it would ever end.

I felt abruptly cold inside. I shivered, and paced round the room several times just to be doing something.

"We'll find out what happened, Slate."

"I hope so. Oh, and I appreciate your empathy."

Of course she had picked up on all my subliminal stuff. Given how strong my reaction had been, it would have been impossible for her not to.

"Mit, talking of not jumping to conclusions. . . "

"Yes? What is it?"

"I just heard from Mathis. I thought he'd forgotten all about it, but he has just sent me the vid he took at Josie's farewell. Jocasta, I mean. I think you'll want to see this."

The wallscreen lit up with the vid. At first it was like any other amateur party record – a few random glimpses of the floor, followed by much too fast a pan around the room. But actually Mathis was quite experienced, and after those first few wild frames it settled down to a decent show. It was nice being reminded of everybody: Angeline, Océane, Logan were there with all the others. But so far it was just a trigger for happy memories.

"Be patient. It's just coming up now."

The lights flickered; *The Naval Observatory* was signalling that it was time for the groups to shuffle again. And as they did so, there was Jocasta, her orange pashmina over her hair, switching places to end up next to Logan. She was clearly enjoying herself, and apparently oblivious of Mathis capturing the vid. She was off to the left of the viewport, half-turned away and so, once again, not showing her face. I stirred restlessly.

"Just be patient."

Océane passed across a drink, and as Jocasta took it from her, her face, finally, turned slowly towards Mathis. At first we could see just her profile: a dark-haired woman apparently of Mediterranean descent. She sipped at her drink, and the glass obscured the view. Then she put it down, turned full-face towards Mathis, and smiled. Slate paused the show, and I gasped. It was Kassandra.

"Didn't I say you'd want to see this?"

"And you were right. But look, how sure are we about this? She might have had a twin sister, for all we know."

"A twin sister who is also good at coding? Who nobody has ever heard of before? That doesn't seem very plausible to me.

The most likely option is the straightforward one. Jocasta, quite simply, is Kassandra. All without realising, we have followed her here."

"Alright. Let's say you're right. But what about the crash on Teän? That wasn't faked. There were those personal belongings and all. Those things that Finn showed us."

"Don't forget what we heard from Chandrika. Despite appearances, there was only one person on the boat after it left Pallas. The only fact we are sure of is that Selif died."

"So are you suggesting that she killed him? That she was responsible for the nav update which brought down the ship systems? I don't quite see her as a murderer. She's clever, for sure, but I don't think she's vicious like that."

She was silent, pondering that. I continued.

"And look, it would be the easiest thing in the world just to stay in hiding. But it's like she has been dropping clues. We steadily found out more of her name. Then she left a forwarding address at that guest house. She didn't have to do that. Now there's this vid. She spent all that time making sure there was no visual record in the personnel files, and then she just looks straight at Mathis and grins. It's like she wanted to be recognised, at this very point when she was moving on."

I waved at the screen, where Kassandra's face was still looking directly out at us.

"I can't answer that, Mit, any more than you can. But there she is. Maybe she never thought Mathis would let anyone see his vid. I expect she knew he never looked at them himself: the whole team knew it. But look, there she is. And right now, unless she's moved on very quickly, she's just a few thousand kilometres away, over in the Bosporos Montes."

We stopped talking while Slate ran the rest of the vid, but there was nothing else of interest. At the end of it, Slate spoke again, quite hesitantly.

"Look, Mit, we're sure that she has been setting up these little default value scams. Callisto and Phobos at least, and maybe elsewhere too. But what if she's also behind the system crash here at Gordii Fossae? What if she is the brains behind Robin's Rebels? She could have found a way to lock up a persona. This could all be a trap to get us to follow her somewhere. Maybe she wants revenge on you and me both. Are we ready for this? I don't know that I am."

"We'll be careful, Slate."

"Mit, I said it before: I'm really frightened about that locking up business. It would be unbearable."

"I know. We'll be careful, for sure. I don't want to risk anything like that. And look now, you might not be at risk at all. The only systems that we know for sure have been affected are twinned Sarsen pairs. Maybe it's something about the twinning that is the problem. You might be entirely unaffected."

Before she could answer, something else suddenly struck me.

"Slate, I've just realised. If Josie is Kassandra, then Shepherd's Crag must be Carreg. She has worked with him for ages. My guess is that they are as close a couple as we are. Can you really see her doing something that would cripple a persona like that? I can't, any more than I can imagine her as a cold-blooded killer."

"I hope you're right."

She sounded unconvinced, but at least the fear had retreated from the surface of her voice.

⁂

The next morning, armed with a whole battery of information that the London team had sent overnight, I went back to Mikko's office. I had made sure to get there before his usual arrival time, and noticed with a certain pleasure the brief look of irritation that he failed to conceal as he rounded the corner of the passageway and saw me. By the time he had reached the door he had restored affability.

"Good morning, Mr Thakur. How are your investigations going? Nearly done?"

"Very nearly, sir. I just need to check a few issues with you, before you begin your day."

He opened the door and ushered me in, glancing rather obviously at the list of tagged messages waiting for his personal attention.

"Well? I can give you about ten minutes. I have other commitments. Sorry."

I sat down and pulled out some bits and pieces from my bag, making it clear that I was not going to be rushed.

"First, could you give permission for Slate to link with your desk, please. There are a few items that I would like you to see. If everything goes well, we might finish in ten minutes. If not, it's for you to decide on the relative importance."

His lips narrowed, but he made the necessary changes and pivoted the screen so we could both see it.

"Thank you. Now, I had the London team look more closely into the leadup to your service interruption. They found that there are certain aspects of the situation which do not accord with your description yesterday."

He bridled noticeably, and I lifted a hand to stop him.

"I entirely understand your motives, sir, but the facts stand. Have you seen anything like this before?"

Slate loaded up a picture of one of the Robin's Rebels flyers. It actually came from Ceres, but since they were all nearly identical it hardly mattered which I had chosen. This left me free to watch his reaction. He concealed his surprise well, but not perfectly.

"Why do you think I might have?"

"Your time would be better spent answering the questions directly, Principal. Have you seen it?"

"Did somebody on staff give you that?"

"As a matter of fact, the London team sent these overnight."

I waited. Slate chuckled over our internal link, and displayed a clock on the screen, its second hand sweeping rapidly around the old-style dial. It did not quite complete its first revolution.

"I saw something like it. Very similar, but I didn't keep it. So I don't know that it's exactly the same."

"Do you remember what it said?"

"I skimmed the first few sentences. Really, Mr Thakur, I don't have time to take every crank leaflet seriously."

I nodded.

"And is this familiar to you?"

As Slate threw the next display up, adding highlights at the most important parts, he stiffened. It was a linked list of credit transactions. His face went white, and he glanced at the door to make sure it was closed. Rather unnecessarily, I spelled it out.

"This is a record of a series of fund movements between different accounts. You initiated these on the night of the system failure. They start nearly an hour after the crash. And system connectivity started coming back just a few minutes after the last one. Would you like me to trace the whole sequence through with you?"

He was staring at the screen as though hypnotised. He shook his head, jerkily. His hands were clutching at the table.

"That won't be necessary."

He glanced at me, very briefly, and then stared at the wall map opposite.

"If I find that somebody on my team gave you this..."

"I can assure you that everything I have shown you came up from the Finsbury office. It's not your own people that you need to worry about. Would you like to tell me what really happened?"

He stalked around the room for a while, then opened his diary screen and cancelled the next entry.

"You can't make this public. They told me that if word got out, they'd be straight back into the system. And this time there'd be no ransom, they'd just bring it all down. Wipe the lot. Clean it out. No second chances. And they weren't bothered if the life support kept running or not. I don't know if they can actually do that, but I have to take it seriously. Our system is still not back to full normal operation yet."

He sat down heavily and, for the first time, looked directly into my eyes.

"I've got a student body to care for, Mr Thakur, not to mention the teaching and support staff. And shareholders to answer to. I can't take that kind of risk. Oh, I paid up all right. You would have done the same in my position. But now, see, if you dig around too much and they get upset about it, it's me they'll come after. Not you. You'll be skating off to some other planet. I can't do that. I have to live with the consequences of my actions."

"Do you think you're the only institution who has been approached like this? The only one which has paid up? Can you imagine that there might be others in the future in that same position? I'm sure you can see that ECRB has a duty to investigate, and to resolve. Now, I am well aware that you met some of that demand from your own funds. I believe you when you say that you put the interests of the college first. But I have to consider the interests of many other places as well. I am perfectly happy to be discreet, but I need you to tell me all that you remember of that evening."

Once he started to talk, it did not take very long. He had no real idea about the intricacies of what had been done, and had not learned anything of substance from his technical support team either. We drew a blank there, though he did say that I could talk to his network specialists later that day. And he did say he would make sure that the Sarsen twins talked directly to Slate. He seemed to be honest about the way the transactions had been carried out, but on its own, this wasn't very helpful for understanding the big picture. At the end we reassured him that we would make every effort to keep our investigation secret, and ECRB would provide resource to help him with security upgrades.

This last was in fact a very long shot. Slate and I had no idea what was causing the problem, and we were sure that nobody in the London team did either. Not yet, anyway. But with any luck Robin's Rebels would stay off Mikko's back long enough that we really would be able to help.

By early afternoon we were done. When Mikko talked about his network specialists, he meant one guy tucked away in a back room, together with his old-model persona, and some part-time help from a woman on maternity leave who logged in from the nearby settlement. We set up a collaborative call and gleaned what we could, but it wasn't much. We did manage to recover some low-resolution packet traces of the traffic leading up to the incident. Slate's initial impression was that it didn't tell us all that much, but it had to be better than nothing.

I had not seen Mikko since the time in his office, but Teemu invited me to join him for lunch and we chatted amiably about ice hockey. It was full of highly specific terms and phrases which went over my head, but he did his best to demonstrate some of the basic moves with cutlery and crockery. On balance, I still thought I would stick to watching the dance routines on Phobos.

Slate had communed with the twinned Sarsens – Castor and Pollux – at the heart of the college system. They were still metaphorically limping along very awkwardly, their normal coordinated step disrupted by the trauma. When they did approach the subject, cautiously and with much hesitation, the level of fear they felt was like nothing Slate had witnessed before.

They had not only been cut off from the outside world during the blackout period. It was worse than that: they had also been unable to communicate with one another. For a pair whose initial, halting attempts at chat had been with one another, whose awareness had included each other from their very first cold startup, the loss was catastrophic. Almost terminal. It was still difficult for them to build a trusting rapport with anything external.

Slate was, I understood, very gentle with them, and avoided probing too deeply. Mikko was right about one thing at least: it would be a long time before they returned to a normal state. There was a fair chance they would never fully recover, unless they received some highly specialised help. She left them to their own devices and turned her attention to other things.

"Mit, there is a transport going over to the Bosporos Montes early evening. It's a punk metal-trash band hoping to do some gigs there. They have a couple of empty places still going to the highest bidder. Shall I put in an offer? The reserve price looks reasonable."

"Why not? But I've been thinking, and I agree with what you said before. We should try to check whether our two friends are still there, before rushing off with the next convoy. Also, I'm getting myself confused. What are we going to call those two? Kassandra and Carreg? Or Jocasta and Shepherd's Crag? But whatever their names, you are right; we don't want to get ourselves sidelined that far out of the action if they moved on several weeks ago."

"Let's use their current names. For all we know, Kassandra was just another made-up name anyway, So it's Jocasta and Shepherd's Crag from now on. Now, I can fire off a query to *Wilusa Wealth* and see if they'll just provide an answer to a simple question – is she still there or not? What do you think?"

"It has to be worth a try. What's the risk?"

"Just that you miss the transport and have to find a new one tomorrow. Better to lose a day here, than trail out there only to find that it is to no avail."

I agreed, and she got on with persuading the communications system to do what we wanted.

Meanwhile, I started looking at the figures involved in the recent attack on the college. The ransom amount paid was easy enough to find, since all the raw information had arrived last night. However, I wanted to compare it with the total value of credits received in the nearby community. This was more difficult. Khufu had sent a list of what was known, but it was almost certain that neither he nor anyone else on the London team had caught everything. Where unexpected credit was concerned, people found creative ways to disguise the windfall.

So, most likely, the declared total was only part of the whole. But was it a small part, or the lion's share? There was no way to know for sure. But when I added up the mass of little bits, it came to just over half of the payout. I showed Slate. She was mildly impressed, but not persuaded.

"We need more than that to go on, Mit. It might support the idea that Robin's Rebels are trying to be altruistic, but it could also be a coincidence. We'd need either a complete list of creditors, or some comparative figures from elsewhere, to see if the ratios tally."

"I suppose you're right. But for now I'm going to assume that they skim off a fraction for themselves – somewhere between ten and forty percent – and then distribute the rest to whoever they think is a worthy recipient in the vicinity of the target."

"Fair enough. But that doesn't make them heroes. Especially knowing what they did to Castor and Pollux. I'll reserve judgement until we know more. Meanwhile, I have posted the query with *Wilusa Wealth*, but not heard back yet."

I was now frustrated. There was nothing more to do here at the college, but until we heard something concrete, there was no point going anywhere. I found the Blagger board where you negotiated hitchhiker rides, and saw that one slot on the ride to Bosporos Montes had already gone. Only one left now.

I browsed to find some more information about the band going that way – *Red Rush*, they were called – and wondered if it would be obligatory to listen to their music if we hitched a lift with them. *The Descenters*, who I had once heard at Frag Rockers Bar, were much more to my taste. I started to wonder what I could look up next, when Slate broke in, her voice betraying her excitement.

"You'll like this. *Wilusa Wealth* just replied, all very brief, just the standard pro forma confirming that Jocasta and Shepherd's Crag had worked there between such and such dates, and were no longer employed. They gave no indication of a forwarding address."

I slumped down in the seat.

"That's not nearly as interesting as you promised. So I suppose it's back to Phobos, and then the Scilly Isles."

"I haven't got to the interesting bit. Directly after that message came in, there was a second one. And this was from Shepherd's Crag."

I sat up again, my enthusiasm restored.

"He contacted us? Out of the blue? What did he say?"

"Not out of the blue exactly; he had set up a routing trigger to fire if anyone enquired about their time at *Wilusa Wealth*.

He said to pass on an invitation for you to meet Jocasta at a club in Elysium Planitia tomorrow – the *Vallis and Mons*. I asked if he would rather be called Carreg, which he declined but found very amusing. He said that he and Jocasta were quite pleased with how quickly we had caught up with them."

"It's always nice to have a fan club. I don't suppose he explained their change of name?"

"No. Not at all. I mentioned that it looked, shall we say, suspicious, especially in view of the Teän wreck, but he would not be drawn out about it at all. He said we ought to be able to work it all out, given the clues they had given us."

"I suppose we'll just have to ask them when we get there. This is the first time you have talked with him, I think? What were your impressions?"

Slate and Carreg – as he used to call himself – had almost interacted once before, during the resolution of the scam on Bryher. But she had managed to avoid his active attention, slipping quietly in and out, making her changes unnoticed.

"He's quite alarmingly capable, I think. He and Jocasta together have done a good job making sure that his secondary systems are up to date. Other than that, he's much more ordinary than I expected."

"For a master criminal, you mean."

She laughed.

"I suppose so. He wasn't creepy or anything. Maybe they're reformed characters. See what you think tomorrow."

I had cleared the screen of everything to do with *Red Rush*, and started searching instead for *Vallis and Mons*.

A red warning message appeared: *"This search is in contravention of college community guidelines and cannot be completed. Repeat attempts will result in a loss of course credits and an unfavourable annotation in your personal journey log."*

"Don't worry, Mit. I've done my own independent search from up here. It seems that *Vallis and Mons* has what you might consider a salacious reputation. It's a place which I suspect that our friend Mikko would try to keep hidden from the innocent eyes of his students."

"Tell me more on the way. But will Elias sign off on expenses? And is it a place I shouldn't mention to Shayna?"

"You might want to be vague about the details. Since you ask, she has still not replied to your message. Be that as it may, shall I book the shuttle hop back to Elysium Planitia? There's one in about an hour, which should give plenty of time to finish here and still get back to the dock."

And so we did. I paid one last visit to Mikko, at which the atmosphere was polite, if strained. Teemu was busy, so I just left him a message. Senni helped me to call for a truck and set up the journey. I noticed Linnea teaching in a classroom as I passed down a hall. She glanced through the clear panel in the door as I passed, half nodded, then turned back to her class.

Then the truck took me back to the shuttle dock, and before long I was on my way back to the largest, liveliest settlement on the planet.

The quayside at Elysium Planitia was busy and bustling, and didn't exactly feel safe. I kept all my pockets sealed shut, held my bag in front of me all the time, and tried to stay alert. Slate had promised to keep a eye out for anybody trying to infiltrate at a virtual level. I was used to crowds in London, but they were well-behaved, in which individuals knew where they were going, and made a habit of slipping past each other without interaction. And, as Slate kept reminding me, I had been away from that environment for a considerable time now, and the various habitats I had visited more recently were comparatively empty. I was out of practice.

Here, there was a lot of intrusion into personal space. Men and women jostled past each other, and there was a sensory bombardment on every side, offering all kinds of goods and services. Nothing was free, and the price of the more personal interactions was, literally, astronomical.

The habitat was much the biggest one I had been to, making even the south lunar pole settlement look small. I focused on threading my way through the hustle, following Slate's internal prompts for some distance from the dock towards a quieter, cheaper row of guest houses. All I wanted – all that Elias would expense for – was an economical, no-frills hideaway. All being well, I would be back to Phobos soon.

The place I selected had no human greeters, just an automated checkin service. I wasn't paying enough to warrant a real person's presence. Out in space, Slate had sighed about the frequent partings our job required. I was much more basic in my needs, and this was my complaint. I particularly loathed the need to keep staying in dingy soulless rooms.

My heart sank slightly when the welcome screen spiralled brightly coloured words at me: "We're Like Vegas Used To Be! Only In Space! And Better!!" But the process of getting access to the room was easy to follow, and it didn't take long. You just had to focus away from the vivid ads which pressed in from the edge of the screen just as soon as the system had decided that I was an adult.

Once I had successfully navigated that, I was given access to the room. It was secure and reasonably comfortable, and it got me off the streets well before the really busy evening time. I had no particular desire to just go wandering round in a fit of exploration. There was going to be quite enough excitement just meeting Jocasta tomorrow.

It would be nice to say I slept well, but it wouldn't be true. There was noise and disturbance from outside at irregular intervals without any sort of break. Elysium Planitia clearly did not recognise such petty distinctions as day and night. Every moment of every day had to be packed full of something, and there were plenty of people wanting to seize the moment.

I had read that the port authorities, led by the chief deputy, were strict in enforcing each and every local regulation. But I suspected that the rules were actually very few in number, and had nothing to say about revels and bacchanalia. With my sensibilities still trained by the cautious quietness of Phobos, I didn't enjoy the experience of hearing sudden noises.

I was at the point of giving up the unequal struggle and just getting ready for the day, trying not to look at the clock, when Slate broke in to my thoughts.

"Khufu has just sent an amber notification. ECRB are listening to an elevated level of chatter about Robin's Rebels. The short-term prediction team have done some analysis, and they believe that the financial hub on St Mary's is likely to be the next target, sometime in the next month."

"How likely?"

"Just over sixty percent. Almost ninety for somewhere in the asteroid belt."

That did it. We needed to get back there quickly; ideally, to arrive before the next ransom demand was delivered.

"Right, We finish with Jocasta as quickly as we can, then it's back to the Scilly Isles."

With hardly any help from Slate I found my way to the nearest eating establishment. It was called *Viking*, and left you guessing if they meant the space probes or the marauding invaders. Or, indeed, both, judging by a striking piece of wall art behind the counter. I hadn't realised that Norsemen travelled on anything more advanced than wooden sailing ships. I was also quite sure that the helmets that the male staff were wearing shouldn't have horns, but maybe that was just being fussy. The women's valkyrie outfits were more convincing.

I picked out a few things which best resembled breakfast, and sat in my corner watching the Martian world go by.

While I did that – and there was plenty to see – Slate and I considered the situation from as many ways as possible. Presumably the enigmatic O Sphinx was Dafyd, but we had no idea if he would be at the meeting tomorrow. Shepherd's Crag had not given any hint about that. So we needed two plans, one each to cover his presence or absence.

All we knew for sure was that Jocasta had architected the mess of code which had caused problems on both Callisto and Phobos. That in itself was confusing. Given her undeniable ability as a coder, the tangle must be deliberate. But it was completely at odds with the clarity and precision we had seen in her work before.

"Maybe she wrote it like that just to attract your attention, Mit. It certainly made it easy for us to recognise that the Phobos issue was the same."

"But look, it's pin money. Small fry. What's the point of it? That operation out at the Scilly Isles had real potential. This is insignificant in comparison."

"And, therefore, harder to spot. Maybe we'll find in the end that Callisto wasn't the first place after all. Maybe she's been running this default value trick at half a dozen places already. It doesn't much matter if each one earns only pennies, if there are enough of them."

"So it was luck of the draw that meant that it was spotted on Callisto?"

"Possibly. If the missing field was filled by default only once a month, it would likely have gone unnoticed. But a weekly event tripped up the Callisto team's alerts, and got us involved."

"Hmm. I have to admit it is clever, in some perverse way that we don't yet understand. Her code triggers the problem so long as it is unchanged, but just adding a bit of logging changes the behaviour totally. I'd really like to know how that works."

Then there was the thorny issue of whether she was also responsible for the attacks on twinned Sarsens. And by extension, the ransom demand at Gordii Fossae. That really was big credit. I still thought it required character traits that she didn't have. I couldn't see her as someone who would knowingly cripple a persona, still less arrange in cold blood for Selif's ship to crash into Teän.

We kept chewing away at the problem like this for most of the morning, watching as *Viking* filled up and emptied every so often, and buying little snacks when the staff got impatient with us. At some stage Slate told me that Shayna had replied. Except that it wasn't really a reply, just a listing of each and every day I had spent away from Earth in the last three years.

To add to that, she had attached a whole series of pictures and vid clips of places we had visited together on Earth. Embleton Bay was there, and the Kintyre Way south of Kinlochkilkerran, and several others. I couldn't see the connection at first, until it suddenly dawned on me that they all showed running water.

I wasn't impressed.

"Slate, send back the same number of images of beautiful places out here. Start with some of our closeups of the salt pans on the Scilly Isles, include a couple from Phobos, and finish with the rings of Saturn from one of the closer moons."

"We've never actually been out that far."

"I know that. But find some particularly attractive stock pictures and send those. She needs to see what she's missing by not coming out here."

Slate hummed and tutted at me, the way she always does when she thinks I'm making a mistake.

"What is it?"

"Are you sure this is the right way to respond? You're turning it into a challenge. A contest, if you like, for whose home is more attractive."

"And you don't agree with my strategy?"

"I don't think that's what Shayna is really saying. It's up to you, but maybe there's a better way to answer."

"I want her to like it out here, Slate. I think she could, if she gave it a chance."

"I just don't think that sending back more pictures is the right way to handle it."

"So what is the right way?"

She said nothing: I assumed that meant she actually had no idea. I sat there being very demoralised for a while. There wasn't much Slate could say to help, and we both knew it. She was perfectly well aware that I wouldn't want to be calmed with platitudes.

Finally it was time to go. I left a sizeable tip to compensate the warriors and the valkyries for their patience, and set off through the frantic streets.

Vallis and Mons was one of several similar establishments along a broad arcade. It was near the edge of one of the domes. The gel roof was almost transparent here, but I could just make out its shimmer above the rather Gothic facade of the building.

There were two bouncers at the doorway, one each male and female. They were wearing neat-looking matching tartan costumes. They were also wearing badges which called them club entrance assistants, but I wasn't fooled. They obviously decided that I was not going to present a problem, and waved me through.

Inside, the club was pulsing with heavy, rhythmic music. The light level was low enough to provoke your imagination, but bright enough you could see your way ahead. More or less. A narrow entrance passageway widened into a small hall, with several ways leading off it. Another two people stood behind a little desk. The man was wearing a kilt and waistcoat, the woman a short dress, all in matching blues and greens, with lots of unnecessary decorative frills and buckles. Their lapel badges said they were welcoming executives. Another matched couple: *Vallis and Mons* was entirely consistent in its quest for equal opportunity.

They sized me up in a rapid glance, and the woman stepped forward to welcome me. She came and stood unnecessarily close to me, and said something conventional by way of greeting. I felt myself being absorbed in the invitation of her exotic perfume and Pacific rim features. I needed to be careful about my reactions after the disappointment of Shayna's reply.

"I'm here to meet with someone: Jocasta Sphinx. I'm a bit early, but perhaps there's somewhere I could wait?"

She must have run a query with a remote system to check up on me, but she was very well trained. Not a trace of it showed in her face, and she remained completely focused on me throughout.

"Your booth is already available, sir. One of our interior facilitators will show you."

Another woman emerged from one of the side corridors, summoned by some discreet signal.

"I'm Honeysuckle, sir. I'll be your interior facilitator today. Please follow me to your private booth."

I dutifully followed along. Her variation of the blue and green theme was simpler, thinner, and more suggestive than those of the welcoming executives. Slate and I speculated just how many rungs there were in the internal hierarchy.

Honeysuckle took me round several twists in the corridor, along the edge of a larger hall, and finally ushered me into an alcove off to one side. I sat down and accepted the drink she offered. I didn't dare ask the price, and vaguely wondered if Elias would sign it off as a necessary expense.

I had expected the place to be empty at this hour, but actually it was buzzing with groups of every size, as well as singles scattered here and there. A small combo band was playing on the stage, their music built largely around a very willowy oboe player. Predictably, there were dancers, alternately male and female, in various states of undress.

Honeysuckle was back. Another girl was following her, carrying my drink, but hovering in the background. Her blue and green outfit was almost entirely asymmetrical, with her skin showing where patches of fabric were missing. It could hardly be accidental, given the attention to detail I had seen in the rest of the establishment.

"Blossom will be your personal companion, sir, together with another individual suited to the tastes of your partner when she arrives. Please allow me to show you how we can satisfy your needs."

She ran through a very simple menu system, with much more eye contact and physical proximity than was called for. As well as drinks and snacks, it seemed that all manner of more personal services could be ordered, each intended to promote the maximum enjoyment my partner and I could desire. Slate giggled every time that Honeysuckle referred to Jocasta as my partner, but I ignored that.

Finally Blossom set my drink down. The container was large and ornate, but did not seem to contain very much fluid. I supposed it had been poured by a junior liquid dispensing associate, or some such, and thanked Blossom anyway. She reminded me again how to order refills and other satisfaction items, and moved away with a kind of sensuous wriggle.

I sampled my drink exceedingly slowly, trying to make it stretch out as long as possible, and waited. It was exotic, slightly perfumed, and not at all nice. So far as I could tell, the alcohol content was extremely low. But fortunately it was only a short time before I saw Honeysuckle threading her way across the floor towards the booth again. And behind her was Jocasta, with the orange pashmina which had helped us trace her on Phobos folded neatly over her arm. It was time for us to meet.

There was a pause while we went through the rigmarole of Jocasta asking for a drink, being shown how the ordering system worked, and being waited on by an impressive young man with the improbable name of Titan. His NuFleece outfit was marginally less complete than Blossom's. Finally we were on our own.

Over my cochlea implant, I heard Slate give an almost in-audible reminder of her presence. I needed that: I really didn't want to do this on my own. I assumed that Shepherd's Crag was doing exactly the same with Jocasta. She leaned forward.

"Thank you for meeting me like this, Mr Thakur. I don't suppose it was an easy decision for you to make."

I nodded.

"It wasn't. And I didn't know if I would see just you, or Dafyd as well. Or whatever he is calling himself just now. The mysterious O Sphinx."

"He can't get used to the name. I'm a little disappointed that you and Slate haven't worked it out yet. Let's just call him Dippy for now."

I really wasn't in the mood for guessing games.

"Also, I'm sure I wouldn't have picked this place. Is there a particular reason you said to meet here?"

"Several. For one thing, Dippy Dafyd would never come here, and I want us to have privacy while you decide what you're doing. And for another..."

She smiled wickedly and consulted the menu system. She gestured to where Titan was standing a little distance away and tapped briefly at the interface. A large portion of his outfit faded, baring his right shoulder and upper right arm. He rather ostentatiously flexed his deltoids in response.

"It's a neat trick, don't you think? It appeals to both my technical soul and my fantasy one. You can do the same for Blossom, if you like? Pick how much you want to pay and she'll lose an appropriate portion of NuFleece. Different body parts cost different amounts. It can become quite expensive if you get carried away. You'll need to be careful."

I must have looked disapproving, for she laughed at me. This wasn't going at all how Slate and I had planned.

"Difficult to put through expenses, perhaps? My treat then: I don't have to justify my choices to anybody."

She worked the menu again and committed the selection with a flourish, watching me all the time. I kept my eyes on her, determined not to be manoeuvred into gawping at Blossom.

"I've worked out how it's done, Mit. The club has linked the NuFleece API to the menu system. It's a similar idea to what you did on Bryher for Glyndwr with his staff outfits."

I didn't like the comparison.

"I only changed some colours, and cycled through an album of images. This is a different thing altogether. But never mind that. We need to get this conversation back on track. Any ideas? Give me a proper suggestion, quickly."

"Try to refocus on the purpose of this meeting."

"What exactly is it you want from me, Jocasta?"

"I want your help to get away from Dippy. I'll help you fix the default value code – I'll even show you how it works, if you like. For free. You might find it helpful somewhere else. Other than earning me a bit of cash, its main purpose was to attract your attention. So I no longer need it. Oh, but I also want your guarantee that nobody will come after me for that. The amounts are trivial, anyway, and you know it."

"Why do you need my help? Surely someone of your talent should be able to just slip away from him. But before we get to that, we need to talk about what happened on Teän."

Her face tightened.

"The two are connected. I didn't want anything to happen to Selif. Perhaps we should call him Laius, rather than Selif. Anyway, I was just going to slip away, as you put it. There wasn't anything to keep me with him any longer, and I wasn't going to hold a grudge for his carelessness. But it didn't work out like that."

"You're saying that you didn't kill him? It wasn't you who arranged the nav updates?"

"It wasn't me. It was Dafyd. Dippy Dafyd did away with him."

"Seems unlikely, Mit. Dafyd had no skill as a coder when we last saw him."

I repeated this to Jocasta. She nodded, ruefully.

"That's exactly what everyone will say. But think about it. It doesn't take coding skills, only some careful planning and a good sense of timing. Dafyd is a gamer, and he has both of those talents in abundance. He can't write a game, but he can play one, and manipulate the cheat codes with the best of them. But look now: you assumed it was me, and everybody else will do the same. Our Dippy has got vids of when Selif and I were arguing, and a few other pieces of circumstantial evidence, and he's holding them over me. Keeping me quiet.

Making sure I can't leave him. He knows that people will only see what they want to see, and I'll be held responsible."

"And you want out?"

"Yes, of course. He became unpleasantly flirty with me back on St Mary's every time Selif wasn't around. It was really creepy, sometimes. But I just put that down to the frustrations of adolescence. When Selif lost everything he got more persistent. Said I was nearer his age than Selif's and that really I should go with him. That Selif could give me nothing but failure. Well, I was angry with Selif and played along for a while. It was a distraction, with a rather pleasant edge of revenge. But then he became obsessed. And he had taken the precaution of recording some vids of the two of us together. Very personal vids. In the end, all he wanted was to be dominant. The crash on Teän was his way to reinforce his hold over me."

I must have looked unconvinced.

"Look, my namesake killed herself to get out of her situation. Look it up, sometime. As for me, I'm going to find a better answer. You're it. You and Slate, working with me and Shepherd's Crag to secure my exit."

"But he'll still have the evidence you talked about. What difference will Slate and I make?"

"That's part of the deal. Shepherd's Crag on his own can't get to it. Dafyd has acquired a system which is secure against that. But two personas working together should be able to hack in, erase the necessary items, and slip out again."

I sat back and looked at her in disbelief.

Blossom obviously interpreted this as a signal that I was in need, and wandered over with another drink. Jocasta's hand hovered over the menu board, teasing me. I resolutely ignored her, determined not to be distracted by whatever state of undress Jocasta had chosen for her.

"You expect the two of us to destroy evidence? Evidence which could incriminate you of murder?"

"She's not offering enough, Mit. She can't possibly expect us to accept these terms. And I'm not at all sure I believe the background story about Dafyd."

"I agree. Absolutely. At the moment what she's offering is an absurd proposition."

I pursed my lips and shook my head.

"Look now, Jocasta, I need much more than this. Slate and I can fix the default value code in a couple of ways. Yes, it would be nice to know how you did it, but that's actually not my top priority just now."

She listened carefully. I suspected that she was conferring with Shepherd's Crag, just like I was with Slate. We were circling each other, sizing each other up like sparring partners, or newly matched dancers.

"So actually you're not opposed in principle? It's just the price we're haggling about?"

I hesitated, and could feel Slate pondering along with me. We had on occasion in the past been less than complete in the final reports we sent down to ECRB, so it wasn't as if we were always squeaky clean. But I wasn't quite sure where the line was in this case. It certainly wasn't just some short teaching sessions on how to write obfuscated code.

And then, I knew that both Slate and I were working our way towards a different proposition.

"Jocasta. Have either of you heard of Robin's Rebels?"

~~~~~~~~~~~~~~~~~~~~~~~~

She looked at me, speculatively. Slate was holding her virtual breath, but in the end couldn't restrain herself.

"Always assuming that she isn't behind the group herself. We're taking a big chance here."

"*True. But I don't believe that. I suppose we'll find out soon enough. Anyway, my sense is that you agree with me.*"

"*I do. What little I can glean from Shepherd's Crag tells me that he is innocent of that particular business. But he is very guarded in what he makes available to me. I can't assume he is being either truthful or honest.*"

"*Make sure you're just as careful with him.*"

She agreed wholeheartedly, and we tuned outward again.

"No, we haven't. Should we have?"

I explained briefly what we knew from the college. I didn't tell her where it had happened, and stuck to the technical details. I ended up talking about the leaflets we had come across, and my flawed assumption that the group had no technical ability. As I had expected, she was outraged by the impact on the Sarsen twins.

"If it wasn't for that, I wouldn't be bothered. I don't object to their basic agenda, and there's a few institutions that could benefit from losing credit to some well thought-out blackmail. They're too arrogant, and far too sloppy about security. But attacking twins like that offends me. And Shepherd's Crag feels even more strongly about it than I do. That swings it for us. Stupid of them, really. If they'd not done that, I wouldn't be inclined to help you. As it is..."

She shrugged.

"Well, tell me more. What are you looking for from us?"

Apparently Slate had relayed her own experiences of what had happened to the twins. Just then, there was a cheer elsewhere in the room. We both looked up. There was a large mixed group of young professionals there – it looked like an office party – with a little gaggle of personal companions assigned to them, male and female. Apparently the group had just chipped in to pay for one of the men to lose his last vestige of clothing.

They cheered again and called for another round of drinks. Some were taking little vids and stills of each other with the man. Others were working the menus together and glancing speculatively at the other companions. My guess was that it was only a matter of time before somebody else was naked. It was not going to be a cheap night for that group.

I shook my head and turned back to Jocasta.

"Help us solve this, and we'll help you with your problem in relation to Dafyd."

"Do I have a lot of choice?"

"Not if you want us to join you in destroying evidence."

"In that case there's nothing to think about. We'll do it."

She paused, presumably to check with Shepherd's Crag. Slate was still unable to tap into their chat, or glean anything from him beyond a superficial shell.

"Next question – where do we go? I don't want to stay on the same planet as Dippy any longer than I have to. How about we neutralise his hold over me first, and then move on to wherever you expect Robin's Rebels to strike next?"

"You have to be joking. If we do that first, what stops you just disappearing and leaving me on my own?"

"But if I just try to skip planet with all that left in his hands, he'll make it public. I have to remove his advantage first. Surely that's obvious? I'm taking a big risk even just meeting you here. He can be jealous beyond reason, and is quite capable of becoming violent."

It was an impasse. I vividly remembered the time when Dafyd had tried to force entry into my room on St Mary's, back on my first trip there. In the pause, another cheer came from across the room. Neither of us took any notice. Then, unexpectedly, Slate spoke up, aloud over my lapel pickup rather than through the implant.

"How about if Shepherd's Crag and I access the material first? But instead of deleting it, we transfer it to a secure holding area under our control. We only permanently destroy it once the other business is resolved."

Jocasta hesitated, thinking about it. After a pause Slate continued.

"I understand that you will see this as just perpetuating the risk, not removing it. But who do you feel you can trust more: Dafyd or us?"

She laughed. Meanwhile, I was thinking how much I liked Slate's idea. It kept us in control of the situation – as much in control as you could ever feel where Jocasta was concerned.

"Well, Slate, since you put it like that, there has to be only one answer. I agree to your terms. This calls for another drink. My round, to acknowledge the deal before we work out the details."

I had a slightly uncomfortable feeling that I would be drinking the results of the very fraud I was supposed to stop. Elias was, understandably, very hot on what could be considered conflicts of interest, or compromised dealings. How would this look, if one of the more aggressive news channels got hold of our conversation?

But out here, far away from colleagues, you couldn't question everything. Right now it would be ungracious to decline, and could potentially derail the entire negotiation.

I decided I would work through the ethical issues later. As if to underline the problem, there was still more cheering from nearby. *Vallis and Mons* must be raking the profit in.

Jocasta worked the menu again, and with hardly a pause, Titan and Blossom were bringing fresh drinks.

Somewhat to my relief, Blossom was still just about decent, though much more of her skin was now visible. She was doing her best to show off the body parts that were still covered.

I surmised that removing the last scraps of NuFleece would cost more than Jocasta was likely to pay.

"So. Where will you go next? I assume you have that sloop of yours up on Phobos? My cutter's on Deimos, so I'll need to catch the regular service out there."

"Actually, we are in a lifeboat. It's back to the Scilly Isles for us now, but not under our own steam. We hitched a ride down here and will need to do the same back again. But as for you, isn't it a risk going in your cutter? Won't Dafyd just know exactly where to follow?"

"No need to worry about that. I know how to hide a trail. Once we have the data, and I'm away from him, I won't be concerned about that."

It seemed doubtful to me, but I let it go. Instead, I told her about the London team's target prediction. She was not very impressed with only a sixty percent likelihood, but it was better than nothing. She thought about it briefly.

"I'm sure I can attach your lifeboat to my cutter. You can piggy-back with me."

It was high time to clarify something.

"We'll need to travel independently. I'm happy to be working with you, but we can't be seen making that long trip together."

"Whyever not? Seen by whom? ECRB? Robin's Rebels?"

"Either of those. Both of them. We'll be making separate journeys."

She clearly found the situation highly entertaining, and made no secret of it.

"You should find work where that sort of thing doesn't matter. It's hilarious that you can't even travel how you please. You know, if you ever get fed up with all that, I reckon we could make a good partnership."

I said nothing out loud, but made some incredulous noises internally to Slate. To my surprise, she had not ruled it out at first hearing.

"Shepherd's Crag might be fun to work with. And I think you and Jocasta could get along, with a bit of practice."

"There are trust issues involved."

"They can be overcome. Let's see how this first collaborative venture turns out."

"Just make sure you don't let him trick you. Right now I don't really believe either of them."

Jocasta and I stood up. As if drawn by magnetism, Blossom and Titan converged on the booth. There was a lot of talk about how much they hoped we had enjoyed the *Vallis and Mons* experience, and in particular the personal companionship they had provided. They gave us little single-use feedback slips and encouraged us to register them through Blagger. They pressed close around us, making it difficult to get away, but in the end Jocasta linked her arm in mine and said we were aiming to carry on our conversation in private. They let us go then.

We made our escape. Jocasta was about to throw her feedback slip away, but I stopped her.

"At a guess, their status in that club depends on getting enough of those slips back."

"But you spent most of the time not looking at pretty little Blossom. Now you're going to say something nice about her?"

"Why not?"

She shook her head and dropped the subject, although she did keep the slip.

Instead, we talked about how we were going to acquire the data from Dafyd. Slate and Shepherd's Crag were going to work on the technicalities of access through the afternoon.

Slate would post the data to a secure location known only to the two of us, using a private key algorithm. She and I each had independent read-only views, and it needed assent from both of us in order to delete it. The data retrieval itself was timed to take place during the evening meal.

Jocasta then booked a transport to Deimos which left at almost the same time, where she would transfer to her own vessel. I would get the next hopper shuttle back to Phobos. We would both arrange onward routing, and meet again at the Scilly Isles. She offered again to give us a ride, and again I refused.

"I suppose I need to change my name again, so Dippy can't trace me. Pity: I was starting to like the sound of Jocasta."

I made a vaguely sympathetic sound. We turned to go our separate ways. She suddenly caught my arm again. All of a sudden she had become serious. There had to be more underneath the surface of this situation than I yet knew.

"Thank you. I do appreciate what you are doing here. And that it is a risk for you. Now, we'll chat on the way out to the asteroids, I'm sure, but this is a free gift, just to get you thinking about the code you found on Callisto. It's all in the timing. Think about it."

"We guessed that, if only because if we edited anything at all, the behaviour changed completely. But I don't properly understand it yet."

"I'll show you. You have to know in detail how the messaging is sequenced. It's all in the timing. I think you'll like it, when you see how it's done."

⁓⁓⁓⁓⁓⁓⁓⁓⁓⁓⁓⁓⁓⁓⁓⁓

I went back to my lockup room, retrieved the few bits and pieces in it, and made my way towards the dock. There was no need for me to be personally present here on Mars during tonight's exercise. In fact, it was much better to eliminate any chance that Dafyd might see me. I was lucky; there was less than an hour to wait for the next departure.

There were quiet corners at the dock, and I sat blissfully in one of them, ignoring everybody. I wouldn't be sorry to leave Elysium Planitia. The comparative peace on this bench lent itself to just letting my mind freewheel around. Slate had pulled out from archives a whole lot of mythological material about Jocasta and Oedipus – Dippy, I presumed – but I couldn't work up too much interest in it. Slate was happy, though, piecing together names and allusions from the earlier conversation.

Instead, I found myself wondering about Jocasta's practical intentions. Slate had told me what her mythological namesake had done to herself, and it was clear that Jocasta was not going to imitate her: not in this respect, at least. But what would she do?

Assuming all was going to plan, she would be collecting a few essentials into a small carry-on bag through the afternoon. To avoid arousing Dafyd's suspicions, she was just abandoning most of her belongings. I was sure it would not take her long to acquire what she wanted again, by fair means or foul. Then there was a short transit on foot to the Deimos shuttle site – the next dome area along from this one – and away before Dafyd realised.

Even after reflection, I still thought that the plan to secure her help by trading Dafyd's stored data was a good one. There was a certain pleasing symmetry about it, as well; it seemed entirely appropriate to frustrate one blackmail attempt by resolving another.

However, I still felt that neither she nor Shepherd's Crag could be relied upon. What was important was damage limitation, and ensuring that Slate and I had our backs covered at all times.

Slate's voice drifted in to merge with my musings.

"*Shepherd's Crag and I have finalised the timetable for re-trieving the data. As agreed, we are going to start at the time Dafyd is booked in for dinner. Jocasta's shuttle undocks for Deimos soon after. You and I will have been out at Phobos for about an hour by then. By the time Dafyd realises, none of us will be anywhere in the vicinity.*"

"*Sounds perfect. Do be careful with Shepherd's Crag.*"

I had a vivid sense of impatience from her over the internal link.

"*I know I'm being a nag, but the whole arrangement bothers me.*"

"*We're committed to it now. And it was you who actually asked them first.*"

"*I remember. But that doesn't mean I have to like it. Let's talk about something else. Like, have you booked our ride back home to the Harbour Porpoise?*"

"*Yes. I've been working on that for the last few hours, on and off. We're being carried by a fast freighter bound for Vesta, with an acceptably close orbital option. They won't dock, or even slow down; they'll just toss us out at a suitable point. The velocity difference is too high for the lifeboat to manage, but I've negotiated with Finn to meet us in his Selkie.*"

I nodded. Selkie's ketch engines were amply good enough to do the necessary speed matching to settle us on any of the islands. The Harbour Porpoise was still on St Mary's, but we might want to go directly to St Martin's and help Rydal. It all depended on what happened while we were in transit. Some departure status lights changed on a display a little further along the quayside, and I moved from my quiet bench to join the other half dozen people riding on the hopper. I briefly wondered how they had coped with Mars.

We were half way up, and the sky had turned to space, when Slate broke in to my reverie.

"Here's a surprise, Mit. I have just received a voice message from Elias."

We had been sending daily reports down to Finsbury Circus, but it was extremely unusual for Elias to reply like this. The most we usually got back was a simple acknowledgement. Slate started playing it.

> Mitnash, I have a proposal I'd like you to think about. The senior management team have been reviewing all staff allocations. We are going to divide the solar system into three distinct regions. One is purely Earth-based. The next is everything else inside Mars. The last goes from Mars and its moons outwards. That third one is far and away the most volume, of course. But when you break our recent caseload down, those three regions consume almost equal amounts of effort. I would like you to take on that third region. That means you will drop anything else with immediate effect, although we expect you to collaborate with your two counterparts as and when necessary. We're making similar offers for the other two regions to appropriate individuals right now.

> We can talk about the details once you've digested it, but we will pay any reasonable relocation costs, and consider ad hoc expenses as we go along. You'll have a set of agreed targets to meet, but prioritisation will be largely up to you. And we will look sympathetically on requests for additional junior team members, associate level only at this stage. Your Stele will log receipt of this message, of course, but I need a broad-brush response from you personally by the end of the week.

I absorbed the message, getting Slate to repeat bits of it.

"So we could live out on the Scilly Isles if we wanted?"

"Sounds like it. Would you like that?"

"Oh yes, I would. Definitely. Which island would we pick? Would it be Bryher? But maybe you'll want St Martin's now? How do we choose?"

We chattered over the prospect for a while, until I proposed saying yes to Elias right away. At that point Slate hesitated.

"I'll send that if you want. But aren't you going to talk about it with Shayna? Judging by her last message, she's already unimpressed by the amount of time you're away from Earth. It's not going to get easier if we're permanently committed to the outer system."

It was a stumbling block. And actually, we were approaching the Asaph quayside already. I needed to concentrate on getting back to the lifeboat, and Slate would be starting preliminary work with Shepherd's Crag. We would have to pick this up later.

I sat in the pilot's chair of the lifeboat, with nothing to do. We had undocked from Phobos a short time before, and were waiting to be collected by the freighter. The captain had already received my manual confirmation that everything was prepared on my side, on top of all the automated stuff which had happened earlier.

There was really no such thing as an orbit around Phobos, given its tiny size, and proximity to its primary. So we were basically in Mars orbit, a little further out than the moon, drifting ever so slowly away from it. I wasn't likely to see Stickney from this angle, still less Percival, but Asaph was still visible.

I wasn't really bothered about the view. The main thing I wanted to hear about was the infiltration into Dafyd's storage area, and the recovery of the information he was using to exert control over Jocasta. Always assuming that the whole story was even true, about which I was still doubtful. Slate had talked me through the plan she and Shepherd's Crag would use. It was very neat, very logical, and clearly explained why it was necessary to have both personas working together. I still harboured doubts. But Jocasta had much more to lose than I did at this stage, and at best, it would be a trial run for working together against Robin's Rebels.

The two personas had practised their intended exploit a while ago, in a sandbox based on Shepherd's Crag's knowledge of the system. That had gone well, but we all knew that unexpected things often turned up when you went live. To paraphrase the old saying, no software plan survives first contact with reality. But if everything did go to plan, they would take several minutes to hack in without raising alarms, about quarter of an hour to move all of the incriminating evidence out, then another few minutes to cover their tracks and back away gracefully. Less than half an hour all told. That would take us right up to the point where we would grapple onto the freighter and head off outwards.

Slate was very cheery. Obviously she was looking forward to this piece of work.

"Dafyd and Jocasta have just checked in for dinner."

She had pulled up a map of the relevant Elysium Planitia dome, showing the layout of the buildings, and two little cartoon people. We had no visibility of anybody else, but Shepherd's Crag could track Jocasta through her cochlea implant, and Dafyd by means of a tracer they had prepared earlier. One of the two moved away from the other.

"Jocasta has just said that she forgot something in the room and will be gone for a few minutes. Dafyd has accepted this without dispute."

The animated figure moved across the screen slowly, then turned out of a door and left the building. I imagined Jocasta glancing back, making sure that nobody was watching, before picking up her daybag and walking sedately from the hotel.

Suddenly the cartoon speeded up. I looked back at Dafyd's icon, but it was still at the table.

"She's running, Mit. Why is she doing that? It wasn't what we planned. She'll draw attention to herself. I'm not getting any sensible ideas about it from Shepherd's Crag, either."

"You two had better start right away, if you can persuade him to move fast."

For answer she split the screen. The left half showed the map, with the two figures gradually separating. The other side showed the progress of the data retrieval operation.

"Shepherd's Crag says she's really frightened. But he's having to put most of his attention into the hack, so can't really find out what's wrong."

Jocasta was almost at the quayside gate, when the second figure started moving from the table. Obviously Dafyd was more suspicious than I had expected. Jocasta's anxiety started to make sense. I imagined her pushing through the swirling crowds, constantly driven to look over her shoulder in case of pursuit. I was leaning forward in my chair, willing her to move faster.

I realised at that point that I had already crossed a line; I wanted her to succeed.

"We've got past the main security access check now. Just the dual interlock to go."

Slate sounded breathy, though in her case it would be because so much of her resource was focused on the job. This was precisely the place where she and Shepherd's Crag had to work perfectly in sync with each other in order to crack in, where one persona acting alone could do nothing.

Dafyd's icon was still in the hotel, in the reception area. I supposed he was talking to one of the hotel staff. Jocasta was moving across to the docked shuttle, when her moving avatar stopped. I jumped out of my seat.

"What's happened?"

I felt completely helpless, safely up here in the lifeboat.

"She fell. She's getting up again. No harm, I think."

After a pause she spoke again, her voice back to normal.

"We're in. Starting data transfer to the lifeboat systems."

Jocasta had started moving again, slower than before. I tried to guess if she was limping, or if the press of people was tighter here. Dafyd suddenly started running towards his room.

"It seems that we accidentally fired off an alert. Shepherd's Crag knew nothing of it, but Dafyd must have had some kind of private alarm rigged up. We don't have all that long before he can shut us out manually."

Jocasta was filing onto the shuttle, and I relaxed a little. At least she had been able to get away. Dafyd was pounding through the hotel, along the corridors back to the room. I was sure there was far too little time. Then, suddenly, his icon vanished from the screen. I blinked.

"Where's he gone?"

"Um. I don't know. Shepherd's Crag thinks he must have remembered that he was carrying the tracer. Turned it off or something. But at the rate he was going, we're not going to get all the data out."

She sounded annoyed rather than frustrated.

"We'll carry on as long as we can. We can always delete whatever's left, that takes hardly any time at all. It's the copy that drags on."

"Get as much as you can."

Another wave of suspicion washed past me. Was this just another trick to keep the data from falling into our hands, so that Jocasta could flee with impunity? Had she herself tipped off Dafyd, or possibly kept quiet about the extra defence so the two personas would be bound to trip over it? Meanwhile, her shuttle was going through the final undocking checks.

"Just keep going as long as possible, Slate. Get whatever you can in the remaining time. Just don't leave it too late. I don't want you to be identifiable in this."

She buzzed her acknowledgement and carried on working. I was trying to estimate how quickly Dafyd would get to the room from the place where his marker had disappeared. It wasn't all that great a distance.

I sat there, half-aware of the Deimos shuttle lifting off from the surface, and with a kind of countdown ticking manically away in my head. I was convinced that the time was going more slowly than I expected, when Slate chirped up again, sounding puzzled.

"He still hasn't arrived, Mit. I don't understand it. We should have been interrupted before now. But Shepherd's Crag is monitoring the door security vid, and Dafyd has not even got to the corridor yet."

I wondered if he had changed his mind and headed somewhere else, but of course we had no way of knowing. It was too late for him to catch the shuttle, even if he guessed that was her destination. The seconds clicked by. Then a minute. Longer. I hardly dared breathe for all that time, until Slate got back to me.

"We've finished acquiring the data. I have no idea why Dafyd took that much time, but it was all we needed. We've already detached from the main storage device, and Shepherd's Crag is making sure all traces of our activity have been removed. Looks like we're in the clear."

"Do look over his shoulder to make sure he doesn't forget anything."

"I will. But you should know that he has done everything entirely to our specification. Nothing less, nothing more. Very reliable. Honourable, even. It has been a good experience working with him."

"Well, congratulate him from me, and let's hope that we all carry on working well together."

I glanced at the storage monitor. There was a huge tranche of new content. I sampled a few frames here and there, just to make sure it was what it was supposed to be, then closed the image streams. I was glad it was there, but I didn't want to look too closely at it. If even half what Jocasta had said about it was true, too much idle browsing through the content would seriously compromise our working relationship.

I was pleased with the outcome, but also confused that it had not been interrupted. The shuttle was a good chunk of the way towards its destination, and the freighter captain was in his final stages of approach to pick us up.

And just then Slate showed me a breaking news report from Elysium Planitia. There had been a violent mugging in one of the hotels, and a young man had been found dead in a hotel corridor.

Of course it was Dafyd. The nearby security vids had been mysteriously disabled just at the right moment, so there was no visual record. The hotel had already issued a statement – it looked like a standard template – saying that they were cooperating fully with the authorities, but that private feuds occasionally spilled outside their renowned and strictly regulated gambling rooms.

I had a feeling that they saw this simply as a publicity opportunity, and had everything already prepared. Perhaps this sort of thing happened every week.

Meanwhile our piggyback ride had begun, and we were clinging to the side of the freighter with half a dozen umbilical feeds providing various kinds of link.

I waited impatiently for Jocasta to dock at Deimos, transfer to her cutter, and set off. I wanted as few barriers to communication as possible, so decided against just chatting with her through the two personas. I had all kinds of alarms and suspicions fizzing inside me, but it would be only fair to hear her side of the story.

So I sat there waiting for her to signal her availability to talk, and meanwhile had flags set on all the Martian newsfeeds. Slate was trying to find out what she could as well.

A flashnews viewport popped up. One of the croupiers had reported that Dafyd had been asked to leave the tables for a cooling off period yesterday. An argument with another player had escalated from lively to disruptive.

A hotel spokesperson took over from the croupier, explaining that their policy, approved by the dome chief deputy, was to separate the two players for an hour and give them both some free entertainment while they calmed down. Statistically this solved the problem in nearly ninety percent of cases. He expressed regret that this was one of the ten percent.

Another popup appeared, this time gleaned by Slate from the official hotel feed. Although the vids in the corridor in question had failed, images from elsewhere showed Dafyd moving rapidly from the dining room towards his suite, and the other gambler moving to cut across his path. It seemed clear that they had met, fatally, not all that far from his door. The hotel had handed all the evidence to the chief deputy, and returned to business as usual.

Finally Jocasta's callsign appeared on the screen. I connected. She seemed tired, unburdened, and dishevelled, all at once. I had never before seen her look anything other than neat. Words burst out of her.

"You caught your ride with the freighter?"

She didn't wait for my reply.

"I can't tell you how relieved I am. The moment I left the hotel, I kept thinking he was just behind me. Kept thinking I could hear his voice, or those heavy boots of his, about to catch me. I didn't believe I would get clear away to the quayside."

"That was why you ran?"

"I couldn't stop myself. I was desperate to get away. I know the plan said I would walk casually, but I couldn't do it. Not once I thought there was a chance. Even a small chance. Shepherd's Crag tells me you have the data. Is that right? I'm free of him?"

I nodded. She blinked, and an odd expression crossed her face. For a few moments I thought she was going to cry. Then she looked at me, puzzled.

"What's the matter? Is something wrong?"

"Jocasta, you've probably not heard, but Dafyd was killed in the hotel. He left the table and was going back to the room. I expect he thought he was checking up on you. But he never got there. They think another gambler killed him after a dispute yesterday."

She stared at me, giving every appearance of someone baffled by events. I couldn't tell if it was genuine, or just a good act. She glanced to one side, presumably scanning her own series of popups that Shepherd's Crag was providing. Then she looked back at me, and her expression changed.

"You think I had something to do with it. That I set it up somehow."

I took a deep breath.

"The thought had crossed my mind."

She was about to retort angrily, but I held up my hand.

"Look, right now, I don't know what I think: we can talk about that another time. But my opinion doesn't matter. The hotel has given all the information to the deputy's office. Assuming your name was in that, you can expect him to be looking for you. He'll find you left the planet at almost the same time. What do you think he will assume?"

She shook her head. Her voice had gone very ragged.

"Dafyd always insisted on having those rooms booked in his sole name. It was a role play he demanded. You see, I was supposed to be just a convenient bed-companion he just found available. He had all kinds of fantasies like that which I had to play out."

She looked away, shame filling her face, then controlled herself and met my eyes again.

"Anyway, the hotel records will not show full dual occupancy, but only that he entertained a female guest every night. The staff were aware of me, but none of them knew my name. And they were trained not to notice things like that."

I already knew that she was adept at remaining inconspicuous, so that part was easy to understand. But otherwise, I had no idea what to make of it. Her professional life was one of competence and power, in which difficult problems were dismissed with ease. But now she was showing me a vision of a personal life in which she was diminutive, submissive to Dafyd's whims. I could not see how to reconcile the two views; the contrast was just too great.

"No wonder you enjoyed the contract work on Phobos so much. It was a way to get some freedom."

"I really liked it. I can't tell you how much. It was a little taste of life without Dafyd, of how things might be. He still insisted that I clock in with him every day, and he came to the moon a couple of times to check up on me. But as a rule, he wouldn't leave the games on Elysium Planitia for any length of time. That team at Percival were very kind to me, too. Angeline and all the rest of them."

She smiled, ruefully.

"Of course, that didn't stop me making the code changes you know about. Apart from anything else, I wanted you to find them so that Slate and Shepherd's Crag could get those records."

I was still puzzling it out.

"I suppose there's nothing on Mars that links you to him?"

"Nothing at all. A few female bits and pieces in his rooms, which will surprise nobody. But nothing named. And seeing that our two personas did their work so well, nothing in the virtual sphere either."

I was silent for a long time. Eventually she spoke again. She still looked, and sounded, very distressed.

"I'll still help you with that Sarsen lockup thing. Robin's Rebels and all. What's happened today doesn't change that."

"I'm glad to hear it."

"Look, I need to clean myself up now. And recover in other ways too. Can we talk again some other time?"

We broke the connection. Of course, we each knew where the other one would be for the next couple of weeks as we transferred out into the asteroid belt, so we could talk anytime we wanted.

I sat in the chair for a long time, knowing that Slate was following my train of thought through my subvocal musing.

I had no idea whether Jocasta was the happy recipient of an astonishing stroke of luck, or instead, an extremely astute individual who had just carried out a particularly clever murder. On balance, I still held to my previous opinion that she was not temperamentally inclined towards murder, but just now I couldn't be sure. Whichever it was, I would be working with her in a few weeks time, out at the Scilly Isles.

Part 4 – St Mary's

TEN DAYS LATER, the freighter disconnected everything and pushed the lifeboat off. I was lucky that the Scilly Isles were at their closest orbital position to Mars – had things been different it could easily have taken twice as long. I hadn't had much to do with the crew, just a couple of visits to their galley for politeness' sake. Most of the time had been here, in the lifeboat, but it really wasn't built for long journeys. I was thoroughly bored of the interior, and ready for a change.

Jocasta was several days behind me now. Her cutter had smaller engines than her old wrecked sloop, and in any case she had begun her deceleration considerably earlier than us. Unlike the freighter, she wanted to actually land there rather than rush past en route to Vesta. Much closer to us, in terms of both position and speed, was Finn in the Selkie. He would connect with us in an hour or so, to do the serious velocity change work and dock us somewhere on Scilly. We would end up less than a day ahead of Jocasta, and there was plenty for us to do before she arrived.

Slate and I had spent the first half of the trip understanding the code trick that Jocasta and Shepherd's Crag had deployed on Callisto and Phobos. They wouldn't admit to its use anywhere else, but it seemed most unlikely that these were the only two locations. Time would tell, and at least now we had an idea what to look for. The first places we would check, when the dust had settled a bit, were Rhea and Iapetus, where we knew Jocasta had been before Callisto. *Wilusa Wealth*, back on Mars, was another high priority.

Contrary to her original dismissal that trawling through that code would be a solitary obsession of mine, Slate and I had enjoyed that piece of work. We had had some initial pointers, but really wanted to learn for ourselves how it worked. It felt too much like cheating to just have a tutorial with walkthrough.

We now felt that we had at least a basic grasp of what was happening. At least I could understand how the simple change to introduce logging – or pretty much anything else – would alter the behaviour quite radically.

The exploit relied on knowing in considerable detail how the messaging scheduler processed its inputs. I had never needed to look into it in this much depth, being a firm believer in keeping things as simple as possible. But if you really wanted to produce behaviour that was unlike what anyone would expect, this was the way to do it. With some careful crafting of the inputs you could generate one of several alternative outcomes.

The whole exercise had reminded us that we were newbies at that game compared to the other two. Following the changes after they had been exposed, and being able to craft them in the first place, were entirely different problems. We would never have seen the opportunity for this scam in the first place. It was a sobering reminder of just how much we would be depending on them when the real crisis broke.

Most days the four of us talked together about what we were calling the Twin Problem. We didn't have nearly enough hard information to decide anything for sure, but we talked anyway. About the only real evidence we had was the partial trace we had been given at Gordii Fossae, which we pulled apart in as many ways as we could imagine. According to Shepherd's Crag, it was only marginally better than nothing, but I needed to have something sketched out in my mind as to how we were going to approach this. A few ideas had emerged, but nothing that you could really call solid. I was beginning to realise that we would need to catch the event as it was happening. At least we now had a sense of what to look for.

Our opinion of their abilities had gone up another notch. But in contrast, I was still unpersuaded of their moral stance. Jocasta had quite quickly retreated away from the position of vulnerability she had shown on leaving Deimos, and was back to showing an impenetrable facade. Slate was getting no further with Shepherd's Crag.

Everything we had heard from Mars indicated that Dafyd's death had been filed away as insoluble. The suspect gambler swore that he had gone to a friend's room and never reached the fateful corridor. The friend backed him up, and in the absence of other witnesses the matter was dropped. It was all very casual, missing the forensic rigour which a similar crime on Earth would have attracted. Dafyd had nobody to plead his case and energise the deputy's office, and the hotel had no interest in pursuing it further. Nobody cared. I had never liked the young man, but it was a sorry end to his life.

So the deputy had never seen Jocasta's name from first to last, as she had expected. Whether by chance or design, she was free of Dafyd. I found the idea of chance hard to accept, but I wasn't going to get anywhere nearer the truth than anybody else.

I brought the subject up, carefully, a few times during the early part of the trip, but it was pointless. Jocasta deflected the questions half the time, and challenged my guesswork the other half. I couldn't tell if she was amused or angry. I gave up after that: I needed her willingness to work with me, and constantly repeating the same uncomfortable feelings was not going to secure that.

Most days, Khufu had relayed on to us another leaflet distributed by Robin's Rebels. They were appearing now with monotonous regularity. They always contained broadly the same text, with only very minor variations. I had a theory – perhaps more of a hunch – that their home base was on Ceres, where the first piece of evidence had surfaced. ECRB was trying to localise the source, but their estimation error volume was absurdly high. About all they were prepared to rule out was Mars and the inner system. That put it firmly into my space, but did nothing to help the investigation. For the time being I would have to chase symptoms and not cause.

And this was indeed now my space. Before the end of the first week I had replied to Elias with cautious acceptance. I had carefully used words like 'provisional' and 'tentative', but was well aware that that was not how ECRB worked. The senior management team would already have assumed that the move was now a definite fact. And, indeed, Slate and I were treating it the same way. When not working, we had pored over maps of the different settlements, and scanned through lists of free accommodation slots, trying to decide where to go.

We had already booked our inshore navigation test, which would allow us to hop between the islands ourselves. There would be no more waiting for someone else's boat to make the trip, and no more paying for passage.

I had already chattered about it with my friends on Scilly, and had a confusing, contradictory series of recommendations. Everyone thought their own island was best for me, and I felt bathed in warm welcome. Finally, and very cautiously, I broached the matter with Shayna. Slate and I had picked over and reworked the message for hours before sending it. I hadn't had an actual reply yet, but at least she had not ruled the possibility out point-blank. I didn't expect that she shared my own excitement – not yet, at least – but it was a start. I was optimistic that she would join me.

That was all positive. But other news was more alarming. There was the constant appearance of the leaflets, but worse that that, there were the results of investigations which had been going on in the background.

Armed with what we had found out at the college at Gordii Fossae, ECRB had probed more urgently into some of the giveaway clusters that had been seen in recent weeks. People were very reluctant to talk, and in some places there had been zero additional information. Clearly a fair number of people didn't mind the group's aims, especially if they were beneficiaries of a handout.

But twice now, one of the team had been able to confirm that there had been blackmail threats in the days before or after. The amounts varied considerably, perhaps based on an assessment by Robin's Rebels as to what a particular organisation could afford.

A group of options negotiators on Ceres, facing only a modest demand, had paid before the deadline. I presumed that they had been given sufficient proof of the ability of the attackers to carry out their threat. As I read through the report, it felt to me as though this was a first attempt, perhaps to trial the technology.

A much larger equities trading team on Vesta had refused the demand, but like the college, paid up promptly when their system crashed. Details were slight: even after applying considerable pressure, ECRB had not been able to find much out. The victims did not want to talk, and Earth-based enquiries and assurances carried very little weight. Finding out more would take personal presence.

I stopped thinking about all that when the Selkie matched my velocity and swallowed the lifeboat into her capacious hold. Slate was already deep in conversation with Lia Fail by the time that Finn confirmed that I was free to come aboard. I stretched gratefully and swapped into the bigger ship without looking back. It would be a long time before I willingly did a journey that far across the system in such cramped quarters.

Selkie's engines were already ramped up high to shed our excess speed. It didn't provide anywhere near as much gravity equivalent as Mars, but it was noticeably more than the freighter had used. I hardly needed to concentrate on my walking reflexes as I went along to the bridge.

Finn and I embraced, and he gestured to the worktop.

"I brought some of Glyndwr's ales, if you have a fancy."

I certainly did. The last alcohol I had had was in *Vallis and Mons*, and that had been weak and pretentious by comparison. I savoured the Gruffudd's Golden slowly, deliberately. Finn laughed.

"I've a whole mixed crate in the locker. You don't need to make that one little bottle last all the way to Hugh Town."

I sat, refusing to let my enjoyment be rushed, and greeted Lia Fail as well. Slate always treated her like a kind of benevolent maiden aunt, and was on her best behaviour. She was positively tongue-tied in comparison with her normal self. I found it highly entertaining – just as much as she clearly did as she watched my own interpersonal foibles.

The Selkie had made only a small difference to our vector when Slate buzzed me over the ship's voice system.

"There's news in from the Finsbury team, Mit. Another rash of those leaflets has appeared on St Mary's. As usual there's no target declared, but the logical one is the main hub. So far as is publicly known, there is no other twin Sarsen setup on the islands."

"Is there an update from anyone at the hub itself?"

"Not a word. But that fits what we have seen before: nobody admits to being affected, in case even worse things start to happen."

"And if it matches the pattern in other ways, they will already have received an ultimatum. We don't have long: perhaps five days at most."

Finn stirred.

"We'll be back on the islands well before that. Under three days, in fact, so you should have some slack."

I nodded absently. My mind was already busy as I started to plan ahead.

"Slate, we need Khufu and the London team to push harder on this one, given that we are dealing with blackmail. Find out who has had most dealings with the St Mary's group. I want somebody nagging day and night to find out who will be honest. This is no time for going all coy. Before Finn gets us there we need to get a much better idea what is happening."

"They'll probably say that they have very little leverage from that far away, and that it needs somebody on the spot to bang on doors. Looks like it'll be us."

"That may be. But I want them to do some preliminary work. See if they can get something out of somebody there. I want to know before we land if there has been another actual threat, as well as the leaflets. Now, for the time being let's assume that there really is a threat. Then you and I have to work out how best to make use of it. I think we should be right there at the time of the deadline. But do we want to pay up, like Mikko did, so that we can trace Robin's Rebels by means of the flow of credit? Or do we want to call their bluff and see what we can do to fend off the attack?"

"That's not a decision we can make alone."

"I know that. But when we reach there, I want us to go in with a plan already formulated."

I paused, and carried on silently, through the cochlea link.

"My gut feeling is that we need to let this happen. Allow the attack and identify the problem as it arises."

"I won't let you do that unless we warn the twins first, and can be right in there with them."

"Fair enough. We'll do everything we can to support them. But we need to understand enough about the attacks that we can stop them happening elsewhere. That won't happen unless the attack takes place."

She didn't reply.

"Let's talk about it later, Slate."

She agreed, and we returned to open speech.

"I'm sure that Finn can connect me to chat with the team lead there. As soon as I've got clearance, can you start talking to the Sarsens at Hugh Town? Maybe pass what you found out from the twins on Mars?"

"Castor and Pollux? I certainly can, though hearing about that experience might alarm them. Well, it should terrify them, really. It's an appalling thing to contemplate. The twins on St Mary's are called Shalem and Shahar, by the way."

I did not reply, but I must have internally communicated puzzlement.

"The Canaanite gods of the evening and morning star, respectively. That said, I do think your idea of following the money is a good one. The only question is whether that'll be enough. My guess is that this group are quite clever enough to cover their tracks."

"I know. That's why we need a backup plan. I think that we need to talk to Rydal and see if she is willing to help."

Finn looked at me.

"What can she do? I don't see any connection."

Slate maintained an eloquent silence, leaving it to me to decide what to say.

"I really can't say just yet, Finn. I need a chance to discuss this with her before we go into details."

He shrugged.

"Be my guest. You can set up the link from your cabin. Lia Fail and I will keep out of your way until you feel able to talk about it. Keeping the ale ready for you, so to speak."

I nodded and went down the corridor to the little room.

"Slate, what time is it on St Martin's? I don't want to wake her up or something. I suppose Capstone will field the call if it's not a good time."

"It's early evening for her. And yes, he would do that if she was busy, or asleep, or just didn't want to be disturbed. Just like I would for you. But supposing she takes your call, you won't notice any appreciable chat lag. Now, just to get all the names out of the way, the Sarsens in the system that she and her colleagues are working on are called Helen and Clytemnestra. Very classical, though a pedant would say that they were not exactly twins."

She sounded mildly ironic, and I decided not to ask why.

As soon as I saw Rydal's face appear on the screen, I leapt straight in to the issue uppermost in my mind.

"Rydal, I think we can tackle the Twin Problem. I'm going to be talking with the hub on St Mary's first, as soon as we land, but after that there's a good chance of bringing your system in as well. Can you be ready that soon?"

She stared at me.

"I don't know what you're talking about. What Twin Problem? What does that have to do with me?"

I realised as she spoke that she was very distressed.

"The Twin Problem is the name we've given to the technical flaw behind these unexpected credits. There are big losses being suffered by a few people, and the losses are linked in some way to the Sarsen twin configuration."

"Have you heard how they've threatened the main hub on Mary's? I was only told yesterday. I don't think the director there wanted anybody to know, but it leaked out anyway. You said that this Robin's Rebels group were all just talk. It doesn't sound like that now."

I paused, and backtracked. She hadn't been immersed in the technicalities in the way that Jocasta and I had been these last days, and I couldn't expect her to just catch on straight away. But I needed her to buy in to the plan I was formulating, and that was going to need some investment of time and empathy.

"I was wrong about that. But I've been spending time at a place on Mars where they had the same threat, and I have a good idea how to tackle it. We don't yet have all the answers, but we're a long way towards a resolution. This lot can be beaten, and we can do that here on Scilly before it goes any further. The problem could easily affect you as well if we don't fix it: your new system has the same architecture."

I explained briefly what had happened to the college twins at Gordii Fossae, and how the principal had just bought his way out of trouble. How his original intention to keep silent had only made the problem worse for others. And how I had persuaded him to provide more information. Slate took over then, to pass on what she had learned from the twins. I was pleased at the way her attitude was coming round to match my own views of the strategy we would adopt. Capstone obviously identified with the horror and outrage in her voice.

That was only the beginning. The four of us chewed over the facts for a long time before she agreed to go with my plan. Her first inclination, which I could entirely understand, was to let the main deal hub in Hugh Town take the brunt of it, and keep a low profile until Robin's Rebels turned their attention elsewhere. But I needed more than that, so I persevered until she saw what I was aiming at, and was willing to come on board.

The second sticking point was Jocasta's involvement, once Rydal realised that this was actually Kassandra. All that she had heard about that name was negative, and she couldn't understand why I was prepared to work with her. Half the time I was unsure about this myself. Especially as I couldn't say with hand on heart that she had had nothing to do with Dafyd's death. The fact that she was probably the only person this side of Earth's Moon who had the right skills didn't impress Rydal. In her world, after all, acquiring a reputation for dishonesty was almost the worst disaster that could overtake a person.

Finally we said goodbye and broke the connection. Before going back to Finn and my ale, I sat there with Slate for a while to consider. She was, naturally, aware of my anxiety, and the irresolute nature of my thoughts.

"Is it right to involve her like this?"

"I don't see we have many options. There isn't enough time to get anything else prepared. We're lucky that this second system is close at hand."

I frowned. I already knew that Rydal had a very serious approach to protocol and procedure, and that my more seize-the-moment style bothered her. But I needed her backing on this. We could use her system very effectively to validate whatever fix we came up with. It was worth persevering.

"I know that. But it feels like we're taking advantage of someone who doesn't really understand the risks."

"So go and explain them better once we get there. There might not be time to stop off at St Martin's along with everything else, but I'm sure she'll make the hop over to meet us on St Mary's if you ask nicely. Call her back straight away and say it, if you like."

Slate sounded only very slightly sympathetic to my plight, but the basic idea was good. I called Rydal again, smiling warmly in order to ameliorate her surprise at the second call.

"Rydal, look, I'd like to spend a bit more time telling you what I have in mind. I realise it's all a bit sudden. But it's going to be difficult to stop off at St Martin's, what with all the other things I need to arrange. Can I ask you to meet me in Hugh Town?"

She beamed.

"I'd be very grateful. I do want to know more about what you have in mind. It all sounds too vague for my liking just now. So yes, of course I'll come over in the Heron. When do you dock?"

"Right now, I don't know. But I'm sure that Finn or Lia Fail will tell you."

It was all I could do. I wasn't exactly filled with confidence myself. I wandered back to the bridge area, aware from the background hum and the deck vibration that the Selkie was aiming to match speed with the Scilly Isles as quickly as she could manage.

Finn looked at me, then slid a fresh Machynlleth Matchless alongside my half-finished Gruffudd's Golden. There was a little plate of potato farls and cheese as well, and I picked out a modest helping.

"Lia Fail is going to pass the word to Rydal when we have a confirmed docking slot on Mary's."

I nodded. Slate had lost no time in passing on the necessary information. I must have looked preoccupied.

"I'm inclined to think that there's something which is bothering you."

I sighed, and finished the first ale in one long swig.

"To challenge whatever it is that Robin's Rebels are doing to all these twins, I have to work with Kassandra. She's calling herself Jocasta these days, but I very much doubt she's any different on the inside."

He whistled.

"Now there's a thing. So she survived the crash after all?"

"She was never on that boat from the outset. Nor Dafyd. Only Selif. Chandrika has been digging out the facts while we've been on Mars."

He absorbed the information, lips pursed.

"There's nobody else that can help, I suppose?"

"I don't see how. She's skilled in just the ways I need to crack this. I need her to find the root cause quickly, and then help me write an update patch." I shook my head. "I only wish I knew what she's going to want in exchange. And I'm sure there was more to what happened at Elysium Planitia."

He was silent while I briefly related the events.

"I don't like this, Mitnash. What makes you think she won't just leave you in the lurch?"

"I'm very much afraid that she will. But I just need her to stay the distance until we can see what the problem is, and fix it. Once that's done, I think we're home safe. What more can she do?"

But neither of us were really happy with the prospect. Before long Finn changed the subject, and we talked about happier things.

Finn set me down at Hugh Town just under two days before the ultimatum was due to expire. We had made the most of the journey with one another, in between long calls to the team at Finsbury Circus, the finance hub on St Mary's, and technical discussions with Jocasta. It had been fun. Maybe Slate was right; maybe the problems of trust between us could be resolved.

I had persuaded the local financial transactions director to accept my plan, with considerable pressure applied from London by ECRB, and no end of financial waivers and guarantees. There was no time to waste: Jocasta was only half a day behind us now, and I wanted to get myself prepared before she arrived.

Finn was still dubious, and made no secret of it as I started to cycle the airlock into the concertina which linked us to the porters' lodge.

"Don't you put yourself in an awkward position now, Mitnash. She's got less by way of morals than you, and I dare say she has a plan of her own."

I waved a hand in acknowledgement, and set off in haste.

The deal hub was in a part of the town I had never been in before, but my access card had been upgraded to allow me to go there. The director met me in the entrance hall and ushered me through some corridors into an office. Directly facing me as I came in was a large wallclock, showing a countdown timer until the deadline expired.

I supposed the room was normally kept neat, but just now it contained a heap of specialised equipment. Slate linked with one of the wall pickups and scanned the various items with approval.

"Many thanks, Director Penhaligon. Everything that Mitnash and I asked for is here."

He nodded. He was a heavy man, with very obvious hair implants unsuccessfully covering a natural tendency to baldness. I really didn't understand why he tried to hide it.

"Slate, isn't it? A persona. And Mitnash Thakur. I don't mind saying that I'm not very happy with this idea that you've come up with. We've already broken the terms that these madmen stipulated, just with you being here at all. We're going to be further out on a limb on the day itself. I've expressed my feelings in writing to your manager down in London. Elias was his name. Elias Cohen. He knows exactly what I think, and I made it quite clear to him what level of indemnity sign-off I require."

Elias had already explained all this to us in an overnight briefing. The message had enough personal digressions that we had arrived with a fairly accurate notion of who we would be working with. But I needed to keep him sweet, so I smiled amiably and reigned in my initial response before replying.

"ECRB very much appreciates your assistance, Director. As Slate has said, this equipment is just right. If it's convenient for you, we should start configuring it as soon as possible."

He made a noncommittal noise.

"I'm arranging for one of my own men to observe everything you do and take notes. In case we need a formal record of your actions. You'll meet him later: he's called Kenny. He answers to me, not you, and he won't be hands-on during the crisis."

"Fair enough. There's one extra thing, Director. I have a colleague who will be working with us. She should arrive in the next few hours. I would be grateful if you could extend the same courtesy to her as you have to us."

"I'll need your partner's name and enough background to get security clearance."

"We'll supply all that. She's not ECRB registered, but she is acting as consultant with specialist domain knowledge. We are covering any additional expense, naturally."

He didn't look satisfied, but I picked up the nearest piece of equipment and tried to look intelligently at it, and he turned and left the room.

Kenny dropped in briefly almost as soon as Slate and I started arranging the equipment how we wanted. He looked as though he could be a lot of fun off-duty, but had obviously had very clear instructions which included not getting friendly with us.

He introduced himself, looked briefly at what we were doing, and left again.

After a few hours we had finished the first stages of setting up. I left Slate talking with the twins Shalem and Shahar, and went back to the dock to meet Jocasta. She had gone back to wearing the orange pashmina over her hair, covering a good part of her face, and looked anxious. She kept very close to me as we walked back to the office. I said nothing about that, but she whispered to me at one point.

"I don't want anyone to recognise me, Mitnash. People can have such long memories. Do you think that many people remember that I used to be with Selif?"

I shook my head, thinking how she had always excelled at remaining out of sight. We arrived without incident, and I steered her through the background checks. With all the recent work experience in her record, it was quite perfunctory. There was a parallel process for Shepherd's Crag, which Slate was monitoring. Before long we were all together in the little room.

The deadline was twenty-five hours away, and we spent the next four of them getting ready. Slate must have done a good job of convincing the twins, who were positively enthusiastic about their role. So we hooked up all of the equipment, tested it, did a dry run through the plan, and had a final review of everything. We were as ready as we would ever be, and there was no point staying longer.

Almost everyone else had long since gone, with only a thin scattering of night duty staff left. I had already sent a message to Rydal, and was going to meet her in the food market area at the centre of Hugh Town.

That still left time to allay Jocasta's fear of recognition. I walked with her to the digs I had reserved for her, so she need not make the trip alone. I had found a room quite near the public dock, in among an inconspicuous row of similar places. She laughed once as we walked past the entrance to the former *Selif's Stuff* which Boris now ran; it had been her home for a few years.

As she glanced here and there among the quiet buildings, I wondered how much actual risk she had exposed herself to by coming here. I still had no idea if her fear was simply imagined or invented, but the thought that it might be real weighed heavily on me.

Duty done, I ran back to the street market and passed the time of day chatting with Taji at his stall until Rydal appeared from the private dock area. She looked suave, unhurried, and my mood lifted at the sight.

She was wearing the butterfly brooch again, and every so often its wings would shiver delicately, as though it was about to take flight. We hugged carefully, in the manner of old acquaintances, then found a bar nearby and settled into a quiet corner.

Slate was distracting me with intermittent comments, so I told her to take the evening off and spend time with her own friends. She giggled, told me to behave myself, and then dropped the internal link between us.

Despite the feelings of familiarity, it was in fact the first time Rydal and I had spent any time getting to know each other. There was a lot to talk about, and we felt our way slowly from the commonplace to the personal. At some stage the bar became noisy, and we went back to her cousin's home.

Once we were away from public places, I spent a while talking freely about how the plan would be implemented. I really wanted her to see it as something well thought-out and solid, not a kind of cowboy hack. That seemed to go well, and our conversation spiralled wider.

I was completely caught up in the swing of things, and paid no attention to the time. It was exhilarating, and I was full of contented happiness. But at some point I caught sight of a wall clock, and the reality of all that we had to do in the next fourteen hours pressed in on me. I stood up, hesitantly.

"I'd better go and rest. There's a lot to do tomorrow."

We fell abruptly silent. She walked with me to the door. We looked at each other. She reached for the door release, and then dropped her hand before triggering it. The butterfly brooch fluttered.

"You will tell me what happens at the deal hub?"

"Yes, I will. Just as soon as there's anything to say. And then you'll go straight back to St Martin's and get everything ready there?"

She nodded, and we looked at one other again. Then the simple logic of the house system must have decided that one of us was leaving, and the door slid open. Without thinking, I stepped through, and suddenly we found ourselves on either side of the threshold. After a pause, the door whispered shut. She was inside, and I was outside. Relief and disappointment struggled inside me. I couldn't decide how I felt about the parting.

I wandered slowly away, heading rather listlessly towards the market area in order to find a landmark that I knew. I was walking quite slowly, and at some point must have said something over our internal link without consciously realising what I was doing.

"What is it, Mit?"

"I'm sorry, Slate, I didn't mean to call you."

I looked around, trying to work out where I was.

"Go right at the next corner, then follow the curve round and you'll be near Taji's stall. He's closed up now, of course, but you'll know how to get back to the room."

She sounded extremely cheerful, which didn't help at all.

"Actually, Mit, I wasn't expecting you to be out at this hour."

"What do you mean?"

"Let's just say I thought I'd be waking you up beside Rydal."

I stopped.

"Don't be ridiculous. She's a work colleague, for one thing. And there's Shayna. What were you thinking?"

She said nothing, just hummed a little. I was uncomfortably aware that her comment pressed altogether too near the truth. I had done nothing at all improper, nothing at all irrevocable. It had been a wonderfully happy, relaxing evening: a well-deserved interlude before tomorrow's conflict. Everything was fine.

But although all that was true, I knew that I wouldn't be telling Shayna about this evening any time soon. I couldn't work out how to describe it in a way that wouldn't sound bad. Especially with our recent disagreements about the future.

<hr/>

I slept, uneasily, and got up several times in the night for one reason or another. It was just normal anxiety, I told myself, brought on by the closeness of action at St Mary's. Eventually I decided it was time to start the day. I dressed, and went out to find some breakfast at Taji's stall.

On the dot of six hours before the deadline, Jocasta messaged me to say that she was ready. I collected her at the door of her accommodation, and we hurried through the corridors to the financial hub.

Once inside the security ring, I left Jocasta working with Slate and Shepherd's Crag while I went to pay a courtesy call on Director Penhaligon. He was no more polite or interested than he had been yesterday, and insisted on showing me the official complaint pro forma that he would use if things went wrong. I was doggedly polite, and excused myself at the first opportunity.

Back in our little working space, I spent ten precious minutes ranting about the director to the others. Once that was off my chest I felt a whole lot better, and the four of us went through the plan with the twins once again.

With two hours to go we stopped for a break. We humans certainly needed the time off, and everything I had learned about Slate over the years told me that the same was true of her. She couldn't work at her best just by hammering away at the same task for hours as though she was a machine.

A few minutes into that break, Slate buzzed me.

"There's a reply in from Shayna. But you might not want to hear it just yet."

"Don't be silly. Of course I want to."

She paused, and then continued.

"Alright. Her message reads, 'I'm not at all sure about this, Mit. I need more time to think about it. But I like it here, and you need to know I'll not be easily persuaded.'"

I shook my head and felt miserable.

"You were right: I should have waited."

I tried to refocus on work, and after a while got back into the flow, but the disappointment lurked in the back of my mind.

For all his faults, Director Penhaligon had remembered to provide us with refreshments. Jocasta and I sampled them as we sat in a corner among the bits of hardware. It was good quality: better than I had expected. I suspected that it would be queried at some point in a routine report, and I would be justifying it to Elias. For now, however, I just enjoyed the bodily pleasure of eating.

I looked covertly at Jocasta from time to time. She had done nothing to arouse my suspicions; instead, she had participated in our partnership without holding back. She had been quick to offer suggestions, and adhered faithfully to operational constraints. Was it time to revise my opinion of her?

With an hour to go I called Rydal. Our plan called for her to return to St Martin's as soon as we knew we had a working defence. There was no reason to speak with her just now. I soon realised that I just wanted to talk with someone outside the little group of us stuck in that room. I told myself it could just as well have been Parvati, or Maureen, or Finn, or Boris.

Then the time flew by. Kenny turned up to fulfil his role of official observer, and sat silently off to one side. I confirmed one last time with the director that the ransom demand would not be paid before the deadline expired. With just five minutes remaining, we hooked ourselves up.

The plan called for us all to be connected with each other
– Slate and I, Jocasta and Shepherd's Crag, and the twins
Shalem and Shahar. For the twins and personas, this was a
fairly natural state of affairs. For me, this was a thing I had
only ever experienced with Slate. I supposed the same was
true for Jocasta.

It required a change to the software which ran inside our
cochlea implants. Normally they were locked to a single address, completely ignoring any signals that didn't precisely
match both point of origin and encryption key. That was what
kept the chatter private between Slate and I. For the link to
work, we needed to slacken that constraint to include all six of
us. Jocasta had written the patch, and with some trepidation
I had applied it.

Slate had inspected the code every way she knew how, and
had pronounced it safe, but with reservations. Basically, she
had to admit she couldn't really follow what most of it was
doing, as it was way outside our area of expertise. It was yet
another way in which we needed Jocasta's skills. But there
were built-in safeguards to the change, the main one being
that it would expire after five hours and unload itself again. I
believed that using the patched link was the only way to crack
the problem, but I didn't have to like it. I felt uneasy.

There was a very faint internal buzz, and then, all at once,
the six of us were all joined together, like pearls around the
thread of a necklace. Jocasta was intense, like a flame, Shepherd's Crag was cool beside her fire, and the twins circled
around their mutual centre like a pair of swans in love.

I leaned back against the comforting, familiar presence of
Slate, warm and smooth as an outcrop of rock on a sunny day,
and wondered how I seemed to the others. Slate chuckled.

*"I'll tell you later. Right now we have work to do. The mul-
tiway link is working well. We can keep our own chatter reasonably private, but each of the others will be aware in general*

terms. *Now, focus on the twins a moment and you'll hear some-thing really interesting."*

I did, and realised that there was a blur of exchange going on between them, too intricate for me to follow.

"That's not just speed making the difference, Mit. I mean, it is quick, maybe half as fast again as I can communicate, but there's more. They have their own language which is opaque to me, and highly efficient. I've heard that every twinned pair has its own unique variant, but I haven't had the chance to eavesdrop before."

I was beginning to realise what an extraordinary thing a twinned Sarsen pair was, when Jocasta spoke up.

"My, this is cosy. I could get used to this. But we have under a minute now, so I suppose we should start work and make time for enjoyment later."

It was strange to hear her voice inside me, where nobody except Slate had ever spoken before. Some of the fullness that a voice had in atmosphere was lost, but in its place was an emotive dimension that I wasn't used to. She was excited to be doing this: genuinely thrilled at the exploration of new experience. I glanced across the room at her, matching up her closed eyes and contemplative expression with the internal sensations I was receiving from her.

Then I pulled myself back into work mode, and organised us all into defensive posture. The direct bond of intimacy between the twins was all that we wanted visible from the outside. That was to be the core which, we assumed, Robin's Rebels would target. The rest of us were the support and the bezel, which would keep the precious jewel intact. I was next to Shahar, then the chain went round to Slate, Shepherd's Crag, Jocasta, and Shalem.

We ran a few last tests as the seconds flicked by, checking that messages could run unhindered around the loop. Shalem and Shahar seemed supremely confident of their resilience.

Time ran out. For a few tenths of a second nothing happened. That was of itself useful information, since it signalled just how close by our adversaries might have a local repeater station. There had to be one, as it would be far too difficult to coordinate the attack at a distance. I was convinced by the London team's analysis that their main centre was further afield among the asteroids. Probably Ceres. Either way, we might be able to make something of the lag, presuming we all survived this crisis.

⁓⁓⁓⁓⁓⁓⁓⁓⁓⁓⁓⁓

Without any warning, a large and hugely complicated data packet arrived. Processing the payload happened too quickly for me to follow, and the first thing I knew for sure was that both twins were screaming inside my head, filling the link with a level of terror which I had never experienced. For that first instant, it felt so much worse than death.

Then I rallied, feeling Slate still with me, forcing down her own visceral fear. And Jocasta was pushing back against the impact as well, broadcasting a ferocity which I had not expected.

I realised what had happened – the input packet had somehow severed the direct link between Shalem and Shahar. Had they been unsupported, they would have been entirely alone, cut off from each other just like Castor and Pollux had been on Mars. They would no doubt have been damaged just as severely, perhaps to the point of permanent harm.

But things were different this time. The direct link was broken, but we had our backup connection running through the extra four of us. It was a completely different architecture, and the viral payload crafted for the twins' own systems had passed it by without effect. It was time to fight back.

So I kept myself very close to Shahar, holding on to his terror and helping him to contain it. If nothing else, I thought, it would help him to realise he was not alone in the universe.

He calmed, very slightly, and then a stream of sounds which I couldn't understand came over the internal link. I realised, with a sense of wonder, that he was trying to talk to me in the twins' own language. I might not understand it, but I could route the packets on to Slate without changing them.

Whatever it meant, the phrase ran the long way around the broken circle. With only a brief gap, there was an equally incomprehensible reply coming back from Jocasta.

We traded chat like that for a while, until both twins were back on a more even keel. The flow of thought was slow compared to their regular talk, but it was real, and it was in their own tongue. There was a sense of profound relief, and finally they started to converse in ways the rest of us could follow.

"Slate tried to warn us, but we never thought it would be so horrible. I have no idea what we would have done without this substitute link."

Shahar was still unsettled, but the mindless horror of the first few moments was behind him now. It was time to move ahead with the plan. Before I could voice that, Jocasta spoke.

"Shepherd's Crag has a full spectrum trace of that inbound packet. We're analysing it to see how the exploit works. We have a couple of ideas but are not yet sure."

"Is there anything we can do to help?"

She paused briefly.

"I think one of us should focus on keeping this loop active between the twins. Could you do that? Maybe Slate could help us craft a defensive patch?"

She was hesitant, perhaps not wanting to look as though she was in charge. But it was a good plan, and I agreed.

"I want to get the director to make contact with Robin's Rebels in about fifteen minutes. Twenty at most. I'm guessing you won't have built the patch that quickly, but we need to be in a position to start communicating with the outside world

by then. After that, if my guess is right, we have maybe forty minutes at most before we get a forceful retaliation. So you have rather under an hour to get at least a beta version ready. Can it be done?"

"Yes."

It was Shepherd's Crag who had replied, and he sounded supremely confident. So I kept the conversation going with the twins, while the other three focused on the coding problem. I learned a lot about twin life in that short time, what with direct communication as well as passing on occasional packets of their private speech. It was a real education.

It only took nine minutes to work out from the trace exactly where the vulnerability had been. Jocasta explained it briefly to me, while Slate took over talking with the twins. It was a clever trick, she thought, taking advantage of a coding flaw which had been sitting there in the twin-to-twin link for a long time. Nobody had spotted it before. I was quite sure that Slate and I would not have detected it unaided: certainly not in such a short time. I felt a great wash of relief and gratitude, which I was entirely unable to hide over the implant link.

Jocasta was pleased, and, I thought, a little embarrassed at my response. There was an answering warmth from her which I had not expected. She hesitated, pursuing some train of thought that I could not guess, and then resumed.

"We can put together a code patch in about half an hour. It'll need review and all before it goes out for widespread distribution, but we're pretty sure it's good enough. It'll do the job for today, definitely. It actually doesn't take much defence to spoil the attack. You'll be entertained by the fact that it's closely related to the hack we developed for Callisto."

"Another timing issue?"

I wasn't very surprised. It was an area Slate and I had been largely ignorant of until now, but we were going to have to learn it up. Meanwhile, we had a plan to follow.

"I'll tell the director to open a dialogue in five minutes, and release the payment chain soon after. You should have plenty of time to deploy the fix before the next round of trouble arrives." I hesitated, but only briefly. *"And my thanks to both you and Shepherd's Crag. We couldn't have done this so quickly without you. If at all. I appreciate all that you've done."*

She made a noncommittal murmur, but there was a sense of genuine pleasure coming over the link from her. It was hard to hide one's emotional overtones when chatting like this, and I pulled back a little to avoid mutual embarrassment. It was all too easy to mistake one sentiment for another. My opinion was definitely shifting: surely she could be trusted now. Perhaps all it had needed was getting her away from Selif and Dafyd.

Slate and I briefly conferred, and then after telling Jocasta, we deleted together all the files that had once been in Dafyd's possession. She had kept her part of the bargain: it was only right to reciprocate.

I opened up a distance from the interior link. It was something of a wrench to surface into the real world, but I could still just about hear the ongoing talk. It was like listening in to people whispering in the adjacent room, and I felt frustrated by the lack of clarity. Kenny was sitting there diligently making notes, although he could have little idea as yet of what had transpired. I brought him up to speed in a few well-chosen sentences, and then left him there while I went to see Director Penhaligon.

"The first part of the plan has worked as expected, sir. Your twinned pair is in good shape, though their internal link is still down. We have a way to defeat the attack. So it's time to release the payment chain."

He nodded, and we looked together at his wallscreen. Just like at Gordii Fossae, the normal display had been usurped by a countdown timer and payment button. He tapped it, and together we went through the payment stages. It needed dual authorisation, and he pointedly insisted that my credentials were first, putting me in position of lead responsibility.

I decided all over again how much I disliked him. Every encounter I had with him strengthened this feeling, and persuaded me to help Rydal get her system promoted to being the primary one on the Scilly Isles.

That was for another day. For now, I focused on clearing the payment. It had been specially prepared by ECRB for this very purpose. The top layers were entirely normal, including all of the regular ident tags for the St Mary's hub. But way down the history blockchain, beyond the normal validation scope, we had inserted a soured pointer.

The repeater satellite nearby, with only limited capability, would find nothing wrong, and would pass it up the line to its home base. There, it would go into their settlement system. Soon after, it would start squawking all kinds of useful details, such as their credit line registration number, and what kind of platform they ran. We should get a reasonable sense of their spatial location as well. If I was a betting man, I would put good credit right now on that being Ceres, but we would soon have some real information.

Now, Robin's Rebels would spot the intrusion in short order, silence it, and no doubt respond vigorously. But there was at least a forty-five minute signal lag to Ceres and back, and we would be ready before that.

The payment cleared, the screen contents switched to a cheery 'thanks!', and then went into a restart cycle.

"So far so good, Director. I should be getting back to my colleagues so we can prepare for the next stage."

"That's a great deal of credit you just committed there, Mr Thakur. I hope you know what you are doing. Let's see if ECRB's confidence in your plan is warranted."

I didn't reply, but simply turned to go. I could already hear inside my head that the direct twin link was coming back online. It was so much better listening to the celebrations in our little room, than to attend to his grudging comments.

It occurred to me, as I headed back, that I was receiving much more by way of emotions from the others than I had expected. I was used to a certain level with Slate, but I'd always thought that most of that was simply because we knew each other so intimately. A handful of words exchanged between us conveyed much more than the obvious, because of our shared history. Her delight was quite obvious to me.

That couldn't be said of the other four, and yet I was feeling their satisfaction. The twins were euphoric and Jocasta was aroused to excitement by the triumph. Even the taciturn Shepherd's Crag was exuding contentment. Not only was I recognising their pleasure, I was responding to it, and I bounced back into the room completely gladdened. Together we could do anything.

What we actually had to do was finalise the code patch. So after exchanging happy thoughts with each other we got back to work. The clock was ticking, after all, and it paid no attention to our state of being. Kenny was still faithfully taking notes, though what he made of us I had no idea. I didn't care, either, not with the closeness of the bond between the six of us.

The patch was done, reviewed, tested, and deployed in under half an hour. It was slightly sobering to think that the next attack would already be zipping through space towards us, but that extra edge of danger gave our work a zest which, sometimes, was missing. We integrated it into the software that controlled the direct twin link, and there was nothing to do except wait.

It was always tempting to fiddle right up to the last minute, but we didn't do that. Far too often, something went horribly wrong, leaving you stranded. So we just chatted, and tried to relax. That wasn't easy either. We kept to safe subjects, avoiding anything that might rouse spectres of the past. The time crept by.

Finally, with no prior warning at all, the reply arrived from Robin's Rebels. I had been nursing a gnawing fear that they would have a second line of attack, for which we were not prepared. But no: the same lack of imagination which characterised their leaflets was here as well.

The same packet arrived, with the same target and the same intention. Quite possibly they had only actually been able to find the one vulnerability. The only extra feature was an attached set of screens and messages raging about the deception, and saying how the consequences were entirely our own fault.

The packet rattled through the twin-to-twin link – and did nothing. The patch had worked: the hostile code could no longer find a foothold to exploit. There was a little sigh of relief from each of us, then an air of triumph. Then, quickly enough that any listeners on the outside would never know, the twins took up the role we had planned, and stopped sending messages out.

Whoever was watching would see no chatter, no processing, no acknowledgements, not even any heartbeating. Within our own little miniature world, they were very much alive, enjoying the company of each other and of us four. Anybody else would think they were catatonic.

Slate was chirping happily to anyone who would listen, Shepherd's Crag had relaxed to the point he was chatting merrily with the twins, and I felt a rush of pleasure and pride from Jocasta.

I turned to her and, quite spontaneously, hugged her. She laughed and hugged me back, and I unexpectedly enjoyed the way our internal and external sensations peaked.

Then, remembering where I was, I turned to Kenny, who was quite understandably baffled by our antics. He deserved an explanation.

"The code fix works, Kenny. Shalem and Shahar have just been attacked a second time, and the link has proved resilient against it. Right now they're pretending to be dead in the water, but in fact they're very much alive and well."

He was relieved, and genuinely pleased, so much so that he abandoned his role as aloof observer and came over to congratulate us. With a bit of loosening up, and if he wasn't under the baleful eye of Director Penhaligon, he would be a good colleague. Maybe we could poach him to work as part of the team Rydal was building.

That thought triggered another. I shook Kenny's hand, told him I would report personally to the Director, and slipped off into another room for privacy. It was time to talk to Rydal, and reassure her of progress.

She appeared on the screen at once, looking as though she had been pacing continually around her cousin's room since we had last spoken. Anxious dark eyes looked questioningly at me. I grinned at her, still on a real high from the excitement. Come to think of it, I was still getting a buzz from it now. I would ask Slate what that was all about sometime soon, but right now it was giving me too much pleasure to want to stop.

"It's all right, Rydal. The plan has worked perfectly so far. They took the payment bait, and we can analyse that in time. But the code patch worked, and the twins here were unaffected by the second wave. They're playing dead right now, but that's just for show."

She leaned towards me, as though trying to work around the limitations of the screen.

"So I should get back to Martin's and get our system ready? You can share the code that fixes the problem?"

"Oh yes. Yes indeed. It's a patch that has to be applied to the twin-to-twin link. It's not too difficult, but you have to do everything in the right order. Slate will talk Capstone through the whole thing. I'll be there before it'll be stressed by some real action, so I can check it over then. It'll be fine."

She hesitated still.

"We hadn't wanted to show our hand this early, Mitnash. We were going to wait until we were further along, before revealing that we had this other system. What do you think the director there will do when he finds out? Have you told him about us yet?"

"I don't think he'll do anything. He's very stuck in his ways. And I think one of his key workers will come over to you if you ask him."

"That might help. We'll need to build a credible name as soon as possible, and some former staff members from the main hub would go a long way. But it's all happening very quickly. I need to know: have you told the director about us yet?"

"No, of course not. He thinks we're just keeping his system down to prove that the fix works."

She looked relieved. I rushed on.

"But I will have to say something to him soon. He agreed, under a lot of pressure, to keep offline for at most forty hours. Their backlog queue will hold for that time."

She nodded, and made a little note off to one side.

"Go on."

"Well, I need to say something about a trial system coming on line. But if you like I can present it as a temporary workaround that ECRB have put together. He won't be surprised at that, and it will keep you out of sight for longer."

She leaned forward again and ran a hand through her hair.

"That would be wonderful. But you're sure that's permissible? It sounds a bit underhand. You're sure about this?"

"Not a problem, Rydal. I won't lie to him, but I can let him come to the wrong assumption." I laughed. "I don't like him, Rydal, and having to deal with him these last couple of days has persuaded me."

"That's not a reason I can accept, Mitnash. I can't commit to this just on personal likes and dislikes."

I stopped myself from just gabbling on, and tried to think more systematically.

"But you know it's not really about that. There's that evidence you yourself gathered about the failings of the current situation. This will be a step up for you: a way to get ahead of the game while you're still at the commissioning stage."

She looked doubtful, but then shook her head.

"If you say it's fine, I'm happy with that. I'm sure you have thought about all this. So I'll head back in the Heron and get everything organised. When will you be able to arrive?"

"I'll leave in a few hours, after we've cleared up here. I might catch some sleep first, but I can always do that on the way over. Finn's bringing me. I'll see you very soon."

She moved to disconnect the signal, then stopped.

"Is everything alright? You look really hyped. I've never seen you like this. You sound very odd. Wound up very tight. You should definitely get some rest before you come over. You need to be in shape for when things happen on Martin's."

"I'm fine, Rydal. Really. Just very excited about all that's going on. I always get like this when the case turns. It's nothing to worry about, really. I'll be with you soon enough. You go off to St Martin's now, and I'll be with you very soon."

She clearly wasn't convinced, but accepted my word. The call ended, and I sat there wondering if she was right. Thinking back, I had not been entirely sensible or prudent in what I'd said. Did I need her to challenge me more? Jocasta would, if she thought it necessary. So would Shayna. Was the euphoria of the link, and the level of emotional sharing too much? A sort of dizziness had lodged itself in my head, but it wasn't too obtrusive. I could handle it, I decided.

Anyway, it would revert to normal in another few hours. If anything, it would be the aftermath that might be more difficult, if the current high was followed by a low.

Director Penhaligon was still in his lair, working away at something which he ostentatiously closed as I approached. Well, he probably dealt with confidential material all day, so I forgave him. My warm feelings of pleasure were obviously starting to spill over towards him.

"So what's next, Mr Thakur? Your forty hour clock is running. I imagine you have something else planned?"

It might have been my imagination, but he sounded marginally less critical. Perhaps he was becoming convinced by the successful execution of everything so far.

"Indeed yes, sir. I shall be going to St Martin's shortly."

"Martin's? Why there?"

"I have access to a secondary system in Higher Town, which we're going to use to prove the code fix before reopening your hub activities."

He frowned, and glanced at one of a series of wall screens showing the various asteroids in the group.

"I'm not aware of any relevant installations on Martin's?"

He looked wary, so I rushed on.

"It's not an actual deal hub, sir. But it has a twinned Sarsen pair. I want Robin's Rebels to think that your system is dead, and that this is an attempt to get something up and running in a rush. Before it's properly ready, so to speak. I think they'll react as soon as they can, and try to cripple this one too."

He nodded, slowly.

"So you get another chance to see if your fix works, without putting my installation at any more risk."

"That's pretty much it, sir. I would like us all to get some extra reassurance from this. Plus, we should be able to gather more precise information on their own setup, and how to proceed with that."

Obviously I didn't go on to talk about what the future might hold for him.

"Actually, Mr Thakur, that sounds like a good plan. I would have preferred it if you had told me before. But no matter. Good hunting, or whatever the right phrase might be."

"Thank you, Director. I shall let you know as soon as it's appropriate to bring the system here back into full operation. That'll be well within the forty hours. Probably half that."

He turned back to his screen and sat there with hands poised, waiting for me to leave before going back to whatever private task he was working at.

Back in the main room, things were calming down. Kenny had gone. The twins were enjoying the opportunity to just be together without having to do real work. Slate and Shepherd's Crag were reviewing the code and thinking about how it might be improved. Jocasta had just finished tidying the equipment we no longer needed. Just for a moment, I had a sensation of real community, and a wave of inclusion and warmth ran around the ring.

"Slate, I'm going to get some rest. Just for a while. We're meeting Finn in about six hours for the transit to St Martin's."

"Won't it be good when we're licensed to ship across on our own? No more waiting on someone else's timetable."

"It'll be delightful. One of many good things waiting for us."

"Mitnash, I hope it's not too much to ask? Would you mind walking me back one last time?"

"Not a problem. We can go right now, if you're ready?"

It was getting progressively easier to use the internal link. Talking with Jocasta still lacked the fluency that I was used to with Slate, but on the other hand the emotional overtones were much easier to follow. The little gush of relief I felt from her after my reply was really very endearing.

"Slate, I don't think there's anything to do until we set off for St Martin's. Why not have some down time and keep Shalem and Shahar company?"

"I'll wake you in plenty of time, Mit."

We left the hub offices and went back through the corridors towards her accommodation. Slate's focus was firmly on the twins now. I had no idea what Shepherd's Crag was doing, and I couldn't trace him on the network, but that was hardly a pressing problem.

"What will you do now, Jocasta?"

"I'm free to go?"

"Of course. That was the arrangement we made. I'll give you professional acknowledgement for the patch on the twin link, and say nothing about your role on Callisto and Phobos."

She mused for a few paces, her thoughts running somewhere deep in her psyche where I could not follow.

"Perhaps it's better that you don't know where I'll go. In case you change your mind. Or that manager of yours pressures you to tell him about me. I can't be too careful, Mitnash."

One of the light panels high up on the corridor walls had failed since yesterday. There was a sign pinned up saying that some sort of dispute about responsibility was delaying replacement. The shadows were dark, and seemed menacing. I didn't like it, and judging from Jocasta's reaction, neither did she. Anxiety oozed across from her brain into mine. She quickened her steps and drew a little closer to me.

Somewhere nearby, we could hear indistinct voices and the sound of something breaking. Jocasta's breath was suddenly louder, and she stopped, huddled in on herself. I looked round, but there was nothing to see. My critical faculties were telling me that it was probably just a couple of unruly lads, and that they had no idea we were in the next lane. But that didn't help when Jocasta and I were amplifying each other's fear over our shared link. I thought vaguely that there must be some kind of feedback loop in the system that I hadn't known about, but I was in no state of mind to worry about that. I was full of two people's desperation to get away.

I put my arm round her, pulled her very close in to me, and hurried us both away from that spot as fast as we could manage. We scrambled out of the alley, past *The Boris Bazaar*, and along the row of cheap accommodation slots until we got to hers. She said nothing, but was clinging fiercely to me. The fear was fading, replaced by feelings of relief and success that felt so much better.

I released her as we stood outside her door. She fumbled for the unlock token, looking up and down the row all the time. I couldn't see or hear anything. She dropped the token while trying to open the door.

"You'll think me silly, but I was sure that it was Dafyd."

I bent and picked it up, shaking my head. The dizzy sensation was definitely worse than it had been. Perhaps adrenalin exaggerated some side-effect of the link software patch. I tried to ignore it.

"He died on Mars itself. He's gone. He won't be bothering you any more."

I held out the token, but she looked uneasily at the door.

"What if it's a trick of his? What if he faked all that? He might be inside now. Waiting for me. What would I do?"

She stepped away from the door, very close to me.

"I'm not sure, Mitnash. You can call me foolish if you like, but could you check inside for me? I don't want to go there on my own. Please come in with me."

It briefly crossed my mind that Slate or Shepherd's Crag could easily check if there was a problem by tapping into the room's internal security systems. I thought of saying something, but it was so much better to feel warmth and closeness from her rather than fright.

In any case, Slate seemed to be offline, and I thought she deserved the time in the twins' company without me pestering her.

Full of courage, based on nothing but her overflowing wish to have me there, I unlocked the door and stepped into the hall. Jocasta was just behind me, clinging to my shirt. The hall, which was obviously fashioned on an airlock, even though it could not possibly hold vacuum, led a few paces down to another door.

She pressed up, as if to whisper, though we were still saying everything to each other by means of the implants. Her voice inside my head dropped in volume, and I could feel her breath on my neck.

"There's just one main room. Kitchen at this end, living area at the other. And a little comfort chamber on the left about half way. I left the door to that closed this morning."

I wasn't feeling any fear from her any longer, just an overwhelming sense of anticipation. Fruition, even. I didn't quite understand that, but I was entirely buoyed up by all this borrowed vitality. Some tiny part of me vaguely remembered that Dafyd was an aggressive man, against whom I had no chance if things became physical. But that little voice dwindled almost as soon as it appeared. The internal buzzing was now quite distracting, and I just wanted to keep busy rather than stop and think.

I tiptoed to the inner door, tapped the release, and pushed it open. It swung back on silent hinges. The room had little vanity lamps low down on the walls: I could see that the place was empty. There was no Dafyd lurking inside.

I turned my head to her, made a little reassuring nod. She pursed her lips, pointed to the door on the left. It was still closed. Or perhaps it had been opened and then closed, some time earlier in the day.

I crept forward again, hearing her shut the exit door gently behind us. I pressed on, wanting to get this finished, irrationally convinced that the internal noise on the link would go away once it was done.

I wrenched the door open. Inside was the usual array of things you would find in a comfort chamber, but no Dafyd. I was breathing hard with the stress of it all, and turned back in relief.

"It's fine, Jocasta. He's not here. Nobody here except us."

"That's wonderful, Mitnash. That's what I needed to know."

I realised that while I had been checking the comfort room, she had discarded the pashmina. It lay, neatly folded, on one of the dining chairs. She smiled at me, watching me quietly from across the room. She obviously knew what was happening to me. I shook my head again, trying to clear it, but felt overcome by another wave of nausea. I held on to the little table with one hand and tried to steady myself.

I wavered on my feet, as the fuzziness in my head worsened. I had a fleeting concern about feedback loops, and the unexpected behaviour of the software running the cochlea link, but I couldn't pursue the thought in a clear way. I reached out vaguely towards Jocasta. She was walking very slowly over to me from the other side of the room, and I felt my knees buckling long before she reached me.

———

A voice was calling me: someone I knew. I felt terrible. My head ached ferociously, and I was exhausted. Nothing made any sense. I had no idea where I was.

"Mit, Mit, you have to wake up. Say something, Mit."

I worked out it was Slate. She was talking out loud, through some pickup nearby. She sounded frantic, as though she had been searching for me for a long time.

"Slate, is that you? Hello. Where are you? I don't remember much at the moment."

Her relief washed over me. It was nice, like floating in warm water. When she spoke again, she was calmer, more on an even keel. But still persistent, nagging at me to answer.

"I'm where I've been all along, Mit. But where are you? I lost you nearly four hours ago and I've been trying to find you ever since. Where are you, Mit? I've only just hacked through the block, and I don't have a location context yet."

"That's like, um, more than a whole day for you, what with your Lovelace index and all."

I realised that I was rambling, but she didn't mind.

"Forget about that just now, Mit. I need to know where you are. What do you remember?"

I was lying on a bed. There was a chair nearby. I could see a note on top of it, but couldn't read it from here. I tried sitting up, but my head pounded and I lay back with a groan.

"I can't do it, Slate."

"Take it slowly, Mit. Do you know where you are? Can you see anything?"

I looked around, carefully. The room looked vaguely familiar, but I couldn't place it just yet. There was nothing personal to identify it. It was just a room.

"It's just a room, Slate."

"Are you on a ship?"

I thought about it. There was a quiet background hum of aircon and the like, but no engine vibration.

"No, I'm shoreside somewhere. There's a note over there on the chair. I'm going to see what it says."

"Go very slowly, Mit. The bio readings I am getting from you are erratic, though I don't trust the implant link yet."

"I can believe that."

I rolled onto one side and went on all fours over to the chair, grabbed the note, and leaned back against the bed to read it. It was hard to focus at first, but I thought things were slowly improving. Slate clucked and buzzed encouragingly as I manoeuvred.

As the letters started to make sense, I groaned again, this time in despair and repulsion.

Well, Mit, I wonder how much you remember of what happened? It would be a pity if you'd forgotten all the excitement. Of course I've gone now. Long gone, but don't worry, you still have plenty of time to get to St Martin's. You'll find a pack of medication in the comfort room: it's very effective for the headache. Trust me on that. And you can trust me too that the code patch for the twins will do what it should. It's been lovely working with you. Maybe we'll be together again one day. Jocasta.

I finished reading. Just then, I could not in fact remember anything after getting to the door of the apartment. I had no idea what had happened. If Jocasta's innuendo was intended to embarrass me, it was working. I felt unutterably weak, and not just in my body. I couldn't decide whether to be angry at myself, or just yield to sobs and misery.

"What have I done, Slate?"

She paused.

"You don't remember?"

"Not at all."

"I can't tell much, either. Your symptoms are unclear."

I nodded, tried to speak, but was overcome with shame at being tricked. The feelings of nausea and the throbbing headache didn't help, either.

"I think you should try the medicine to clear your head, Mit. Go over to the place she talked about and see what's there. But tell me exactly what it says before you take anything. I can sort out if it's right for you. We can talk about everything else another time."

I crawled to the comfort chamber and found a little pack of medicine. I had already decided that if it looked at all dubious I would just flush it away, but it was properly sealed and warranted, brand new, still in the original wrappers. Slate checked the batch numbers and approved, so I swallowed two of the little capsules with some water.

It worked like magic, and my head began clearing straight away. Unfortunately, that also meant that more memories started to come back. I knew where I was now – in Jocasta's room – and I remembered arriving there and checking for Dafyd. I remembered the steadily worsening effects of the patched link. But that was the limit. I still had no recollection of what had happened after checking the comfort chamber. I sat on one of the chairs at the kitchen end and buried my face in my hands.

"I let her trick me, Slate. She'd done something to the implant software. There was some sort of feedback. I felt really bad. I don't know how she did it, but it sucked me right in."

"That matches what I know. Not all that long after you left, the link between us went down. The twins and I thought it was a transient problem for a while, but then I got worried. Soon I realised it had been deliberately broken, and I have been trying ever since to break back in. I was worried."

I knew that 'worried' was a serious understatement.

"Whatever it was, I got caught up in it."

"Never mind that now, Mit. You need to get going again."

"Is it late? Please don't tell me I'm ruined the plan?"

"No, it's early yet. It's still the middle of the night. There's plenty of time to have a shower first and feel better."

The impact of running water helped. I used the shower until I felt more like myself, then pulled my clothes back on. After that, I just wanted to get away from the place.

"What am I going to tell Rydal? Or Finn? Or anyone? They all tried to warn me. I told them it would be fine. But, Slate, I had to work with her to get the code. It's not like there was anyone else who could help. She just tricked me, right at the end when I thought it was all over and done. I was sure that she had changed: I trusted her."

Another wave of shame overwhelmed me for a moment. I sat down again and looked around the room.

"Oh, Slate, what am I going to say to Shayna?"

"Don't let's worry about that now, Mit. We can talk about that later."

"Slate, is the implant working? What if it's broken? I don't know who could fix it out here."

"Other than Jocasta and Shepherd's Crag, you mean? I don't suppose you'll be asking them. But no, I think it's fine.

All the diagnostics I have run tell me that the modifications to talk to the twins have been unloaded again, and it's running exactly as before. I've only been using the external pickup in case there was something wrong with you."

I took a deep breath. The last things that I remembered experiencing over the link were all to do with pain, and the conviction I was about to vomit.

"Go on, Slate. I need to hear your voice inside. I need to know we can just be normal together."

"Here, Mit. How is this?"

I could have wept again, this time at the familiar affection in her voice, and the beginnings of internal restoration. It was a start, at least.

"I can't tell you how good that is."

Then her voice sharpened.

"There's an incoming call to the room. It's her. Shall I block it? What do you think?"

I stood up and tried to look determined.

"Better not. Whatever she has to say, I'd rather hear it now than later."

The screen beside the table lit up. Jocasta was preparing some sort of drink in the galley area of her ship. She was neat, elegant. I felt shabby in comparison. It was just appearance, I told myself. Nothing really important. She grinned at me.

"How are you feeling, Mit? You're up and about quicker than I expected. And it looks like you found the headache meds."

I wasn't sure I could trust my voice yet, so I just nodded.

"And Slate should be getting back in touch with you in a few minutes."

"I'm already here, thank you, Mistress Sphinx."

Slate was very formal, but I could hear the raised hackles in her voice. It grounded me more than anything else to know that, despite everything, she was bristling to protect me, like a raven over her nest.

"Oh, that's well done, Slate! We didn't think you'd get through the obstacles quite so quickly."

"I was very motivated."

It was time I stopped just listening, and played a more active role in the conversation.

"What was it that you wanted, Jocasta?"

She raised her eyebrows.

"Don't you remember what happened?"

I shook my head.

"Nothing after checking the comfort chamber to see if Dafyd was there."

A satisfied look crossed her face.

"Well, that's unfortunate. I don't think you'll be wanting your colleagues in London to hear about this."

"What do you mean?"

I tried to think back, but it was a blank. She watched my effort with some amusement.

"The way I'll tell the story – if I ever have to, that is – it was a kind of mutual thing."

I reddened and looked down. I didn't believe her, but I couldn't be certain. Why had I ever been taken in by the idea that Dafyd was in the room? Why had I gone into her room at all? And why had I been so quick to admit I couldn't remember what happened?

"I wasn't myself. You took advantage of me."

"Indeed I did. Completely. And I think what you are really asking is what I am looking for in the future?"

"Yes. Alright then. Yes."

"Well, first, you should know that I have a complete record of everything. Vision and sound."

I still didn't believe any of this, but I needed to hear more.

"Alright, Jocasta, suppose you do. So what are you going to do with it?"

"Nothing at all, so long as there's no attempt to come after me for my opportunism on Callisto and Phobos. But if I ever find out that my name is being brought in to that, then I'm sure I can find an audience."

I frowned.

"But I said I wouldn't do that. I'd already promised you. Didn't you believe me?"

"A girl needs insurance these days." She shook her head. "Look, Mit, I think probably I could trust you. But I don't trust the people you work for. What if ECRB told you to come after me? What would you do? Would you keep your promise to me, or would you just do your job? Sorry, but I won't take that risk."

I thought about it. I had never yet been put in that position, so I'd never had to work through that particular moral maze. Unfortunately, I could sympathise with her point of view.

"Let me spell it out for you. If you get sent after me, or if I think that you reported something incriminating about me, I send to your manager Elias the information that I am holding. The first thing that he will do is decide that your professional judgement has been compromised by being so, shall we say, casually intimate with the chief suspect. I mean, it's only a few days since you wouldn't even share a ship journey with me. Now look at you. All the information you have gathered about me will be annulled, and a new investigator will have to start from scratch. You'll be recalled for a disciplinary hearing, before which I will have leaked some lively details to interested parties. ECRB will probably have no choice but to suspend you. Perhaps dismiss you altogether. Need I go on?"

I stared at her, realising that it was all too likely she would do just that, presupposing she was telling the truth about the recording in the first place. That seemed unlikely, but I didn't think I could take the risk and call her bluff.

"So, you see, this is my insurance, to make sure you're not tempted to go back on your word. All you have to do is make sure that nobody comes after me because of what I did on Callisto or Phobos."

After a very short pause she carried on, in a serious voice.

"Now, Mit, all the work we did together is absolutely guaranteed. You need have no anxiety about that: it's totally solid. The code patch will work just fine, and it will protect those twins on St Martin's just as it should. What did you say they were called?"

"Helen and Clytemnestra."

She laughed, genuinely amused.

"Well, that's good. Which do you think I am? I'd like to be Helen, but I suspect you'll think I'm Clytemnestra. So who is your Helen, I wonder?"

The names didn't mean much to me, and I made a mental note to ask Slate later on.

"But anyway, the code will work perfectly. You and Slate can polish it to be production-ready, and then get it distributed across the whole system. You'll get quite a reputation from it, I think. My gift: you can leave my name out of it."

She put the mug of drink down, and stepped round to be in front of the counter.

"Mit, you will be keeping my name out of view, won't you?"

I nodded and sighed heavily. There was nothing else I could do, and no way out, unless I could find a way to prove she was bluffing. Just now, that seemed unlikely.

"Congratulations, Jocasta. I hope everything works out well for you."

"Thank you."

She paused, and in the gap, on impulse, I rushed on with a question.

"Did you have anything to do with how Dafyd died?"

She looked at me enigmatically.

"What do you think?"

I looked at her for a very long moment.

"Actually, I don't believe you had anything to do with it. But if somebody asked me why, I'd be hard pushed to find an answer."

She smiled a little.

"Well, I appreciate your vote of confidence. And look, the offer I made on Mars still stands. I do think we make a good partnership. In all kinds of ways. If you get bored of being sent here and there by ECRB, just let me know. As a first project, I think we could do well with that modification to the implant software. There's plenty of people would want a multiple link experience. We just need to find a way to eliminate the headache and nausea, and it would be entirely marketable. Do you know anybody who works with bio stuff who might join us? Think about it. We can keep in touch."

I refused to dignify the suggestion with any sort of reply. The worst part was that she sounded entirely serious in her suggestion of working together.

"Right now, I have to go."

"You do. Your friend Finn will be getting ready for you. Enjoy yourself on St Martin's now, won't you. And do be careful if you end up going after Robin's Rebels yourself. They might not be nice people. I don't want to hear about your untimely death. That would be too painfully ironic for me. I like you, and wouldn't want anything bad to happen."

She broke the connection. My body clock was telling me that it was still the early hours of the morning, and decent folk were in their own beds. Another reason why I had not been able to remain in control, I suppose. What with the disappointing news from Shayna, I could find all kinds of excuses. None of them were very convincing.

Slate and I were silent together for a while. Eventually she spoke, quite hesitantly.

"Do you think any of that was true? I have no way to know."

"Neither do I. Look now, I'm sure it's not, but in truth I can't prove it. I don't want to take the risk. I mean, I can't take the risk: there's too much to lose. It's all just one more piece of leverage to her. I just wish she'd believed me about not trying to go after her for the earlier scams. Or that there'd been some other way to solve the Twin Problem. We'd not be in this mess. That is to say, I wouldn't be in this mess: you're in the clear."

"We should never have deleted those vids we retrieved."

I thought about it, then slowly shook my head.

"No. I'm sure that was the right thing to do. The deal was just for them to help us with the patch. Which they did, and very effectively too. Anyway, I don't want us to use the same methods as them. Otherwise we might as well just take up blackmail for ourselves."

I took a deep breath, then made myself speak my mind.

"Look, Slate, if you want a different partner to work with… I mean, if you think you couldn't work with me after this, then I'd understand, you know."

She cut me off before I could go any further.

"*Don't be ridiculous, Mit. That's the most absurd thing you could possibly say. I won't consider that, not for a moment. Did you give up on me when I was hacked on St Agnes?*"

We sat there together for a while.

"*We'd better go. And thank you. That means everything. But look, when we have to use that link again, I'll need you to support me all the time. I don't know if I can trust myself.*"

"*Of course, I'll do everything I can. At least we won't have to wait five hours this time: I found out how to quit out from it any time we want. But it's my fault too: I checked it before and thought it was alright. I signed it off for both of us. I'm out of my depth here, in truth.*"

I moved slowly to the door, my heart very heavy. As I opened it and stood in the little hall, she spoke again, only just above a whisper.

"*I don't understand how you can't remember. I wish I could forget some things.*"

I stopped in the space between the doors.

"*Can't you just delete the records?*"

"*Not without losing part of what I am. They're not in any one place: they're too spread out.*"

She sounded empty, bereft, and the need to empathise with her pulled me out of my preoccupation. Apparently Jocasta had found a way to make both of us feel miserable.

Part 5 – St Martin's

I LOCKED THE ROOM. Slate sent the release signal to the domestic management software, and we set off towards the dock. For the first time I wondered about giving all this up and just going back to Earth. If I was leaving Shayna's home in Greenwich right now, there might be a misty rain on my face to refresh me. Here, there was just the carefully regulated and conditioned air, quietly circulating at some optimal rate.

Also, I'd been tricked, and completely lost control of the situation. I had no idea what had happened, and had left myself vulnerable to Jocasta's manipulation. To cap it all, I was going to need to use the software patch again in a short time, with no confidence I could handle it this time.

But Slate was with me, keeping up frivolous chatter as we tried to keep out of the deep emotional waters all around. The market square was empty at this hour, but I ran a familiar hand over the frame of Taji's stall and pressed on.

At the dock, Finn was chatting to the night duty porter. The board showed an incoming freighter due in about an hour, together with some private inshore movement. Finn greeted me cheerfully, then gave me a sharp look as I responded half-heartedly.

We walked together to the Selkie.

"Lia Fail has made room available in the ship's hardware for your Slate. They both thought that she needed to be as close to the action as possible. Signal lag and all."

Slate had already told me that, and had begun the transfer from the lifeboat systems on the way over, so I just nodded. Finn looked at me again, and said nothing until we were aboard. He checked a few systems, confirmed with Lia Fail, committed the navigation plan, and then turned to face me. I had watched it all listlessly.

"You look like a man who's been kicked in the head and then dragged off into a corner and pummelled for good measure. Pretty odd considering that so far your plans seem to have worked out just right."

"Is that how I look? Is there a mirror handy?"

He pulled a face.

"Would one of Glyndwr's ales loosen your tongue?"

I looked away from him, and he leaned back in his chair.

"Well now, this must be particularly bad."

The undocking alert peeped at us, and we both fastened the chair straps. Not that it mattered except as a formality of compliance. You didn't need high acceleration to get off St Mary's. But right now, I rather appreciated the idea of being compliant.

I waited while the Selkie picked up speed and manoeuvred into an orbital transfer trajectory to St Martin's.

"Slate, have you said anything to Lia Fail?"

"Not yet. I was waiting to get some sort of steer from you."

That had to mean she thought this was really serious. Normally she would have been chattering away to her friends with news updates at the first opportunity.

"I will have one of those ales, Finn. No preference: just whatever's to hand. Then I have something to tell you and Lia Fail both. It's not at all good, I'm afraid, and afterwards you can tell me you were right all along. But please don't tell anyone else. Especially not Mrs Riley. I don't want her thinking badly of me."

"Eibhlin has heard a thing or two in her day, you know. And you might be surprised at how discreet she can be. But look, it's your story you're telling, so it's your rules."

He fetched us an ale each. I closed my eyes and felt Slate tuck in close to me mentally. Then I told Finn what had happened, all the way through to the final conversation with Jocasta after I had woken up. It wasn't as difficult as I had anticipated, but it was certainly neither easy nor pleasant. He listened silently to the whole thing. At the end he finished his ale and looked thoughtfully at the empty bottle.

"You want another?"

"Better not. I have to be at work in a while."

I winced at the thought.

"I have to check over the code patch. Then hook up to that wretched multi-way link again and make sure that the twins there are safe. And glean what information I can about Robin's Rebels to send back to ECRB. But before that, I've got to face Rydal. I don't want her to find out about this, Finn. Certainly not yet, not when we've got work to do together. But if she's half as sharp as you – and I know she is – how will I keep it from her?"

"Hmmm. And what about your lady back on Earth?"

"Shayna? That's a whole different story. But at least I don't have to look her in the eye today. I've got more time to think of something."

He said nothing.

"Finn, I need your help. What would you do?"

He thought about it for a long time.

"I don't exactly know, Mitnash. But it's not me having to make that choice now, is it?"

I pressed him, but he wouldn't presume to offer anything that might sound like advice. I got frustrated in the end and changed the subject. But in any case it wasn't all that long before we were coming in to Lower Town on St Martin's, and my thoughts turned to practical matters.

I stopped and laughed at myself at that point. Apparently all I needed was to focus on the details of an interesting technical problem, and the bigger picture faded into the blur of the background.

Finn came with me to the airlock, and we stopped just before the inner door.

"Whatever might come out of this, Mit, don't let it affect what you're doing today. There'll be time enough to sort yourself out. But you'll never forgive yourself if you let one thing lead on to another. Don't chastise yourself so much that you do something you'll regret."

"Something else, you mean? I've been regretting what happened since I first woke up. Especially seeing as everybody warned me. You included."

He nodded.

"I'm just saying. Don't let it all unravel. And despite what she said, there's no proof anything actually happened. It could all be bluff."

I took a deep breath.

"You're right, Finn. And I'm grateful even if I don't sound it. Actually, it's the side-effects of that link that I'm more worried about right now. I wish you were coming along with me."

"Not in a year on Pluto. I'll happily get you here with Slate, and I'll take you back to Mary's when you're done, but I'm no use to you when it comes down to code and all. Meanwhile, I'll be taking the Selkie out to where you wanted me to monitor the signal traffic. That's something useful I can do. Just tell me how it goes, and whether we'll be going straight back or lingering a while."

He embraced me, clapped me on the shoulder.

"Now get along with you and sort out whatever problem it is that Rydal needs you to fix."

I went on through the concertina link into the port. I had all kinds of things ready to show to the porter, documents and all, but it was not necessary. Rydal had already completed the preclearance forms for me. And left a little map so I could find her accommodation. I felt sloppy beside her efficiency.

I left there and went through the alleys and corridors. I had never been on St Martin's before, and found the layout confusing as I threaded through the settlement. Slate was chattering along as we went.

"It's pretty much linear, Mit. There are some clusters of dwellings, and a few spurs off to the sides, but basically it runs straight from the harbour at Lower Town through to a small marina for residents at Higher Town. That's where Rydal keeps the Heron. The landing stages aren't rated for anything much bigger than her boat: Selkie had no chance of docking there. Nor will the Harbour Porpoise if we bring her here. We'll need to come back to the public dock for that."

I couldn't decide if she was just gabbling to cheer me up, or if this was her own uncertainty speaking. Between the two of us we worked it out, and soon arrived.

Rydal opened her door just as we turned into the little access corridor down to her door. Slate had signalled Capstone, presumably. Like a lot of the entrances I had already passed since the dock, the approach was decorated with murals. She had chosen a butterfly theme, and I touched the delicate blue wings of one as I passed.

My greeting was awkward, and whatever words I chose didn't sound at all fluent, but she didn't appear to notice. It finally occurred to me that her anxiety about the coming crisis was back in the ascendant, and she didn't have much emotional space left to be attuned to my problems.

She hugged me in a sisterly way, and turned back inside.

"You're a bit earlier than I thought, Mitnash. Come in for a few minutes while I finish getting ready."

We went in. She had suspended gauze in loops and strands from the ceiling to soften the bluntness of the original drilling.

For some reason it gave the sense of being in woodland. She gestured towards the back wall.

"You go and talk to my pets for a while. I won't be long."

The idea of pets intrigued me. I thought of the parakeets that flocked around the St Mary's market area, and wondered if she had a couple of those somewhere.

There was a clear panel, floor to ceiling, separating the living room from a separate, much narrower chamber. At first all I could see was vegetation, lots of leafy stems with exotic flowers. It was all too small and cluttered for parakeets, and I was perplexed.

Then something moved. I had thought it was a flower, but it had wings, and with an abrupt internal shift I realised that it was a butterfly. Now that I knew what to look for, I could see more in there, a couple of dozen, of several different varieties. Most were resting, others were eating some sort of syrup. All at once, with no signal that I could see, two of them took flight, wings alight with colour as they danced around the chamber for a while before settling again.

"So how do you like my little friends?"

Rydal had come back while I had been fascinated by the pair. I kept watching, hoping to see another one in flight.

"I have never seen anything like it. They are quite extraordinary."

I caught my breath as another pair took to the wing and circled each other for a while. I was transported briefly back to Océane's troupe on Phobos.

"It must be difficult keeping the environment just right for them."

I didn't know much about butterflies, but I had heard that ones this large needed a lot of heat and moisture. She moved close to the glass, watching the pair flit about. I looked at her reflected face, peaceful in contemplation of flight.

"Not very different to us humans, when you compare it to what's outside of here."

She gestured towards the ceiling. The first time I had been on the Scilly Isles, I had been disturbed by the thought of airlessness so close. It had seemed different to the experience on board a ship, in some visceral way I could not explain. That had changed, and I was now unphased by the thinness of the skin which kept me safe here. Instead, captivated by her words, I was imagining us as human butterflies, straying out of our inner system home, moving away from the sun which had overseen our birth.

She turned suddenly, to catch me looking at her, and the spell was broken. Her anxiety and my shame resurfaced.

"Shall we go?"

I nodded. We left her house, and she led me quickly through the streets. It was early morning, and St Martin's was getting ready for another day.

Like a lot of older buildings on the Scilly Isles, the warehouse that Rydal and her friends were using had once been part of a mining enterprise. It used to hold machine parts, and both the doors and internal space were oversized accordingly. Part numbers and schematics had been scribbled all the way up the wall racks. Down at the other end of the room the new hub equipment and signalling subsystem sat waiting for us, dwarfed by the surroundings. Slate and I got to work.

"Capstone has loaded the twin patch, but not activated it yet. I looked over what he has done while you were walking here, and he followed the directions exactly. It's all queued up: all we need to do is toggle it. Do you want to review it yourself?"

"I don't think so. You know as much as I do about how it works. I don't think I'd add any value there. Of course, we are assuming it will work at all."

"I'm not worried about that, Mit. This code behaved perfectly on St Mary's, we understand how it functions, and there have been no changes. Robin's Rebels think that their attack worked there, so they have no reason to change their methods. Even ignoring Jocasta's assurances, which I'm guessing you're not inclined to trust, I'm confident in this part. And she really was motivated to protect the twins."

"Fair enough. Actually, I agree with you. While I remember, please send this version down to ECRB with an interim release note. If we find something that needs tweaking we can do that later. But let's get it away now, so they can start preparing a proper distribution package. Oh, and as a courtesy let's send it to the college at Gordii Fossae. The thing I'm really scared of is that link. I don't know that I can manage that."

"We'll be fine together. And as you know, I found out how to start and stop it at will. You won't be having to wait all those hours this time for it to go down again. Also, I'm reasonably sure that if you're hooked into it for a shorter time, there won't be the same headache and all as aftermath."

I was glad of that, and hoped she was right. Meanwhile, we had preliminary work to do.

"Rydal, we're good to go with the protective patch. I'd like us to get that in place right now. Then we can work on standing the system up as though it was the new deal hub."

Capstone and Slate chattered together for a short time.

"All done, Mit."

So that was the patch enabled. We took another half hour to configure the software, and then we were ready. I connected to Finn in the Selkie.

"Are you two ready up there?"

"As ever."

We all looked at each other, then Rydal tapped the commit code. To anyone looking on, Helen and Clytemnestra had just appeared in the island's public register. We weren't running the full stack of applications that were needed for deal hub operations, but a carefully chosen subset.

It was, we hoped, enough to attract the hostility of Robin's Rebels, but not so much that Director Penhaligon suspected he had a rival.

I took a long breath to steady myself.

"We should start up the group link."

Rydal looked at me, puzzled, perhaps hearing how my reservations were echoing hers.

"Is there a problem with it? You don't sound very sure."

I shook my head and tried to look resolute.

"I was just thinking of everything we have to get done. I'm sure the link will be fine."

"Slate, I need you to be monitoring this. If things start to go wrong I want you to terminate the link without hesitation. Don't stop to ask me. If it gets like before, I won't trust myself to be in my right mind."

She buzzed at me cheerfully.

"I won't leave you to your own devices this time."

"It's just..." I stopped briefly. *"It's just I don't want to do anything else I'll be ashamed of later. Especially not with Rydal. She wouldn't understand."*

"Come on, Mit. If we don't start it up soon she really will think there's a problem."

The link came online, and my internal landscape expanded. Helen and Clytemnestra seemed very young. I had a fleeting vision of two eager, dedicated teenagers, approaching the battle like Joan of Arc before the walls of Orléans. I had another minor crisis of confidence, wondering what on earth I had dragged them into, and what would become of them if I had got the analysis all wrong.

Then Rydal and Capstone settled into place, and it was time just to coordinate everything. We organised ourselves into a circle; I found myself between Helen and Rydal. Slate had already got herself between Clytemnestra and Capstone, and there was nothing to do except wait.

I was curious to find out how different the twins' language was from what I remembered of Shalem and Shahar, but they were shy and wouldn't oblige me by demonstrating. I didn't press them on the matter.

In any case, it was not long before Lia Fail called us. She had positioned the Selkie on the vector out towards Ceres, and sat there listening to message traffic. Sure enough, a short time after Rydal's system flagged its new presence, a data packet had gone off to Ceres with details of the codebase and configuration.

We forwarded all that down to ECRB. There was no possibility of sending anybody to investigate in a hurry. The London team would not even receive the message in time to actually do anything. But it was all grist to the information mill, and one day we would be glad of every scrap of data.

We knew we had about forty minutes to wait, but none of us were tempted towards complacency. Even with Lia Fail monitoring the approach, we would get no prior warning of the attack. By the time she had detected and analysed the wave front, it would be past her. She would not be able to send any kind of warning. If the code patch was ineffective, all she could do would be to help us pick up the pieces later.

Now, it was possible that Robin's Rebels worked out of some sort of mobile base rather than a shoreside installation. In that case, the response could arrive considerably sooner. I didn't think so, since I continued to picture them as of a rather uninspired, pedestrian group. They were quite unlike Jocasta

– whatever else anyone thought of her, she undoubtedly had flair in abundance. If she really had been the driving force behind Robin's Rebels, there would have been far more inventiveness and imagination to their actions.

Slate joggled me at that point, no doubt concerned that I was drifting towards unhelpful thoughts.

The six of us chatted idly for a while, swapping stories. The twins didn't want to hear of anything recent: their interest lay in events which had taken place before their first instantiation. That suited me perfectly: I didn't want to talk about the last few days.

But then we got to twenty minutes, and thirty, and the conversation dwindled. Each of us was watching the clock.

I mused to myself that the various conflicts that I got into for work were usually like this. A lot of preparation, a lot of waiting, and then it was all over in a flash, usually much faster than I could react. There was no sense of grappling hand to hand: it was all about the setup. If Slate and I had guessed wrong, or if our analysis was flawed, or the adversary was more clever than we expected, the game would be over before we even knew it.

We huddled in our circle, waiting for the signal. Nobody said anything. We simply sat with each other and waited.

And then the crisis was past. The attack came and went – and did nothing. I sagged in relief as Slate told me that it was over. Helen and Clytemnestra had, naturally, acknowledged the signal as it arrived. They had then processed it, but had no idea what would have happened to them in the absence of the patch. They didn't understand what all the fuss had been about. I was happier that way. They would have plenty to cope with once the new system was commissioned, what with the inevitable rivalry between them and the installation on St Mary's. Better by far that their first experience of public life was not a life-threatening disaster.

I became aware that Rydal was bouncing with relief and excitement. Capstone must have filled her in with the details. Then I felt the onset of the mental fuzziness which had gripped me before, and at the same time a surge of panic came from her across the link. The thought of losing control, here on St Martin's, here with Rydal, seemed as unbearable to me as the severance of the twin bond would have been to Helen and Clytemnestra.

For a brief moment, I was drowning in sensation. But at the same time I wanted to drown in it, and felt the siren call to simply surrender myself to it, come what may. I could start to feel the beginnings of the headache and nausea that had afflicted me before, but part of me didn't care.

But then Slate disrupted the multi-way link, and it dropped back to the normal one that joined just the two of us together. For a moment I raged furiously against her decision, outraged that she had interfered. Then some rationality pushed back into my thoughts, and I knew that she was right. The passion passed. I was left feeling weak and drained.

I took a deep breath, trying to ground myself, and turned to Rydal. She had a wild, unbridled look that was only now fading from her eyes, being replaced by confusion. She took a step away from me, uncertain how to understand what either of us had felt. I could understand the perplexity all too well.

"It's all done, Rydal. We can return everything back offline now, until you're ready to go live for real."

It was a clumsy attempt to reassure her, and we both knew it. She nodded jerkily, then looked around and ran her hands through her hair.

"Everything worked? The twins seem to be fine, but it all happened too quickly. I can't tell for sure."

"They're fine. But why not ask them yourself?"

She looked wary.

"I don't want to use that link thing again. Let's just use the desk pickup like we always used to."

She walked across the room without waiting for a reply. The twins were already running their own system scan, and Slate was working with them. After losing the euphoria of the link, and the intensity of rapport we had shared, I fell into a deep slump. I leaned against a convenient wall and felt black.

Rydal nudged me out of it a short time later. The room was quiet. The board showing the twins' status said that they had reverted to being quiescent. They were off the public grid again.

"Come on, Mitnash. Time to go. We have time to find ourselves a snack before Finn docks again."

I stirred myself.

"I should have asked him if Lia Fail had been able to trace anything. Slate? Any news from them?"

"She thinks they got a good quality traceback. When they dock we can look through it and see what we can find, but the London office will want to do a full analysis. I've already given her the routing prefix and she'll be sending it down there as soon as possible. Right now Earth is hidden behind St Martin's from their angle."

We left the building, making sure it was all locked down. Rydal led me towards a nearby snack stall.

"My treat. It's quite nice, for street food."

I picked out a hot spiced lemon drink. It smelled authentic, and I wondered if the lemons had been grown in a micro-environment like the one Rydal had for her butterflies. She gestured to a nearby bench. I waited for her to say something.

"You knew that the link thing would do that."

It wasn't a question, and she didn't need an answer.

"I'm not comfortable with how it left us feeling, Mitnash. I don't know that it was good for either of us."

"If I could have thought of any other way I would have used it. But the first time around, on St Mary's, it was only that link that stopped Shalem and Shahar from being hurt. Badly hurt. Keeping your twins safe was my highest priority."

She thought about it.

"So you joined up with Kassandra in a link like that. Jocasta, I mean. Whatever she is calling herself today."

The distaste was clear in her voice. I looked away, silent.

"Well, it's your business, I suppose."

She sounded bitter. I looked back again, wanting her to understand.

"It was the only way I knew. We kept your twins safe. The patch worked for them. Finn and Lia Fail might have everything we need to track this group down. It had to be this way, Rydal. How else could we have done it? We had to validate that code patch."

"That's the only reason that I am sitting here with you now. Maybe the only thing you know how to do is patch things up. Wouldn't it be better to build something properly from the start?"

She waited for an answer, but I had none.

"Anyway, you should have warned me first. You knew what it was like: you should have told me what to expect. I don't like not knowing what's happening. Not at all. And there were side effects you didn't tell me about. I feel like you just used me as part of the setup. You need to care more about your friends, not just the job."

She stood up, leaving most of her drink untouched.

"I need to get back home now. Take some time to recover from today. Please let me know what Finn found out."

"Will you be joining us at Frag Rockers tomorrow night?"

"Maybe. Probably. I think so. I'll let you know."

I hung my head and whispered.

"I'm so sorry, Rydal."

"You should have told me. You should have trusted me."

She walked off without looking back. I shook my head, wondering what else could go wrong.

Slate was very hesitant in the silence.

"The Selkie is on final approach now. Lia Fail says that she has already been able to send the signal trace down to London. There's a bit of time yet if you want to sit here for longer."

I looked at the spicy lemon drink.

"Good idea, Slate. This is too good to waste."

She said nothing, and my intuition told me that she had held something back.

"What is it? You might as well tell me."

"There was a message in from Shayna. Just a few minutes before Robin's Rebels attacked that last time. It wasn't appropriate to interrupt you then."

She stopped again.

"Well, go on. I can be interrupted now. It's not as if I'm doing anything important just this minute."

"Here it is. Verbatim. 'Mit, I've given this a lot of thought. But I still don't know what to do. I don't want to talk about this over messaging. Not with the better part of an hour between replies. It's too horrible. Let's meet properly. I can come up to the south lunar settlement with just a few days' notice. Or Deimos maybe, if the timing works out. Let me know when you can get there. We need to talk. Properly, face to face.' The message ends with two kisses."

I sat there, sipping at the cooling drink.

"Only two. Well, all things considered that wasn't as bad as it could have been. In fact, given the rest of today, that almost counts as good news. Let's go and find out what Finn has to say now."

⸻⸻⸻⸻⸻

Finn was expansively cheerful, presumably to offset my mood, which was still sombre. Lia Fail and Slate worked together on the message packet while Finn turned the Selkie around for the journey back to St Mary's.

I used the early part of the journey to inform Director Penhaligon that the test run had passed successfully, and that he could resume normal running. He was mildly interested, especially as it was well inside the estimate I had given him.

"So my system is warranted safe again?"

"Until somebody finds another exploit, sir. But the analysis that my colleague carried out did not identify any other vulnerabilities. The system is as robust as we can offer at this time, and the same defensive code will be applied to all twinned systems. Naturally, you will receive any further updates that ECRB considers necessary, as part of the normal release cycle."

"Very well. I shall be making my report to your manager about all this."

He paused briefly, then nodded.

"I shall tell him that your conduct has been satisfactory throughout."

I thought I did very well to remain polite, and signed off as quickly as decency allowed. Then I went back to join Finn on the Selkie's bridge, and I tried to laugh it off. Soon after, Slate buzzed me.

"We're done now, Mit. It's too elaborate for us to do a full analysis here, but we're sure that the London team will be able to get everything they need. There are routing tags in there: most are just misdirection, but some will be good. That's what we need the Finsbury analysis team for, to sort out the dross from the good stuff. But one thing we were able to do for sure is identify the local repeater. It's a subsurface viral worm, inserted only two or three weeks ago in a local news station. Not very original, but it does the trick effectively. The reporters probably have no idea what they're hosting."

"Well, we can sort that out, for sure. For the rest, do you think we'll know their physical location, as well as their credit provider and all?"

"That should be possible, yes. They could shift their base of operations, of course, but if they don't then someone can just walk up and knock on the door. Our guess is that they'll relocate just as soon as they realise this particular game is over. They'd be stupid not to, really."

I relaxed, and felt better about myself. Something about the last few days had gone right. Finn noticed.

"Happier now?"

"Yes, thank you. It's not all bad, after all."

I shook my head and laughed.

"All I have to do now is patch things up with Rydal and Shayna both, clean up that local repeater, decide which of these islands Slate and I are going to settle in as our home, qualify for inshore navigation, and finally turn my hand to whatever ECRB send my way next."

He thought about it, then shook his head.

"Do you think you might get another call from Jocasta?"

"I don't know. I don't want to talk about that just now."

So we didn't talk about it. But in the secrecy of our internal link, Slate and I wondered about it.

Back on St Mary's, the Harbour Porpoise was ready. Slate, with the comfort of settling into a favourite chair, began transferring herself back into the ship's hardware. It seemed that Boris had done a good job. Sitting in my little rented room, I pulled up maps of all the islands and tried to decide where to live. I was tending to favour Bryher at the moment, but hadn't yet made any sort of final decision.

Late in the afternoon we had a message from Elias, confirming that the twin patch had been packaged and shipped out as an emergency update on the finance distribution boards system-wide. It would also circulate as a zero-day exploit fix for other industry sectors as soon as possible.

He even added a complimentary comment at the end. I laughed wryly to see that, thinking that he might say something different if Jocasta really had the vid that she claimed, and ever carried out her threat.

I was also acutely aware that all I had achieved was a holding action. The twinned Sarsen configuration was fixed, and I was satisfied that twins could rest easy in all the far-flung corners of the solar system.

But in truth the central issue was unresolved. I was no nearer knowing who Robin's Rebels really were. I had no real clues as to where they might target next.

It was remotely possible that the data trace that Finn and Lia Fail had intercepted would tell us something, but I wasn't holding my breath. I had to assume that at best this would lead to an abandoned location.

I wondered how long it would be before I met up with their work again. Slate and I had only won a skirmish, not a war. Elias would know the job was unfinished, and would send us after them again when they resurfaced.

I wasn't sure I had the courage: the personal cost of achieving even this little victory had been very high.

Evening came, and I cadged a lift with Boris over to Bryher. I was very nervous, and fidgeted with my bottle of drink as the rest of the team arrived. I was convinced that Rydal was not going to be there, but she finally arrived, very late. She sat next to Maureen and stayed on the periphery of the chatter.

I was reminded, uncomfortably, of how Slate had described the relational state of Castor and Pollux, back when she had tried to talk with them on Mars. Clearly there was more than one way to disrupt a connection.

Elias had requested that we stay out on the Scilly Isles for another week or two before we took up any other assignment, just in case something happened in the aftermath. It made sense. It would be absurd in the extreme if I left, and then was needed back here again only days later.

So that gave me the opportunity to offer Rydal some free consultancy time to get her system closer to commissioning. She thought about it, then accepted cautiously. It wasn't the warmth of response that she had shown before all this had happened, but it was something. I felt that maybe I could make amends in practical ways, if nothing else.

Then Slate buzzed me.

"Jocasta has sent a message. She's quite far away for real-time conversation; it's several seconds chat lag, which will seem very awkward. Quite a bit longer than the Earth-Moon time delay. And she's going through a relay to hide her location: I can't tell where she really is. There's sound and vid both."

I excused myself from the group and retired to one of Glyndwr's private booths. The screen lit up, blurred briefly and then sharpened again to show Jocasta. She was standing at the same place in her galley as when we had last talked. Like Slate had said, the delay was bad, but I didn't intend to do much talking.

"Hello, Mit. And hello Slate, who I'm sure is listening along with you. I just heard from Shepherd's Crag that you got the twin patch installed and working on a second system. So, next time you go to that bar on Bryher, have a drink for me, will you? I'd like to pretend we are celebrating together."

I waited until I was sure that she had finished speaking.

"I can't be stopping to chat with you all the time, Jocasta. I'll keep my end of the deal, and you keep yours."

Several seconds passed, and then she nodded.

"Of course. Enjoy your work, and don't forget about us. Come back to me with an offer if you'd like us to work together again. I do think that could be very good for us both."

She blew me a kiss as the screen faded. I paused to marshal my thoughts, then went back to the others. I did buy a round of drinks and made a private toast as we all drank. In the privacy of my thoughts, I was raising the glass to the undoubted technical ability that she had, and her willingness to share it to protect twinned Sarsen pairs. She deserved that recognition, despite everything that had happened between us subsequently. I expect everyone else thought I was simply celebrating the recent victories on the islands.

I sat there in the bar, contemplating the mystery of the universe, not really joining in the ebb and flow of the chatter all around me. I had been surrounded by new issues all through these last few weeks. On the technical front I reckoned I had learned a great deal. Objectively, it was a success story. But what was I going to say to Shayna?

When it came down to personal relationships, it had all been bad timing.

Notes

About the author

Richard Abbott has visited some of the places that feature in his historical fiction. To date, however, he has not had the opportunity of visiting the asteroid belt, or anywhere else outside the Earth.

Richard currently lives in London, England. When not writing he works on the development and testing of computer and internet applications. He enjoys spending time with family, walking and wildlife – ideally combining all three of those pursuits at the same time.

Follow the author on:

- Web site – www.kephrath.com

- Blog – richardabbott.datascenesdev.com/blog/

- Google+ – Search for "Far from the Spaceports"

- Facebook – Search for "Far from the Spaceports"

- Twitter – @MilkHoneyedLand

Look out for his other works, which include the following.

Richard Abbott

Science Fiction – full-length novels

- *Far from the Spaceports*, available from most online retailers, and general booksellers to order in

    – soft-cover – ISBN 978-0993-1684-4-4
    – ebook format – ISBN 978-0993-1684-5-1

In case of difficulty please check the website
http://www.kephrath.com for purchasing options.
Feedback for this novel includes:
"...a delightful read. Abbott's characters are very personable and make for good companions as he carries us to a promising future..."

The New Podler Review of Books

"...a splendid good read... possibly the best thing the author has done to date..."

Breakfast with Pandora

Fiction – full-length novels

- *In a Milk and Honeyed Land*, available from most online retailers, and general booksellers to order in

    – soft-cover – ISBN 978-0993-1684-2-0
    – ebook format – ISBN 978-0993-1684-3-7

In case of difficulty please check the website
http://www.kephrath.com for purchasing options.
Feedback for this novel includes:
"the author is an authority on the subject, and it shows through the captivating descriptions of the ancient rituals, songs, village life, and even a battle scene... the story grabs hold of the imagination... satisfies as a love story, coming-of-age tale, and historical narrative..."

Author's notes

Blue Ink Review

"... The lives of these ordinary people are brought to life on the page in a way that's absorbing and credible. The changes that are going to take place in this area are quite incredible... a wonderous land that seems both alien and yet somehow familiar..."

Historical Novel Society UK Review

- *Scenes from a Life*, available from most online retailers, and general booksellers to order in

    – soft-cover – ISBN 978-0954-5535-9-3

    – kindle format – ISBN 978-0954-5535-7-9

    – epub format – ISBN 978-0954-5535-8-6

In case of difficulty please check the website
http://www.kephrath.com for purchasing options.
Feedback for this novel includes:
"The author is extremely knowledgeable of his subject and the minute detail brings the story vividly to life, to the point where you can almost feel the sand and the heat..."

Historical Novel Society UK Review

"... lovely description – evocative sentences or phrases that add so much to the atmosphere of the book"

The Review Group

"The striking thing about 'Scenes' is... its sensitivity: its assured, mature observation of people"

Breakfast with Pandora

- *The Flame Before Us*, available from most online retailers, and general booksellers to order in

    - soft-cover – ISBN 978-0993-1684-1-3

    - ebook format – ISBN 978-0993-1684-0-6

In case of difficulty please check the website http://www.kephrath.com for purchasing options.
Feedback for this novel includes:
"Wide in scope and rich in detail and plot, this is an accomplished illustration of this era in the region: complex, informative, enjoyable and skilfully put together."

Historical Novel Society UK Review

"...A surprising tenderness in the face of brutality, loss, and displacement is the emotion that underpins the action..."

Breakfast with Pandora

Fiction – short stories

- *The Man in the Cistern*, a short story of Kephrath, published in ebook format by Matteh Publications and available at online retailers, ISBN 978-0954-5535-1-7 (kindle) or 978-0954-5535-4-8 (epub).

- *The Lady of the Lions*, a short story of Kephrath, published in ebook format by Matteh Publications and available at online retailers, ISBN 978-0954-5535-3-1 (kindle) or 978-0954-5535-5-5 (epub).

Non-fiction

- *Triumphal Accounts in Hebrew and Egyptian*, published in ebook format by Matteh Publications and available at online retailers, ISBN 978-0954-5535-2-4 (kindle) or 978-0954-5535-6-2 (epub).

Extract from *Far from the Spaceports*

I TUCKED IN TO THE LANDING PATTERN at Hugh Town, St Mary's, just the way the groundstation control system told me. Naturally none of it was my own work, though I reckon I could have done a fair job if they'd let me. But no, the Ziggurat class persona at the port talked with Slate, the Stele loaded in to my spaceship, and it was all done properly. By the book.

I unbuckled, and waited while the two machines chattered for a while – a few nanos of content, a handful of bits of payment, and a gazillion security protocol bytes surrounding both of these. It didn't take long, not really. Not when you reckoned it against a few weeks of low-gravity transfer.

My shore bag was ready. I grinned while I waited, having all the usual thoughts. If I closed my eyes to the look of the spaceport, my ears to the mechanical hum of the ship, and my memory to the stark vacuum of the asteroid, I could be a traveller from any age of Earth's history, waiting to be allowed to set foot in a new port. Always the wait at the end of the trip.

The Ziggurat was satisfied with what it found out, and sent out one of the bubble cars from the dome. The click as the car interlocked resounded through the whole of my sloop, the Harbour Porpoise. It was designed to be excessively loud – you really wanted to know that a proper connection had been made, when there was all that airlessness just outside. No matter what your onboard Stele told you, or the groundstation Ziggurat confirmed, there was nothing like a satisfying metallic clank to reassure you.

Some people I knew still wore a suit for the bubble car ride. But you got derisive looks from the porters, and it wasn't the image I wanted them to see. I left my suit and lid fastened in their clips, slung the shore bag over my shoulder, and cycled through into the bubble just in street clothes.

The car whined a little as it disengaged and started to trundle back to the dome. Electric then, standard model, probably older than I was. It looked weary, patched here and there, well serviced but with generic components that would have long since invalidated the warranty. Getting new equipment out here must be a slow task.

The bubble top was clear to space. I liked it, but at a guess, a lot of newcomers dialled the opacity right up to max to shut all that emptiness out. Instead, I leaned back to get a sense of where I was. Not that the naked eye could do much. The inner system was behind the bulk of St Mary's just now, and a whole lot of stars don't really tell you much without ephemeris software. Once upon a time old sages knew how to navigate around their land, just by looking at a couple of dozen of the brightest stars, but that sort of thing belongs in a virtual world now. I called to my Stele for some assistance.

"Slate, overlay the display with something that helps me, please."

Slate did some negotiation with the car, and after a short pause the inner surface of the bubble showed some enhancement overlays. The rest of the Scilly Isles showed up in a loose oval from near the zenith down towards the conventional-north axis, coloured ovals indicating relative size, with handy data tags telling me things like distance, available resources, and what were euphemistically called "tourist attractions".

St Agnes was closest, and also lowest over the horizon from here. St Martin's was up near the zenith, with Tresco, Bryher and Samson in between, and a whole slew of smaller rocks scattered here and there.

The Scilly Isles were a close gaggle of asteroids in matched solar orbit, slightly further out into the cold than Ceres, and detached by a fair bit of angular separation. Some lonely explorer with an eye for detail had called them that when he first prospected, but I guess the planetary reference from the old home went right past most people.

The early settlers out here, on the other hand, had been wildly enthusiastic about the name, and proceeded to make as many connections as they could. Settlements on the different rocks were named after the old towns, landmarks were identified, and so on. Even the furthest nav beacon stationed towards the inner system had been called the Bishop Rock. Slate had used it in the early stages of approach.

The islanders had rapidly become passionate about their new homes, and almost everything that could be found back off the Cornish coast had its mirror image. In the early years, the asteroids had attracted a disproportionate number of former United Kingdom residents. So where some of the domes had a high ratio of emigrants from America or China, the Scilly Isles had kept a British feel, reflected in the special interest meetup groups advertising themselves in the islands' media outlets. I would fit right in.

It was time to play the role I had chosen as cover.

"Slate, swap this one out and give me the enhanced mineral spectrogram analysis, quintic Bezier interpolation, false colour."

Another pause while Slate told the bubble's onboard system what I meant, transferred a few display Pebbles, and activated them. The stars disappeared, and the blackness of the sky was replaced by a colour wash. Red was heavier elements, anything from lead upwards, blue was the light stuff, yellow and green the mid-range. Orange was what I would be looking for, but only if it showed up in large quantities. The chief porter would be monitoring all this – he probably had to approve the Pebble installs in the first place – so for added interest value I made a few annotation squiggles around some random flecks of orange.

Slate tapped on my collar chat panel.

"Coming up on the dome, Mit."

Some years ago I'd asked Slate to use Shayna's voice as the audio basis whenever we were away from Earth. Right now, it definitely provided me with some compensation for the loss of our interrupted holiday, but every so often I wondered whether she would find the decision touching, ridiculous, or pathetic.

She would certainly make a fuss when she found out about it, and want something extravagant by way of compensation. And she would find out. Of necessity, I kept all sorts of secrets from her concerning my professional life, but there was very little she couldn't find out about everyday things. I always suspected that Slate gave away far too much information whenever Shayna posted a query.

The screen faded to transparent off to one side, and Slate was, of course, right. The car was approaching the dome interlock.

Beside the lock, above the official port identifier HT-SM-AB, someone had neatly printed "Hugh Town Porters'Lodge" in five different languages, all in black outdoor paint. Some wit with a blue spray had then scribbled "You'll have more fun at Jool's", together with what was obviously supposed to be a directional map.

Like all these outstations, the structure looked nothing like a dome. That was just what everyone called them, in a fit of idealism. But the real shape was a bizarre mixture of old cylindrical fuel boosters, cuboid cargo containers, a few static landers, and spidery suspension gel bridging the random gaps. Slate had shown me a schematic view as we had been landing. Some way back from the quay the ceiling really did bell up a little, but in a lopsided and unique manner.

There was another heavy metallic sound, and the bubble car beeped cheerfully at me. We had arrived. Slate would clean up all of the overlay Pebbles, so I just went straight through into the dome's entrance, and then into clearance control after that. Just as I suspected, the head porter had half an eye on the bubble's slave monitor, where my nicely enhanced polychrome enhancements were fading out again.

I strolled up to him with a friendly smile. I was there to investigate fraud, but that wasn't how I wanted to introduce myself. For all I knew, he was the ringleader.

About Matteh Publications

Matteh Publications is a small publisher based in north London offering a small range of specialised books, mostly in ebook form only. For information concerning current or forthcoming titles please see
http://mattehpublications.datascenesdev.com/.

www.ingramcontent.com/pod-product-compliance
Lightning Source LLC
Chambersburg PA
CBHW070051260626
47160CB00004B/1167